HOLLYWOOD
Skye

Dear Reader:

Whatever Skye Taylor wants, she gets. At least that's the case when she uses her charm as a nineteen-year-old to woo an older soldier on a Kansas army base. After snagging him and convincing him into marriage, she finds she's still not satisfied. Her focus turns from a prize husband to another quest: becoming an actress in Hollywood.

In her tenth novel, Suzetta Perkins displays once again her talent of spinning a suspenseful tale. As with her debut novel, *Behind the Veil*, the military has a key role in the story line of her latest project. Once Skye lands in Tinseltown, she falls into a trap of a con artist who sets her up for challenges along her path toward success. Her life mirrors many young women seeking fame on the West Coast whose lives may start rocky but eventually lead to stardom or a taste of it. Skye's roller-coaster ride ends with an unexpected outcome, and readers will enjoy guessing what's in store in this page-turner.

As always, thanks for supporting myself and the Strebor Books family. We strive to bring you the most cutting-edge, out-of-the-box material on the market. You can find me on Facebook @AuthorZane or you can email me at zane@eroticanoir.com.

Blessings,

Zane

Publisher
Strebor Books
www.simonandschuster.com

ZANE PRESENTS

HOLLYWOOD
Skye

A NOVEL

Suzetta Perkins

STREBOR BOOKS
NEW YORK LONDON TORONTO SYDNEY

Strebor Books
P.O. Box 6505
Largo, MD 20792
http://www.streborbooks.com

ISBN 978-1-59309-556-7
ISBN 978-1-4767-5623-3 (ebook)
LCCN 2015934967

First Strebor Books trade paperback edition December 2015

Cover design: www.mariondesigns.com
Cover photograph: © Keith Saunders/Keith Saunders Photos

Film reel © Igor Shikov/Shutterstock.com

10 9 8 7 6 5 4 3 2 1

Manufactured in the United States of America

For information regarding special discounts for bulk purchases, please contact Simon & Schuster Special Sales at 1-866-506-1949

The Simon & Schuster Speakers Bureau can bring authors to your live event. For more information or to book an event, contact the Simon & Schuster Speakers Bureau at 1-866-248-3049 or visit our website at www.simonspeakers.com.

To my daughter, Teliza;
my nieces, Shonda, Carla, Brittany, Christina, and Miranda,
thank you for being shining examples of young women
who make the world a better place to live.

ACKNOWLEDGEMENTS

Blessings! I deliver to you my tenth novel, *Hollywood Skye*. What a great feeling.

I give all honor and glory to my Father above for bestowing upon me the gift of writing. My life's desire has always been to create and share written word with readers—words, poetry, and lyrics that communicate my daydreams, experiences, and my eclectic thinking on subjects sometimes too vast for even my comprehension. Thank you for taking the ride with me.

As always, I thank my family for their continued support. To Teliza and Walt, thank you for suggesting that I use Junction City, Kansas as the initial backdrop for this story. It gave me a lot of fodder to jumpstart this novel. To my son, Gerald Jr., thank you for always writing and producing wonderful songs to enhance my books while also making me a contemporary rapper. To my nieces, Carmela Mabry and Crystal Carswell, thanks for being loyal and supportive fans.

I'd like to give a shout-out to Patricia Mendinghall for being a loyal fan and sisterfriend, supporting me no matter where she is in the world. To Lois Leggett of SASSY Ladies Book Club in Louisville, N.C., thank you for a splendid event, taking your meeting up a notch by totally getting into character for my book, *Betrayed*. To Rose Wright, president of SAVVY Book Club in Jackson, MS, thank you for making me a star of your show. To

Carmen Crayne, Althea Boone, and Black Pearls Book Club in Raleigh, N.C., thank you for loving me and supporting a sistah's dream. You're the bomb.com! Emily Dickens and Ladies Who Love to Read in Durham, N.C., thank you for embracing me! To Dail McLamb and Sisters Unlimited, thank you for believing in my work. To Veronica A. Wiley, Alyssa P. Leonard, Jeanette Tatman and all the ladies of Women of Focus Book Club in Nashville, TN, thank you for throwing out the red carpet. I'm eternally indebted to you all—from the time I arrived at the airport, breakfast, my tour of Nashville, and the amazing book club meeting that ended up with a Passion Party, I'll never forget. And to my wonderful sisterfriend, Alberta Lampkins, who was my road dawg for the day while in Nashville and treated me with sisterly love, thank you. To David Atkins and Anya Alsobrook of the Montgomery County Public Library in Troy, N.C., thank you for always supporting me and remembering me in your endeavors. The Red Hot Romance Reception was beautiful and I left with a smile. As always, much love to the Sistahs and Sister Circle Book Clubs in Fayetteville, N.C.

To Ella Curry of EDC Creations, you are the best at what you do. You showcase authors and give them a forum to shine. Thank you for allowing me to let my light come through. And LaShaunda Hoffman, you have the same gift. You're so meek and mild, but yet a strong tower. To Ellen Sudderth of ESP Literary, you are a true friend and giver. Newport News has a gift in you. To Karen Michele Bowman and Book Clubs United, you ROCK!

A special thank-you to my fans Pia and Parenthia Days, Jami Taylor, Lysette Brown, Larry (Sarge), Verneyse (Pam) Gordon, Alice Dickens, Penny Rose, Sandy Dowd, and Casandra Belcher Tripp for your continued support. A special shout-out goes to Ann Anderson in Memphis, TN, who I met dialing a wrong number. We talked about books and the rest is history. To Edryce Tucker, you're amazing. Thank you for sharing my work with Mt. Sinai Missionary Baptist Church.

My humble praise goes to my publisher, Zane, of Strebor Books. Again, she's given me a platform to showcase my work. She's a bad mama jama, with television series and hit movies to her credit on top of all the books she's written. I read *Addicted* years ago, and now it's on the silver screen with class A actors, Boris Kodjoe and Sharon Leal, playing the lead roles. To Charmaine Roberts Parker, Zane's right hand, you're the best. And to Zane's right-hand chick, Nakita West, thanks for all you do. To Keith Saunders of Marion Designs, a standing O for always making my book covers pop. To Yona Deshommes and my Simon & Schuster family, thank you. My journey would be nothing without my fabulous agent, Dr. Maxine Thompson. You've always been there for me, and thank you for taking my sister, Jennifer, under your wings.

Last but not least, a heartfelt hug goes to my dear friend and publicist, Lasheera Lee. She's one of the hardest-working women in the literary industry. She's so selfless and caring and I crown her Literary Diva of the Year. I love you!

I did say last in the paragraph above, however my BFF and road dawg deserves this spot. Mary Farmer, I love you! Thank you for always being there for me. You and Lasheera together have made my literary journey one I will never forget.

PROLOGUE

S kye's world came crashing down around her at the sight of the two men dressed in green, Class-A uniforms—one short, the other tall—blocking her mother's doorway, uttering strained words of condolence, as if they hadn't done it before.

"Mrs. Nona Taylor?" the short gentleman asked as he removed his hat from his head.

Nona looked from one to the other and started to shake her head, her hands thrusting forward as if to ward off some evil spirit. "No. No. No. I don't want to hear what you've come to say."

"We're sorry, Mrs. Taylor." There was a momentary pause. "Command Sergeant Major Travis Taylor was killed this morning, at ten a.m. Kandahar time, in the line of duty."

Nona Taylor collapsed to the floor, the words of the deliverer searing her soul like the grenade that had ripped the side of the Humvee Skye's father sat in while granting an interview to a popular news journalist. Tears dropped from Skye's face, like dumplings into a pot of hot stew, as she stood close to her mother's retching body.

"No...not my daddy!" Skye wailed loud enough for all of Junction City, Kansas to hear. She hugged herself about the waist with the men looking on and continued to scream.

The noise and commotion brought Skye's sister, Whitney, and her brother, Jermaine, to the living room, falling to the floor at the sight of their mother's sobbing body. The gentlemen in green tilted their heads, replaced the hats on their heads, and backed away from the door, leaving the way they had come. Soon the entire house shook from the guttural wails that erupted from the family that was left without their loved one—their arms mangled together as they tried to console one another.

Cast-gray skies threatened rain as the mourners with their solemn faces followed the flag-draped coffin to Command Sergeant Major Taylor's burial site at Arlington National Cemetery. Nona Taylor and her children, all dressed in black, stood side-by-side as the military pallbearers lifted the coffin from the horse-drawn carriage and laid it at its final resting place. Last rites were administered and the crowd waited in silence.

Skye's body shook as the first round of the twenty-one gun salute rang out in the distance. She braced herself for Nona, who was taking it hard and unable to hold the folded American flag that was given to her in honor of her now late husband. Life for the Taylors had changed in an instant, but for seventeen-year-old Skye, it had changed even more. She was her father's heart.

CHAPTER 1

*N*ow nineteen, with a smooth chocolate complexion, a five-foot, nine-inch wiry frame, and short, brown locks twisted about her head, Skye reflected on life and what she was going to do with the rest of hers. She felt trapped in a place and time that offered no more than a mundane existence—a small town with no luster, no pizzazz—the town's Super Walmart the gateway to nowhere. She had barely traveled beyond the city limits of her birthplace, save for a few shopping trips to Topeka and Kansas City when her mother could muster up the time away from her job. Skye made a promise that she wasn't going to limit herself; she was going to see the world. And one thing Skye knew beyond a shadow of a doubt: she was getting the hell out of Junction City.

The Taylors now lived in a small A-frame white house that didn't boast much more than an old oak tree in the front yard and a carport that was large enough to house one automobile that sat next to the side of the house. Mrs. Taylor never accompanied her husband on any of his tours of duty outside of Junction City. She'd grown up there, preferred the simple life, and was happy to see her husband on the occasions he'd come home for a long vacation or was restationed at Ft. Riley, Kansas.

Life had changed drastically in the Taylor household since the death of Skye's father, who was a casualty of the senseless war in Afghanistan. After her father's death, Skye's sister, Whitney, married an army soldier and followed him to Hawaii, leaving Mrs. Taylor heartbroken once again. A year prior, Jermaine went to Kansas State University. Having lost three members of her family so close together, Mrs. Taylor led a hollow existence.

Surrounded by paisley-pink walls, Skye lay on her bed and pondered her dilemma. She didn't have many friends and never had a real boyfriend throughout her school-age years. Her parents were strict—Command Sergeant Major Travis Taylor oftentimes putting her and her siblings through some rigorous drill, talking to them as if they were soldiers and he their drill sergeant—as if Whitney, Skye, and Jermaine were his troops and they were in the military.

But Skye loved her father. Even though he had a menacing exterior, his love for his children was apparent; Skye was his favorite. When he'd come home from wherever he'd been stationed, he brought them gifts, and Skye's was always the biggest and the best. She recalled a beautiful sapphire bracelet her father gave her that her mother coveted, although her mother's explanation was that Skye was too young to have such an expensive piece of jewelry.

Most of all, Skye loved what he stood for and his dedication to the United States Army. And she loved how he looked in his military uniform—it seemed to exude some type of power. Skye often fantasized about toy soldiers coming to life, but now her fantasies were daydreams, and like Whitney, she was going to get her one of those toy soldiers, even if she had to bend over backward to make it happen.

Skye had seen those toy soldiers up close at the Post Exchange or when they would come to the house, when they lived on post, to get a bite to eat or shoot the bull with her daddy—she standing in the shadows imagining what a man draped in starched Army green fatigues and tan combat boots could do for her and what magic those uniforms possessed as she was drawn to them like a magnet. She had wondered as she watched her mother iron her father's uniforms with precision, applying enough starch to make them stand up on their own, stroking each piece as if they were made of gold, examining them to make sure the creases were perfect before pulling them to her chest and reliving a moment that was embedded in her mind.

Losing sight of her goal was not an option. Skye picked up her bag and the keys to her mother's car and headed for the front door in pursuit of the toy soldier that had consumed her dreams for many days and nights. She didn't have far to go—only a few miles to Ft. Riley, the large military base in Kansas that was stitched tight at the seams with Junction City.

CHAPTER 2

"Skye Denise Taylor, where do you think you're going with my car in those skin-tight jeans?" Nona Taylor shouted, walking behind Skye.

With keys tucked tight in her hand, Skye ignored her mother and continued toward the door.

"Girl, don't act like you didn't hear me. Give me my keys, now. You're not taking my car anywhere. Since your daddy was killed, I've done my best to keep this family together, and I'll not have a child of mine disrespect me."

"Mother, you're exaggerating. I'm going to make a short run to the store, and I'll be back before you know it. Love you."

"Skye, the last time you *ran* to the store, you didn't come back for hours. I don't understand how you can do all this running around without a job and with no plans of getting one. You're not going to stay here without putting in your fair share."

"Look around you, Mother." Skye's lips quivered. "Whitney and Jermaine are gone, and I've got plans, too. I'm not going to stay in this godforsaken place. Look at you. You have nothing to show for all your hard work. You work like a Hebrew slave at Walmart, hoping one day they'll give you a managerial job."

Slap! Slap!

Skye's hand flew up and touched the side of her face that burned from the blow of her mother's hand. Surprise registered on her face. Nona had never in all of Skye's nineteen years on earth put a hand on her.

"Don't you ever speak to me in that manner or tone ever again, young lady. It's been over two years since you graduated from high school, and I've tolerated your skinny, sulking behind sitting around on my furniture without job the first or taking the initiative to further your education. There's a good college thirty minutes away in Manhattan that you could enroll in. But you prefer to sit around this house and do nothing while I'm making an honest living at Walmart so you don't have to go without."

"You don't have to shout."

Tears formed in Nona's eyes. "You make me sick, Skye. Give me those keys. At three dollars and thirty-eight cents a gallon, no unemployed freeloader is going to be using my car, driving out the gas that I need to get to my honest job."

"Mother, I'm sorry I upset you. You've been through a lot, and I've been through a lot, too. I miss Daddy so much. I feel a kind of disconnect to the world since he's been gone—no disrespect to you. I've got to get away from this place, so much so that my head is about to explode if I don't do so soon. I'm not sure what's going on with me."

"How long have you felt like this, Skye?" Nona found a seat in the nearest chair and sat down. "I haven't stopped crying since your daddy was killed, but I've got to keep on going or else I'll die myself. Now you want to leave me."

Skye patted her mother on the back. "Something is pulling me in some direction I can't explain. I've got to find out what it is, and I won't be satisfied until I do. Don't laugh; I've had thoughts of being an actress. Anyway, you won't be alone; Jermaine is only thirty minutes away."

Nona looked up into Skye's face. Skye had been a troubled child for some time. Nona recognized it but hadn't done anything about it. She'd been too busy pining over her dead husband, wallowing in her own self-pity. Nona felt that any attempt to offer assistance to Skye now would probably be met with resistance.

"Mother, I need to make that run."

"However you get there, it won't be in my car. And put on a decent top that won't expose everything God gave you."

Skye clutched the keys tight in her hand, walked out the door, and jumped in her mother's car.

Dust from the road flew to either side of the blue Honda Civic as Skye barreled down it for her date with destiny. She made a vow to herself that before sundown, some able-bodied soldier, rank unknown, would be hers. If the plan Skye engineered in her head worked as she thought it should, she'd clutch on tight until the veil was on her head and the pianist was playing the bridal song as she marched down the aisle of somebody's church.

Cows littered the scenery as they grazed lazily in pastures under the hot July sun. Skye jutted her nose in the air and twisted her lips as if to say she was too good for this town. She approached the turn-off for Ft. Riley and drove the road like she had built it herself. She'd heard from an acquaintance that some big general would be on post today—*a change of command*, she had said, which meant that Ft. Riley would be crawling with the military's finest, dressed in dress greens and camouflage uniforms.

CHAPTER 3

*I*t was as if God had dropped a giant bag of green and brown Skittles all over the military base. Skye Taylor's small green eyes gawked as she walked through the sea of soldiers on her way to the Post Exchange, taking snapshots in her mind of each one she passed, as if she were on a shopping trip at an exotic vacation spot. She licked her lips and drew in a deep breath, overcome with this good fortune. The sampling was varied, but there was nothing wrong with having lots of choices. For sure, some of the soldiers were married, but for Skye, whosoever was willing, let them come.

And then she spotted him dressed in green camouflage fatigues and a wine-colored beret sitting on the side of his head. He spotted her too and seemed amused that she was watching him, as he flirted with his eyes.

Skye's feet wouldn't move and her knees began to knock together. Butterflies danced in her stomach, their wings tickling her insides. But his eyes stalked Skye and gave her the courage to move forward.

She worked her jeans and the bright-orange, tight-fitting tank top that plunged at least six inches, exposing ample breasts that spilled over the thin neckline that did its best to keep her intact. Her orange pointed-toe stilettos jutted out from underneath her jeans pointing the way—and point they did as the mesmerized soldier stood at attention until Skye was within two inches of him.

He was as tall as a skyscraper and his ruddy good looks excited her. Although he was covered from head to toe in Army fatigues, Skye could tell he was built. His caramel-colored, oval-shaped face housed a pair of light-brown eyes with lashes much too long and pretty for a man.

"What's your name, pretty lady?" the soldier asked, cocking his head to the side to get a good look. "Walking like that might kill a soldier, especially one that's been battling the Taliban for a long time."

Skye smiled. "What's your name and were you in Iraq?"

"I recently got back from Afghanistan. I'm Sergeant Culbertson… ahh, that is, Sergeant Bryan Culbertson."

Skye ran her first name and his last name together in her mind— *Skye Culbertson. Not bad*, she thought.

"And I'll ask again. Do you have a name?"

Hesitating, her name suddenly burst from her lips. "Skye."

"Skye…uh, like in the sky is blue?"

"Yes, my name is Skye with an 'e' tacked at the end. My full name is Skye Taylor."

"Well, Skye with an 'e,' that's a pretty name for a beautiful woman." Skye blushed. But Bryan's eyes were drawn to the healthy scoop of chest that caused other men to halt and do a double-take.

"Where are you from, Sergeant Culbertson?" Skye asked, ignoring Bryan's gaping eyes, while yet enjoying the attention.

"The Dirty South."

"The Dirty South? Where is that?" Skye asked annoyed.

"Atlanta," Bryan said, trying to ignore Skye's cynicism. "You have heard of Atlanta."

"Yes, I've heard of Atlanta."

Sgt. Bryan Culbertson glanced at his watch. "Look, it was nice meeting you, Skye. You're a drop-dead gorgeous sister and you're wearing that outfit. I've got to move on, though."

"Please don't go," Skye said, grabbing his arm while trying not to sound desperate. "Didn't mean to scare you off; you were chosen."

A severe frown crossed Bryan's face. He removed Skye's hand. "Chosen for what?"

Blunt and bold was Skye's answer. "I'm looking for a husband and you fit the mold."

Sgt. Culbertson stared at Skye without blinking. "Hold on, sister, marriage is not on my agenda, and we've just met. In fact, I'm leaving for Fort Lewis, Washington, in a few weeks."

"What do you aspire to do with your life, Bryan? You don't mind if I call you Bryan?"

"I see myself climbing the military ladder. I'm going to be Sergeant Major of a big platoon one day."

"Well, why don't you let me help you get there? I don't require much—the usual military spousal benefits: government quarters and a change of scenery."

"You're serious."

"I haven't batted an eye."

"You've got to be kidding. What do you know about marriage anyway? And what would your family say about you jumping up and getting married to someone you met only ten minutes ago?"

"I make my own decisions." Skye reached up and fondled the collar on Bryan's fatigues. "Now if you're interested in taking that E-5 rank all the way to Command Sergeant Major, I can help you get there."

Bryan removed Skye's hand from his collar. "You have no idea what you're talking about. What do you know about the military except for what you've seen on TV? And so that we're clear, I'm not marriage material. You're cute, but that's it."

"My father was the best damn Command Sergeant Major the Army ever had," Skye said as if she hadn't heard anything Bryan said. "I was my daddy's favorite and he shared many secrets with me."

"So where's your daddy, now?"

"My daddy died in Afghanistan behind some bull crap that started with weapons of mass destruction that don't exist."

"That was in Iraq. Afghanistan is a different war."

"And you have the nerve to tell me that I don't know anything about the military. Nine-eleven started it all. The United States ran to Iraq and ended up in Afghanistan looking for Osama bin Laden, who was right under the military's nose."

"Well, President Obama took care of that with the Navy SEALs. So what's your point? It's obvious you're bitter about this war."

"That's not the half. If these fool Republicans will leave President Obama alone, he can get this country back on track."

"How old are you?"

"Old enough to have a say-so about how our country is being run."

"Why don't we change the conversation?"

"And talk about what…marriage?" Skye asked seductively, letting the words slide off her tongue while batting her eyelashes.

"Is your head twisted on straight?"

"Is that a requirement for marriage?"

"Baby, you're fine and all, but that doesn't qualify you for marriage. I'm not ready to settle down. I've got more running around to do. No disrespect; straight up…no chaser. I haven't made it to my twenty-fifth birthday yet."

"What if I tell you I'm the only woman you'll ever need?"

"Why me?" Bryan asked, searching for a way to be detached from the situation.

"You were chosen," Skye responded, her face void of pretense.

"Baby, I was on my way to the PX, minding my own business. You shouldn't have been looking so good. Ah-ha…that's how you got me. You were out on a maneuver, and I fell in the foxhole."

"Don't make it sound so repulsive. You definitely liked what you saw."

"You never said how old you were."

"I'm nineteen and I'm way ahead of my time."

"Way ahead of your time and too much for me."

Skye was tired of talking and reached up and brushed Bryan's lips with hers. She swiped her hand over his chest, stopping momentarily to toy with the buttons on his uniform. He removed her hand as a full-bird colonel passed by. He raised his hand to salute.

"We're in a public place, and I don't do public displays, especially when I'm in uniform," Bryan said with a bit of irritation in his voice.

"Well, take me someplace where we can be alone. You know you want this."

"Look, Skye, if that's your real name. While I'd like to be all up in your business, I'm not ready to be tied down to anyone. And the last thing I want is to be somebody's husband. You're too deep for me, girl. It's time for me to move on so you can set a trap for someone else."

"You're already it."

CHAPTER 4

"What's up, Culbertson?" Sgt. Walter Mackey asked, a toothbrush dangling from the side of his mouth and a white towel draping the lower part of his body. He pulled out his travel kit and looked inside. "You look like you saw a ghost."

"Wish it were a ghost I saw. Man, I ran into this fine sister this afternoon. She was strutting her stuff like it was nobody's business—Beyoncé and Halle Berry rolled up into one. And you know how hard it is for me to resist a good-looking sister."

Sgt. Mackey stared at Bryan and shook his head. "That's your problem. Women are going to be the death of you, man. Have you seen my toothpaste?"

"No, I haven't seen your toothpaste. But listen, man, that's not the half."

"The half of what? I've got to find my toothpaste. I've got a hot date tonight, and I'm supposed to meet this sister at the NCO club in a few hours."

"Here, you can use mine. Now listen. This chick wants to marry me."

Sgt. Mackey stopped, turned around, looked at his friend, and laughed. "Culbertson, you're crazy. Who's going to marry your two-timing, three-timing self? Thanks for the toothpaste."

"Look, Mackey, if this wasn't a serious matter, I wouldn't have said anything. This girl is crazy, a true stalker in every sense of the word. I can't get rid of her."

"Did you say you met her today? You're not too smart for a soldier boy who wants to move up in the ranks. Afghan mountains must still be holding you hostage. Treat this like any other mission. The enemy has you blocked in and you need to get back to your platoon. What do you do? You find an alternate route or kill whoever is in your way. Now the lady may be fine and all, but if you aren't trying to commit, walk the other way, fool." Sgt. Mackey took the toothpaste and walked out of the room.

I would if she wasn't waiting outside for me to change my clothes, Bryan Culbertson thought to himself. He sat down on the bed to contemplate what to do.

A knock at the door startled him. It couldn't be Skye. He didn't give her the room number.

Knock, knock, knock. It was louder than before.

"Who is it?"

"Sergeant Culbertson?"

"Yeah!"

"Sergeant Samuels. Open the door."

"Come in."

"What's up with you, Culbertson?"

"What do you mean what's up with me?"

"Some fine chick is sitting outside in a blue Honda Civic asking about you. Why are you making her sit in the car? Look, I'd be happy to take her off your hands."

"Samuels, if it was that simple, I'd say go right ahead."

"What? She's got some kind of disease or something?"

"No, Culbertson says she wants to marry him," Sgt. Mackey said as he reentered the room. He and Sgt. Samuels roared with laughter.

"Can you see that fool married?" Samuels said, choking on his saliva.

"That's what I'm talking about," Mackey said. "He has more women running after him than a receiver on a football field. When he goes for his drug test, he's going to test positive for a venereal disease."

Samuels laughed.

"That wasn't funny," Culbertson shouted. "Both of y'all get the hell out."

Sgt. Mackey buttoned up his shirt. "You're serious, aren't you, Culbertson?"

"That's what I've been trying to tell you. Her name is Skye, and she wants to get married so that she can get away from home. She wants to go to Fort Lewis with me. She's sitting outside in the car waiting for me to come out so we can talk some more. Hell, my mother would freak out if she couldn't be the center of attention at my wedding like she was at my two sisters' weddings. She gets off on things like that. But I don't want to get married!

"I didn't go all the way to Afghanistan, put my life on the line twenty-four-seven, make it all the way back across the water to end up with some crazy chick who wants to marry me next week. I plan to be an eligible bachelor for a *long* time."

"Handle your business, man. You can always pretend you've got PTSD—post-traumatic stress disorder," Sgt. Samuels barked like he was giving orders. He laughed and saluted Culbertson for fun. "I'm out."

"I'm out, too, man. Remember what I said about the mission— abort or kill. See you later on, groom-to-be." Sgt. Mackey slapped Culbertson's arm and choked on his laughter. "Handle your business, son."

"This is not a laughing matter," Culbertson said again, his voice two octaves higher than before. "I've got to get rid of her."

Mackey looked at Samuels and back at Culbertson before he

finally shrugged his shoulders and shook his head. Mackey and Samuels headed for the door and Bryan watched as the door closed behind them.

He pulled his cell phone from his pocket and scrolled down his contact list that was crammed full of female names. He stopped at a name, pushed the dial key and waited for someone to pick up. When a voice came on the line, he politely cancelled his date for the evening and ended the call. He picked out a pair of pants and a shirt from his closet and put them on, and didn't bother to shower or shave. He went to the bathroom, brushed his teeth, looked at himself in the mirror, squinted, and finally gave a big sigh. He looked around the room, got his keys and walked out the door.

CHAPTER 5

S kye looked gorgeous in a simple, strapless satin gown, three-inch satin pumps, elbow-length, fingerless gloves, and a simple silk wrap adorned with beads about her head. Steady hands clutched the fresh bouquet of cut calla lilies that were bound at the stems as she flitted down the aisle of the post chapel. A handful of guests, including Sgt. Mackey and Sgt. Samuels, were assembled in the sanctuary to bear witness to the holy union.

Nona Taylor, dressed in a three-quarter-length, powder-blue suit, stood alone, her face devoid of expression as the organist played the bridal song. Skye hung onto Jermaine's arm and moved past Nona on the way to the altar and into the arms of a man she barely knew. Nona still hadn't been able to grasp until this moment what had taken place two-and-a-half weeks ago when Skye took her car to the store. The minister's message to the bride and groom flew by Nona, the words not resonating with anything she was feeling. Before she knew it, the service was over—short and sweet.

The bride and groom were pronounced man and wife, and Skye pulled Bryan's face to hers and fed him with a passionate kiss. There was laughter from the crowd— those who came to support the groom and to confirm that his bachelor days were truly over.

"What do you know about marriage?" Nona asked as Skye gathered a few of her belongings and put them in a suitcase.

"I'm sure I'll find out, Mother, now that I'm married." Skye wasn't going to allow Nona's taunts to distract her mission.

"You have no earthly idea what it takes to be married or keep the man you hijacked from the military base. I have ears; I heard you tell Jermaine all about how you entrapped Bryan. He's a bigger fool than you. That boy was scared to death when the preacher asked him to repeat his vows."

Skye fingered the simple gold band that circled her finger which Bryan gave as a symbol of his love or lack thereof. "Mother, you exaggerate. You don't want to see me happy. For crying out loud, today is my wedding day."

"Listen here, little Miss think-you-know-what-you're-doing. I can't be happy when I see you making the biggest mistake of your life. That boy doesn't want to be married any more than the man in the moon. Love is one of the foundations of marriage, but that main ingredient is missing from your bridal package.

"Girl, you need to wake up. What's going to happen when your soldier boy comes to his senses? Oh, you'll be fine for a minute. You'll be able to make ends meet on his E-5 pay. You'll get government housing and have PX and commissary privileges. But when the piece of thread that's holding this shotgun marriage together breaks, what are you going to do then? You don't have a job and aren't interested in getting one; go figure."

Skye turned and looked at her mother with tears in her eyes. "Don't take this out on me because Daddy is gone and you've got nobody else; don't try to turn my happiness into your tragedy. You're trying to make this all about you, Mother. You can't stand to see me make something of my life. Bryan and I will be fine. I'm glad to be getting away from Junction City."

"And when it doesn't work out, where will your fast behind go since you don't like it here in Junction City? Don't bother to answer the question. And for the record, I'll be fine." Nona walked out of Skye's room into her own and slammed the door.

Nona sulked in her room after she watched Skye and Bryan leave her home for good even though they weren't setting out for Washington State for another couple of weeks. There would be no one to tell Skye to take off the skin-tight jeans or the skimpy top that she thought inappropriate for a newly married woman to be wearing. "Selfish" was the only word Nona had for her daughter, but what Nona really feared was that Skye would never return home. Maybe Nona was the one being selfish, for now she was truly alone.

CHAPTER 6

*T*he light wind whipped through Skye's locks as Bryan laid his Acura out on Interstate 70 on an early August morning as the newlyweds began their journey to Tacoma, Washington. It was four in the morning and it was already beginning to get hot. As the couple set out to see a world yet to be discovered, the flint hills of Junction City, Kansas flew by and the tower that announced Ft. Riley Army Base became a blur.

"I wish you had stayed with your mother until I got settled at my new duty station," Bryan began not even five good miles out of Junction City. "Two weeks wasn't enough time for me to get things situated."

"We got married so we could be together."

"No, you pressured me into marrying you in order to get away from home. I bought into your little game and helped you out, but no, you couldn't cut me some slack and consider all the things that came with my new responsibility. It's going to cost me extra money to stay in a hotel. If you hadn't come along, I would've stayed in one of the enlisted quarters. I've already had to spend money to stay in the hotel on post since you wouldn't stay with your mother until it was time for us to leave."

"Bryan, you need to grow up. Face it. We're married now. Do what you need to do to accommodate the situation. After all, it didn't keep you from helping yourself every night to my legal goodies."

"Like you said, we're married. I couldn't believe you were a virgin the way you came on to me."

"Why should that have mattered? You don't even recognize a gift horse when you're given one. To marry me unspoiled was a feather in your cap. Not many can claim my status at my age."

"That may be true, but you don't love me, Skye. You're using me, and that's worse than not being a virgin."

"Drive the car. It's much too early in our marriage for us to claim marital problems."

Bryan glanced at Skye, then back at the highway. "What kind of woman are you? You picked me out of a crowd like some kind of hunter stalking his prey. You pretended to be some fast girl, using your body to attract my attention, when all the while, you've never even had sex or a boyfriend, for that matter. Why couldn't you have been one of those pretty girls that like to make a soldier pant, make a soldier want to go AWOL for some booty, make a soldier…"

"That's your problem, soldier boy. You think with the wrong end of your body. You've got one thing right, though. I'm not your ordinary girl; I'm not one of those shallow girls who can't think for herself…who thinks that having sex with every Sean, Peanut, and Ron will make her the prize for the top bidder."

"I don't get you. Why do you think I stopped and looked at you in the first place? You were selling sex like that jean commercial on TV. Your boobs were hanging over the top of your shirt and the jeans you wore looked like they were spray-painted on your behind. Yeah, you were hot and it made me stop and look, which was my mistake."

"I was on a mission, although I'll admit that I loved the way you looked in your uniform. You were wearing yours better than anyone else the day I spotted you."

For a moment, there was silence except for the sound of tires rolling over asphalt or a car flying by. Bryan looked at the gas gauge that read "full" and decided to turn the air conditioner on low.

"You're strange, Skye. It's hard to believe that I was the fool that fell into your trap."

Skye popped her lips, rolled her eyes around in her head, and then looked straight ahead. As if someone had pushed a button, her head turned in Bryan's direction. "You'll never make Command Sergeant Major."

"You may be right about that, but when I do, it won't be on account of you," Bryan said with a sneer.

"How long before we get to Fort Lewis?"

"Sit back and relax, baby. We're talking about three-and-a-half days' drive." Bryan chuckled, enjoying Skye's discomfort.

"You'll get my meaning soon enough," Skye said, ignoring Bryan's attempt at sarcasm. "Don't play with me, Bryan. We may have uttered the words for better or worse, richer or poorer, but there won't be any career advancement if you aren't interested in making this marriage work."

Silence ensued for the next fifty miles.

CHAPTER 7

*M*iles of interstate flew past as the Culbertsons barreled down the highway due west. Without much conversation between them, they breezed through Kansas and rolled into Colorado where they stopped to get something to eat. After a potty break, they were on the road again until they settled in at a low-budget hotel for the night on the edge of Denver. Early the next morning, they were up and on the road again, finally crossing into the state of Wyoming late in the afternoon. They kept on course until they arrived in Salt Lake City and settled for the night.

There were at least six hundred or more miles before Skye and Bryan reached their destination. They started out again the next morning and rolled through miles and miles of Utah desert. Uninterested, Skye reclined her seat, closed her eyes to the world until sleep engulfed her. It seemed only a few minutes had passed, although it had been an hour and a half, when she heard Bryan's cell phone ring and his muffled voice when he spoke.

Skye kept her eyes shut as she listened to Bryan's portion of the conversation.

"Momma, I was coming home before going to Washington, but things got crazy and I ran out of time."

Pause.

"Momma, please. I'm not lying to you."

Pause.

"Who told you that?"

Pause.

"Momma, calm down. I was only doing this girl a favor. Don't sweat me."

Pause.

"Get an annulment? But she's here with me...in the car. We're on our way to Fort Lewis."

Pause.

"Momma, I'm a grown man. There's no need for you to come to Fort Lewis. I can handle things myself. Gotta go before she wakes up."

Pause.

"Okay, Momma, be that way. I love you." Silence.

Skye eased up in her seat and opened her eyes. "So, you're a momma's boy."

"Don't go there. The only person that can talk about my momma is me."

"I wasn't talking about your momma. I merely made a statement about you."

"Look, you've escaped from your momma's house and you're here with me now. Another good five hundred miles, and we'll be at Fort Lewis."

"This isn't quite the life I had dreamed about. I'm not feeling the excitement..."

"Shut it down, Skye. I'm the one who should be pissed and mad as hell. I let you back me into a corner and make the biggest mistake of my life. I'm not exactly feeling you either. I put my life on hold. I felt your desperation...your wanting to get out of a sorry-ass town and away from a mother that held you back. But listen to me and listen well. I'll have your complaining ass on a plane back to Kansas so fast that they'll have to rewrite the ending of the *Wizard of Oz*. Don't mess with the hand that's feeding you."

Skye sat in silence, her insides smoldering from Bryan's verbal attack. She'd let him get over himself; there was no need to abort the mission yet. And if Bryan wasn't going to be on track to make her a sergeant major's wife, although it was a few years down the road, she'd have to dispose of him—soon.

CHAPTER 8

*T*hey arrived at Ft. Lewis the next day, which was now called the Joint Base Lewis-McChord since Ft. Lewis and McChord Air Force Base merged together. It was another military town, but Junction City paled in comparison. The evergreen trees stood tall and commanding and Mount Rainier was picture-perfect, as it provided a majestic landscape far-off in the distance.

"Sit up and give me your military ID card," Bryan said, shuffling through the cards in his wallet. "We're here."

Skye obeyed while surveying her surroundings. She couldn't tell much from her vantage point, but she was ready to get out of the car and away from Bryan, if only for a few minutes. She'd even given a thought to calling her mother to let her know that she was all right and that marriage was agreeing with her; she decided against it.

Bryan gave the security guard their IDs, retrieved them, and plowed forward without a word. The last thing Skye was going to do was speak first. She didn't like how she was feeling, not one bit. She was supposed to feel like a queen who'd met her Prince Charming, but after two weeks of marriage and over a thousand miles away from home, she finally admitted to herself that she may have made a mistake.

Bryan drove on the base and located the Welcome Center.

"We're here," Bryan said again as he pulled the car to a stop and cut it off. "Sit tight. I'll be back in a minute. I've got to process in."

"I guess I'll be here when you get back," she shot back, sensing Bryan's mood. She watched him walk away, laid her head back on the headrest, and closed her eyes.

When a minute became ten, Skye got out of the car and stood next to it. It was cool outside, even for the month of August. Several soldiers passed taking parting glances at the lean, petite frame that posed next to the red Acura. A smile dripped from Skye's lips, and she flirted until she saw Bryan emerge from the building he had gone into—two female soldiers laughing at his side.

Skye snatched the car door open and got in, her eyes fixed on Bryan and the women. As if he suddenly remembered he had left his bride in the car, he sprinted to the car, turning once when one of the ladies called out to him—he giving her a nod. An arctic chill met Bryan when he got in the car.

"Don't even start, Skye," Bryan began.

"What are you talking about?"

"I see the look on your face. I worked with those ladies at one of my duty stations."

"Umm-hum."

"This is the life of a soldier. You ought to know that since your daddy was in the Army. We meet a lot of people in our line of duty. Remember, I was single up til now."

"And don't you forget it."

"Impossible to forget. So, Mrs. Culbertson, why don't we get a place to stay and think about getting something to eat? It might take some of your meanness away."

Skye rolled her eyes. It was Bryan who acted like the stranger.

CHAPTER 9

One day rolled into another and became a week, then two. While Bryan dove back into the throes of his daily duties as a military man, Skye's life lacked the sparkle and thrill she thought was part of the package she'd bought into by marrying Bryan. For starters, she had depended on her mother most of her life for everything she needed. Now, she was in a two-bedroom apartment on base that Bryan told her to fix up, and she had no interest or desire to do so. But on the flip side, Bryan was spending a lot of time away from Skye, preparing for a major military inspection or maneuver that his unit was to be involved in, or so he said.

Skye had yet to call her mother. It was selfish on her part, but she was in no hurry to hear Nona give her the fifth degree about running off with a man she barely knew. Skye had hoped to change Bryan's mind about her—that she was a good catch after all, that they would truly become one, and he'd treat her with respect and adoration.

Things had to change soon. Getting a job of some kind was looking like a better option. Two weeks wasn't a long time, but the walls were caving in on her. Without transportation of her own, she was trapped on the military base. The one thing Skye realized was that she wasn't a domestic. Preparing meals and waiting on a husband who came home late at night only to take off his fatigues and combat boots, leave them in the middle of the floor, and go straight to bed wasn't what she'd bargained for either. Although she hadn't been a sexual being until her first time with Bryan, Skye hoped that he'd teach her about love, romance, and what she needed to do to keep him happy.

Biting her lip, Skye got up from the chair in the living room where she'd been daydreaming, picked up the remote off the kitchen table where Bryan had left it, and turned on the television. The girls of *The View* were talking to a prominent actress about her recent estrangement from her husband. *"I was young when I married Derek. I was trying to break into show business while living on a shoestring budget. L.A. was a big city that I wasn't properly prepared for, coming from a small town in Tennessee. I met Derek at a party that my roommate invited me to, and the rest is history. Derek was a Hollywood agent and I got the movie roles of a lifetime. After awhile, Derek and I outgrew each other."*

Skye stared at the television screen until the network cut away to a commercial. Maybe going to Los Angeles was the answer. True, she didn't have any real acting skills to her credit, but she was a good actress when she wanted to be. While she didn't have a credential to her name, her inner acting skills got her a husband and out of Junction City.

She wasn't sure how Bryan would react to her sudden excitement about becoming an actress. It would mean that she would have to be gone for a while until she could secure a small gig, which really meant that she could be gone for some undisclosed length of time. Bryan would probably welcome this new adventure of hers since he didn't seem to be interested in keeping the fire burning in their marriage. She'd tell him as soon as he walked in from work, and she didn't have to wait long.

Skye jumped at the sound of keys rattling at the front door. She whipped around as if ready to do battle with the unexpected intruder.

It was late morning and way too early for Bryan to make an appearance.

Transfixed, Skye stared at Bryan and the tall, elegant woman who followed him inside. It was fair to say that she was a close relative of Bryan's—the same ruddy complexion with a caramel twist, the same chiseled features, and the same height. The woman had an air of authority about her that put Skye on alert. It didn't take much to deduce that this was Bryan's mother.

"Well, Bryan," the woman said as she slid out of her lightweight trench coat and slithered deeper into their small apartment with her nose turned up in the air, "is this the girl you let borrow your last name so she could get away from home and that godforsaken place called Junction City?"

"Momma, don't start. Skye is my wife. Skye, this is my mother, Mrs. Judy Culbertson."

Skye didn't flinch. "You didn't tell me your mother was coming to visit, let alone that you were going all the way to Seattle to pick her up from the airport."

"Uhh, son, there's no need to offer an explanation about inviting your mother to come and visit you."

"Forgive me, Skye," Bryan said, ignoring his mother. He sighed. "I wasn't sure how to tell you."

"You didn't know how to tell me?"

"You see…"

"There's no need to make any excuses about having your mother come and visit, baby," Mrs. Culbertson stressed again. "You're my son, and I'll come and visit you whenever I feel like it."

"Excuse me, Mrs. Culbertson," Skye cut in. "I may have steered this conversation in the way it's going, but I'm going to redirect it. Please don't talk as if I'm not in the room. I will not be disrespected in my home. My name is Skye and I'm Bryan's wife."

"Are you going to let this country bumpkin, with all those braids going every which way on her head, talk to me like that, Bryan? I remember that you said she was a little off...crazy."

"Okay, ladies. It is a little uncomfortable in here. Let's start over. Skye, I apologize for not telling you about Momma coming to town."

Skye clenched her teeth and didn't utter a word.

Mrs. Culbertson huffed. "Well, that was easy." After giving her coat to Bryan, Judy Culbertson moved throughout the tiny apartment. She sneered at everything and clapped her hands together. "This place needs a mother's touch. I can't have my son living in a dump."

"Momma?"

"What is it, son?"

"Look, Bryan, I'm not going to put up with this bull crap from your mother. No one is going to disrespect me in my home."

"Honey..."

"My name is Skye, Mrs. Culbertson."

"Skye, I'm here to help. You've been here two weeks and you don't have anything in this place to make it look like a home. You're young; I understand that, but Bryan was brought up in a middle-class family with beautiful surroundings. He's used to the finer things in life."

"My father was a Command Sergeant Major who was killed in Afghanistan. My family never lacked for anything, either. And for your information, this is military housing afforded to soldiers of your son's rank."

"My, my, my, you're a feisty one with a little temper. I may have misjudged you. There's something I like about you, Skye. You're forceful, tough, and have a hard exterior. You won't let anyone run over you. But you're not good enough for my son."

Skye looked directly into the face of Mrs. Culbertson and sneered at her. "You may be wearing expensive clothes, shoes, and may have paid a lot of money to have your hair swing around your head with all that body in it, but that doesn't make you or Bryan any better than me. If you want to decorate your son's dump, help yourself. If you want to orchestrate his life as he's allowing you to do, have at it. But you won't be doing any of it while I'm here."

"Talk to that little ingrate, Bryan, before I go off on her."

"And you'll wish that you'd never seen or heard of me. What are you going to say, Bryan?"

"Both of you are making this difficult. Skye, I can't throw my mother out, and Momma, Skye is my wife."

"Stop whimpering and stand up and be the man I taught you to be. If you had, you wouldn't be in this predicament now."

"No wonder you're messed up, Bryan. You have your mother as an example of what a man is supposed to be."

Judy lunged at Skye who stepped aside. Not even Bryan was in a position to keep Judy from falling to the floor. "You little witch, you're going to regret the day you met my Bryan."

"I already do." Skye watched as Bryan helped his mother up from the floor. "I'm going out, and I hope she's gone when I return."

"Skye," Bryan shouted as he watched her walk out of the door. "Don't leave."

CHAPTER 10

*T*wo months into the marriage, Skye was still standing. She'd beaten her mother-in-law at her own game and Mrs. Judy Culbertson had no recourse but to take her uppity, refined ways back to Atlanta on the first thing smoking. Mrs. Culbertson may have pushed her way into their house, but Skye let her know that she was the Queen B in the castle that she and Bryan lived in as husband and wife.

Skye finally landed a job at the Army Air Force Post Exchange (AAFES), the place where the military and their dependents shopped for clothing and household goods—from the high-end to the low-end, Target with a hint of Macy's. Although her job wasn't glamorous, Skye loved being a cashier. And she got plenty of attention.

"Hey, sister, what are you doing when you get off today?" the tall, moderately handsome, dark-skinned gentleman asked.

"Going home to my husband," Skye said, as she let go of a big smile and put the gentleman's purchase in the plastic AAFES bag.

The gentleman searched her finger. "I don't see a ring on your finger."

"It doesn't mean that I'm not married."

"You've got a point, but you shouldn't be looking so good."

"Yeah," his partner said who was in line directly behind him. "You should be working in the General's office."

Skye blushed. "Thank you."

"I'm Sergeant First Class Thomas Milton and this is my buddy, Sergeant Darius Wheeler. Stay fine and if you ever get tired of your old man, look me up."

Skye was flattered but not interested. "Y'all have a good day."

The Post Exchange was busy. Out of the corner of her eyes, Skye spotted the woman she had seen Bryan talking to when they had first arrived at Joint Base Lewis-McChord. She was dressed in military fatigues and her hair was in a ponytail and pinned up on her head by a large metal clip. She got in Skye's line.

Skye swiped and bagged the next three customers. Now, the young lady was upon her and Skye took a mental note of her last name that was stitched on her uniform fatigues—*Ballard*. No pleasantries were exchanged, however, when Skye looked up and gave the woman her total cost of purchase, the woman was staring at her. The woman swiped her card and threw her head back. "You're Sergeant Culbertson's wife."

"I am, and you're…"

"I'm Trina Ballard. Bryan and I were stationed together in Germany several years ago. We met in Basic Training."

"That's nice."

"You're prettier than I thought you would be."

"And why would you say a thing like that?"

"Bryan likes them a little rough around the edges."

"Like you?"

Trina Ballard stared at Skye and then smiled. "Yeah, like me. We were thicker than thieves. Bryan and I were intimate. We shared many secrets and a lot of cold and hot nights together. He was my boo, but it's nice to know that he's moved on, although I'm sure he's never gotten over me. I was supposed to be his baby's momma, but I was playing at being a real soldier at the time—trying to get my E-5 promotion."

Skye wasn't amused. She stared back at Trina and rolled her eyes. "I need to get the next customer."

"That's fine by me. I'll tell Bryan that you said hi. Yeah, we're working together again." And with that, Trina took her stuff and strolled out of the Post Exchange.

Skye was hot, but she wasn't going to allow Ms. Army Soldier to ruin her day. She was making a little money and putting it all in the bank. If Bryan wasn't interested in investing in their marriage, she'd follow up on her dream to become an actress. It was almost time for her shift to end. She couldn't wait to get home and get off of her feet.

There was nothing like a breath of fresh air. Washington summers weren't extremely hot, and Skye appreciated it. Kansas was a hotbed for tornados and violent thunderstorms during the summer, and she relished the cooler weather.

Skye rushed home and prepared dinner. Bryan hadn't come home yet, and it was almost six-thirty. She picked up the mail that sat on the edge of the kitchen table and looked through it. Bryan must have come home for lunch and picked up the mail, she thought.

Setting the mail back on the table, Skye saw cigarette ashes that had dropped on the floor. Bryan didn't smoke, so who did they belong to? Maybe they belonged to one of the guys in his office. Skye thought about her encounter with Sergeant Ballard. She wasn't going to bring it up with Bryan unless he brought it up. The girl was probably trying to make her jealous.

The evening was uneventful. Skye went to work the next day in a good frame of mind, whistling all the way. For a moment, she thought about her mother and how she had ridiculed Nona about working at Walmart to make a living. Now she had a better appreciation for what her mother did. As a cashier, Skye met many interesting people during the course of a day, and she couldn't forget the friendly face of SFC Thomas Milton. If she'd still been single, he might have been someone she'd talk to. Skye wasn't going to let another day go by without calling her mother.

"Culbertson, it's time for you to go to lunch," the head cashier, Ruthie, said. "Turn your light off and close out after the last person in your line."

"Okay. I need to run home and get my wallet I left on the kitchen table. I don't want to get a ticket for not having my driver's license."

Skye finished the last customer in her lane and closed out her drawer for lunch. She only had thirty minutes, but it was enough time to run home and get back. Their post housing area was five minutes away.

She jumped in an old VW Beetle that Bryan had picked up for her from one of the guys in his unit that was going overseas. It didn't cost much, and it gave Skye the transportation she needed to jet around on base or in Tacoma. It wasn't trustworthy for long distance excursions.

Quite a few cars were parked in the parking area of the multiunit base housing complex. Skye dashed from her car to her apartment so she could get back to work on time. Her wallet was right where she'd left it.

Suddenly, she stopped in her tracks. She heard noises coming from upstairs. Pointing her ears upward, she was sure that someone was in the house besides her. Skye tiptoed up the stairway and when she reached the top, she saw that her bedroom door was closed. Still on her tiptoes, she inched forward, not sure of what she might encounter.

Putting her ear to the door, Skye heard moans of pleasure and the sound of the bed she had lain in with her husband only the night before squeaking and squawking like it was being forced to accommodate. The bowels of hate rose up in Skye, and with her right hand, she turned the knob, leaned on the door, and pushed it in.

Sweaty, naked behinds moved up and down oblivious to Skye's cold-hearted stare.

"Make momma happy," the girl that Skye met yesterday said.

"Give me all of your sweet honey," Bryan shouted back, driving his hard, extended penis in and out of Trina's waiting receptacle like a toilet plunger.

Skye picked up Bryan's baseball bat that sat in the corner of the room. She raised it and swung it at his head. Fortunately for Bryan, her aim was off; she barely grazed the top of his shoulder.

"Damn, what was that," Bryan said, stopping in the middle of his sexual exploits to grab his shoulder and look around to see what hit him. His eyes bucked and he jumped off of Trina, his now limp member dangling like an inchworm. "Skye, put the bat down."

"You nasty, dirty, filthy-ass dickhead." Skye swung and missed. "How dare you bring this skanky hoe into our house…our bedroom? And what the hell are you looking at, you piece of slutty trash? Get the hell out of my bed." Skye swung the bat at Trina, but Bryan caught it before it connected.

"Skye." Bryan sighed. "Skye, I tried to warn you that my single, hunting days and ways weren't out of my system. I've known Trina a long time, in fact, we…"

"I know…she was supposed to be your baby's momma. Well, she isn't and when I finish reporting your dirty asses to your unit, you'll wish she had been your baby's momma. Those raggedy E-5 patches you're wearing on your shoulders are going to be Private First Class stripes."

Trina sprang from the bed and held out both hands. "There's

no need to do that, Skye. I'll leave Bryan alone. I won't touch…"

"Shut the hell up," Skye shouted, frowning at the same time. "Ugh, it stinks in here." Skye shook her head and pinched her nose closed for emphasis. "Put some clothes on and get the hell out of my house. And take your cigarettes with you. Your bitch ass has been in this house more than today."

Trina grabbed the cigarettes off of the nightstand, picked her clothes off of the floor, and headed for the door. Skye kicked her in the butt.

"You're a piece of trash."

Trina ran.

"Don't go in the bathroom. Put them on in the hallway and get the 'F' out of here before I kill you," Skye yelled.

Trina jumped in her clothes, took the steps down two at a time, and ran out of the front door.

Skye got up in Bryan's face, pointing her finger that nearly poked him in the eye. She smelled his breath and wrinkled up her nose. "Was she worth it, Bryan? Was that bitch worth everything you're about to lose?"

"Come on, Skye. I beg you not to mess with my military career. I did you a favor; now please do one for me. I'll understand if you want to leave…"

"Is that what you want me to do, Bryan? Do you want me to leave so that you can be free to do whatever you want with that nasty-ass hoe?"

"I tried to be upfront with you, but you pinned me against the wall."

Skye slapped Bryan square in the face. "And you want to be somebody's sergeant major, you spineless, pitiful excuse for a soldier?"

Bryan clutched his face, while trying to catch his breath. "I'm more of a man than you'll ever know."

"You're right about that, Bryan. I am leaving your sorry ass. You can hump, suck, and…never mind. I'm through with you and your sorry-ass momma. I'm going to the credit union and withdraw all the funds except for the twenty-five dollars that needs to be there to keep the account open. I hate you, and I never want to see your ugly face again."

Bryan stood in his nakedness, his breathing labored.

"Go wash your stanking ass and get out of my sight."

Skye jerked her head around at the sound of the ringing phone. She snatched the phone from the base and answered. "Who is it?"

"Skye, this is Ruthie. Where are you? Your lunch break was over twenty minutes ago."

"I had a family emergency, and I won't be back to the PX today, tomorrow, or ever." Skye dropped the phone down on its receiver. Thank God she'd gotten paid a couple of days ago. She'd chalk up her unpaid time to volunteer work. She was going to Los Angeles to become an actress.

CHAPTER 11

*S*kye sat staring out of the window as the Greyhound bus headed south on Interstate 5. With only the belongings she could pack into two suitcases and dressed in a pair of jeans, a striped turtleneck blouse, and a camel-colored, lightweight wool jacket, Skye hopped on the bus and headed for Los Angeles to pursue an imaginary dream that was prompted weeks ago by some actress talking about her life on a television talk show. She withdrew the $200 she had in her checking account and added it to the little less than $500 that Bryan withdrew from his savings—to be rid of her and out of his life forever, mimicking what Judy Culbertson had said to her not long ago in a vile and nasty tone.

The bus crossed the state line into Oregon headed for California. The mountain ranges were majestic and for a fleeting moment, Skye wondered what it might have been like if she and Bryan had taken a trip to explore some of the wonders of the world…of the United States. She'd seen some beautiful country riding across the states from Kansas to the state of Washington. She tossed the thought to the back of her mind, laid her head on the headrest, and fell asleep. The bus made periodic stops, but she never got off, except to make a bus change in Oakland, California.

It took almost a full day for her to travel to Los Angeles, and when she arrived, Skye had no earthly idea where she would rest her head for the night, although it was more or less out of the question since it was late when the bus arrived in the city. She looked around the bus station and was convinced immediately that this wasn't the safest place to be until the sun rose.

Skye exhaled and dragged her two suitcases to a nearby bench to contemplate what to do. She had to use her money wisely until an employment opportunity came her way.

A shadow loomed over her shoulder. Stiff as a board, Skye turned slightly to her left, looked over her shoulder, and up into the face of a young woman who was properly dressed for the warm, Los Angeles weather.

"Hey," the young lady said to Skye. "You got on the bus in Oakland."

"I did," was Skye's reply.

"Are you in L.A. for a visit?"

Skye looked at this woman who asked too many damn questions in the middle of the night. The young lady's preppy look seemed harmless enough.

"I left my husband. We were only married a few months. His evil mother came to town and tried to kick me out of my home, and after surviving that, I found him in bed with an old girlfriend."

"And you left?" The young lady set her carry-on bag on the bench behind Skye and put her hands on her hips. "Look…what's your name?"

"Skye."

"Look, Skye. You should've given mother-in-law a taste of her own medicine. Ain't no way somebody is going to roll up into my crib and kick me the hell out. What did your husband say?"

"He didn't say anything…much. He's a spineless wimp—a certified momma's boy. What's your name?"

"My name is Jaylin Scott, but my friends call me Jaye."

"It has a nice ring to it."

"Look, girl, I'd still be in Oakland protecting my investments."

"You must not have heard me when I said I caught him in bed with another woman—an ex-girlfriend."

"Straight talk."

"Yeah, and I've been riding all day. I came from Washington State. My husband is in the military and stationed at what used to be called Fort Lewis. It has a new name, but I can't remember what it's called."

"Damn, girl. You've been traveling a long way. And where are you staying while in L.A.?"

"Jaye, you sure do ask a lot of questions."

"My daddy always said that if you want to know something, you've got to ask. The only thing a person can do is give you the answer or tell you it's none of your business."

Skye gave up a small laugh but regretted it the second she did so. She wasn't ready for anyone to see all of her emotions, especially since she didn't know Jaylin at all. Jaylin walked around the bench and sat down next to Skye.

"So what are you going to do?"

"I came to L.A. to become an actress."

Jaylin looked at Skye and howled. "Oooh, girl, you might as well be homeless. Do you know how many people come to L.A. every day thinking they're going to be the next great actor to turn Tinseltown upside down only to end up waiting tables or working at a movie theater, rubbing two nickels together to make a dime while they wait to audition for the next gig? And that's after they've been on thirty, forty, or fifty auditions and haven't been called back for a second one. This isn't the place for weak people."

Skye sat up straight. "You don't even know me. I'm not weak by any stretch of the imagination."

"Your mother-in-law kicked you out of your own house and now you're here—many miles from where you started."

Jaylin spoke the truth, but Skye didn't want to hear it. "It's my story, and I'm going to make it no matter how long it takes. And for the last time, I walked out after I caught my slimy husband with his military hoe."

"Okay, okay, I've got it straight now. However, you didn't say where you were staying."

"I'll figure it out."

"You can stay with me until you get on your feet. I'm waiting for my brother to pick me up. Don't make me regret this."

"Do you live in South Central?"

Jaylin stared at Skye. "Why? Does it make a difference whether or not you're going to take me up on my offer? Sit there and be homeless. See if I care. For all I know, you may be running from the law." Jaylin stood up.

"No, no, I…I didn't mean anything by it. I'm from a hole-in-the wall called Junction City, Kansas. The only thing that place has going for it is a giant Walmart and Fort Riley Army Base."

"I've heard of Fort Riley. My father was stationed there years ago when he was in the Army."

"Really? My father was stationed there, also." Skye clammed up, and after a couple of seconds, she spoke again. "My father was killed in Afghanistan and my mother has mourned his death ever since. We fought a lot, but I miss her."

"Why don't you go back to Kansas?"

"I lived in Kansas all of my life and I want to experience something new. That's why I married Bryan…to get away from that awful place." Skye looked up at Jaylin. "It wasn't a marriage anyway. I didn't lose anything; I just left. On paper, we're still married."

"What a story. I've got you for now. Come on. I believe my brother has pulled into the parking lot. And for your information, I live in Inglewood. It had its heyday, but I still love living there. What if I told you I want to be an actress too?"

"You're lying," Skye said, all of sudden feeling giddy. "You're only saying that to make me feel better."

"No, it's the truth. I've made some inroads and maybe I can help you get some bit parts too. My portfolio is growing, one bit part at a time."

"Okay. So you're already an actress." Skye jumped up from the bench. "Thank you, Jaylin; I'll accept your offer."

"Call me Jaye."

"Okay, Jaye. Thank you for being my guardian angel."

CHAPTER 12

S kye didn't get a real sense of Los Angeles. It was late and Jaylin's brother, Bobby, took backstreets to where Jaylin lived. Skye was all set to see bright lights and a city bustling with people. She was disappointed, but there was always tomorrow. Bobby dropped them off and was on his way to a party.

Jaylin lived in an apartment that wasn't much different than the ones Skye saw in her own neck of the woods. Jaylin lived on the second floor that they had to access by stairs at either end of the building. A wrought-iron railing protected them from falling over.

"Well, here it is," Jaylin said, setting her bag down while she pulled her keys out of her purse. "It's not the top-of-the-line in apartment living, but it's home. I plan to move out soon. I work in an upscale beauty salon and I'm able to work in my acting gigs by setting my own time. When I get that one big gig, I'm getting out of here."

The door now open, Skye followed Jaylin into her apartment. For a small, two-bedroom apartment, Jaylin had it fixed up with the latest. A thirty-two-inch flat-screen television was mounted on the living room wall, and her off-white leather sectional, white Flokati rug, and glass coffee table with small trinkets and an *Essence* magazine sitting on top made the room come alive.

"This is nice," Skye said, looking all around.

"Thank you. Let me take your bags. You can sleep in the room that I call an office. I have a day bed in there along with my desktop computer and other stuff."

"If I didn't say it, I'm going to say it now. Thanks. I didn't know what I was going to do. I was a fool to up and leave, but my time with Bryan was over. I married him under false pretenses, and yes, I coerced him into marrying me, but somehow I led myself to believe that I could change Bryan."

Jaylin sat down on the sofa. "If he agreed to marry you, he must've felt something."

"For one lousy moment, I felt that Bryan might have had some feelings for me, but in the real, he got married to shut me up. I was so adamant about getting away from Kansas. He agreed to this farce of a marriage—for me. I had a military ID card so that I could have hospital and shopping privileges. He said female soldiers coerce their counterparts to marry them for all kinds of reasons."

"Well, it was the least he could do."

"But the worst part of it was when he begged me not to go to his commander and report his ass for having sex with that sorry bitch I found in my bed. In my bed, Jaye."

"That was low-down and dirty."

"When I caught them together, I understood at that moment how a domestic situation could become violent—no, deadly. I wanted to kill somebody, and I could've easily done it. His begging me not to tell pissed me off, but I was reminded that he'd done me a favor."

"So you didn't press charges? He deserved to be punished for being a sorry-ass, nigger hoe. He'd at least be unconscious by the time I'd finished with him."

Skye hunched up her shoulders and exhaled. "Yeah, I wanted him to pay, but while riding from Washington to L.A., I had a lot of time to think. I was wrong to put Bryan through all of that nonsense. My mother warned me and I didn't listen to her. I was mad at the world. I was close to my daddy, but he was gone forever. My sister married and left, and my brother went away to college. The walls were caving in on me, and I had to get away."

"Well, you're here now, and the first thing you need to do is get a job. What do you do well?"

Skye looked thoughtfully at Jaylin. "I'm not sure. I was a cashier for a few weeks when I lived with Bryan, but before that, I hadn't worked anywhere since I got out of high school, which was over two years ago."

Jaylin stood up and folded her arms over her stomach. "I want to be straight up with you, Skye. I don't mind helping you out, but you have to get a job. There are no freeloaders on this train. I worked hard for what you see here, and I'm working every day to move up in the world." Jaylin threw her hands up in the air. "Take a few days to get yourself situated. This is the weekend and I'll take you around and show you a little bit of L.A. But if I don't see any progress in a couple of weeks, you'll have to leave."

"That's fair."

"Okay, now that we have an understanding, let's get some rest. You ought to let me tighten your locks up in the morning. It appears you haven't seen the inside of a beauty shop in a while."

Skye began to laugh. "Girl, Bryan was tight with his money. He complained anytime I asked him for a little change."

"How long were you married?"

"A little over two months."

"It seems that you made the right decision to get away from him. From now on, you're going to stand on your own two feet and take charge of your life. You don't need anyone else to survive. I've got a honey, but I make my own bread and spend it how I want to. For now, I live by myself, and I prefer it that way. There is only one dictator in my life and that's me."

"You really have your head on straight."

"I've got to. I plan to be somebody in this world. And you have to know what you want, how to get it, and where you need to go to get what you want. That was a mouthful, but you get my drift. There are no free lunches."

"I like what you said. I'm tired now, but I can't wait to get some more of your wisdom in the morning."

"Okay. I'll get you a bath towel and a washcloth so you can freshen up. Glad to help."

CHAPTER 13

Refreshed from a good night's rest, Skye put on her clothes and looked out of the window. It was Saturday morning, and the street below was relatively quiet. Skye listened for any signs that Jaylin was up, but not hearing any movement, she stayed confined to the room.

Sitting down on the bed, Skye looked around the room. She spotted a picture she hadn't noticed the previous night. Skye rose and picked up the picture on a shelf that housed the monitor to Jaylin's desktop. It was a photo taken at a studio of what appeared to be a happy, loving family—Jaylin's, no doubt. Jaylin and her brother sat opposite each other on a white bench in front of the attractive couple who stood behind them. Skye thought of her mother.

Skye had been gone more than two months and still hadn't called her mother. The odd thing was that Nona had never attempted to call her, either. Putting the picture back down, Skye retrieved her purse and pulled out her cell. It was dead; she'd forgotten to charge the battery.

There was movement outside of her room. Skye stopped to listen and then heard her name.

"Skye, are you awake?"

Skye rushed for the door and opened it. She caught a glimpse of Jaylin as she moved past her door to the kitchen.

"Hey, Jaye."

Jaylin yawned and turned around to face Skye. "How did you sleep?"

"Like a baby."

"I'm going to make us some coffee. You do drink coffee."

"No, but I'll learn today."

"Good. I've got to go into the shop. Saturday is my busiest day. I'll tighten up your hair, and this afternoon, I'll take you around L.A. You need to buy a couple of outfits if you plan to walk the beat to your first Hollywood gig."

Skye's smile was broad, although she hadn't planned to spend any money on clothes. "I'm ready to conquer the world."

"It spins fast in L.A. You'll have to learn to weather the storm. Coffee is brewed. Get your cup. I'm going to jump into the shower, and I'll be with you in a few."

"Okay."

The world looked different through Skye's lens as daylight afforded her a better view of her new surroundings. Since entering Jaylin's apartment on last evening, she now followed her outside to the garage where Jaylin's 2006 blue RAV4 was housed. It was warm for nine in the morning. The low ceiling clouds suddenly evaporated into the atmosphere after being chased away by the sun that pushed its way through.

"I've got eight heads to do today," Jaylin began. "I'm going to do you first. Afterwards, you can either hang out with me or jump on a bus and do some sightseeing."

"I'll be quiet and hang with you today."

"Suit yourself."

They got in the car and drove down the street. The neighborhood was quiet. Palm trees seemed to spring up from the ground everywhere Skye looked. She smiled; she could get used to this city in a hurry.

CHAPTER 14

*T*he hair salon was bustling with activity when Jaylin and Skye arrived. Skye hadn't seen such décor in a salon. Chandeliers hung from the ceilings, glittering as if they were made of precious diamonds. Beautiful art deco in warm colors of gold, burnt orange, and yellow adorned the walls that gave the place a look of richness. Acrylic glass shelves and cases housed beauty products. Skye was in awe. If her mother wasn't doing her hair, she was in the kitchen of one of her mother's acquaintances.

In this salon, Skye felt like a princess. Today, she was going to look like one of Hollywood's A-list divas, and she couldn't wait. She owed it all to Jaylin.

"After looking at your hair, I'm taking it all down, give it a good wash and scrub, and then hook you up with some fresh twists. And you're going to owe me big when you get that first big check of yours. I don't do this for free."

"Thanks, Jaye," Skye said in an appreciative voice. "I don't know what to say."

"Say 'thank you.' I may even give you the Jaye discount."

"I'm down with that."

"Look to your left, Skye. There's the girl from *Glee*..." Jaylin snapped her fingers.

"Amber Riley. She won *Dancing with the Stars*."

"Yes, that's her. We have a lot of celebs that come through here and pay good money, too. At one o'clock, my client is a guy who is a fairly new agent breaking into the business. He got me a few bit parts on several television shows. If you're interested, be in the area and I'll introduce you."

"You'll do that for me, Jaye?"

"I need you to get up out of my apartment." Jaylin laughed. "But in the real, if he can help you get a gig, I won't be complaining."

"Jaye, for the first time in my life, things are looking up for me. I don't know if I believe in God, but if I did, I'd say that He's looking out for me. He put you in my path."

"Girl, it happened how it was supposed to happen. Now, let's get you under the water so I can make you over into the fierce and fabulous woman that you are and the Hollywood diva you're about to become."

"I'm ready."

Skye couldn't believe the transformation when she looked in the mirror. Her locks were fresh and tight and framed her face in a way that made her look as if she belonged in the City of Angels. She was stunning in every sense of the word.

"Put your tongue back in your mouth," Jaylin said, laughing at Skye's antics after seeing herself. "Now you're ready to meet the world and go on auditions."

"I do look fabulous, don't I?" Skye pulled on one of her braids and watched as the elasticity drew the hair back into place. "Delicious."

"Scoot up out of my seat. My next client is on her way back."

Skye watched Jaylin work her magic on client after client. The girl had a gift. Jaye's other gift was the gift of gab. She knew how to talk to her customers, changing her voice inflections or code, switching depending on what station in life the client happened to be. Skye wanted to be like her.

At one on the dot, a thin, dark-skinned, well-dressed brother with a short Afro, with designer shades covering his eyes, entered the salon. He walked with a purpose and headed straight to Jaylin's booth without stopping at the reception counter. His mannerisms said he was gay, and his body language screamed, *I am important and you better recognize.* And when he sat in the chair, Jaylin gave Skye the nod.

"What up, Jaye?" the man said in a cool, calm, and collected voice.

"You're the man with the plan."

"I am that indeed. As a matter of fact, I've got a bit of good news for you, my sister."

"What is it, Jacob?"

"There's going to be an audition Monday morning for an upcoming Ice Cube movie. It's for a leading lady, and you've got the right stuff. I've put your name out there, and if you bring your 'A' game, the part is within reach."

"You're not setting me up, are you?"

"The only thing I'm setting you up for is the real start of your career, girl, and the fabulous commission I'm about to make. Now give me a crisp line and fade so I can work some more magic."

"Thank you, Jacob. Before I do your hair, I have someone I want you to meet."

"They better get here in a hurry; I've got to be rolling out of here in ten minutes."

"She's sitting over there in that chair. She's a friend of mine who arrived in Los Angeles yesterday. She wants to be an actress."

"And so are the other million wannabes." Jacob looked down his nose at Skye, moving his shades down his nose a little to get a better look.

"Shhhh," Jaylin whispered, bringing her forefinger to her mouth. Jaylin motioned for Skye to come over.

Skye got up from her seat and walked to where Jaylin was conversing with the gentleman and stopped in front of him.

"Skye, I want you to meet Jacob Frost. He's my agent and the man responsible for me getting a jumpstart on my acting career."

Skye gave Jacob a half-assed smile and stretched out her hand. "Nice to meet you."

"The pleasure is all mine," Jacob said as he took the liberty to check Skye out further without shaking her hand. "So, you're an actress?"

"Yes," Skye said boldly, dropping her hand to her side. Meeting Jacob made her think about Bryan and how she'd seduced him into marrying her—the one difference was that Bryan was straight and Mr. Frost had some curves in his persona.

"So," Jacob said thoughtfully, still checking Skye out. "Do you come with credentials? What movies have you starred in to your credit?"

"Actually, none," Skye said with an air of confidence. "I participated in school plays and was congratulated on my exceptional talent."

"Oh, were you now," Jacob said with a sneer, his eyebrows arching for effect. "And how long ago was that, may I ask?"

"A few years ago."

"Look…umm…"

"Skye…Skye Culbertson." Skye extended her hand again. This time Jacob shook it.

"Skye, I'm looking for serious talent. You don't even have a portfolio."

"You've got to start somewhere."

"That I do agree. However, you stepped to me as if you had it going on. I half expected you to mention that your credentials included a few B-class movies, that I could accept, but the only thing you've done is high school stuff. And your arrogance…check it at the front door, shugar."

"Let me stop you right there," Skye said, holding out her hand. "Yes, I'm a little forward, but you've mistaken my confidence for arrogance. I'm not a fraud; I can truly act. I told the truth. I don't come with credits to my name, but that doesn't mean I can't act."

Jacob looked at Skye, turning his head slightly. "Why don't you come to the audition with Jaye on Monday? She has the details. Then we'll see if you really have the goods. In the meantime, get a portfolio."

Skye clasped her hands together and attempted to hide the smile that tried to break bad across her face. She pushed it downward and spoke. "I won't disappoint you, Mr. Frost."

"You better not. My reputation is on the line."

Skye let the smile out. "You don't have to worry about my reputation except that it'll be a new name in Hollywood."

"Let's hope so. Remember to leave your arrogance at the door."

"Yes," Skye said. She winked at Jaylin and couldn't wait for Monday to come.

CHAPTER 15

*T*he auditions went well. Both Jaylin and Skye received a second casting call. While Skye didn't get the lead role, she was cast as a secondary character in the movie. Skye was grateful, even though her paycheck would be nothing to brag about. It was a start.

Skye studied her script. Shooting was to begin in two days. The excitement was too much to keep bottled up. Reciting her lines over and over, she was interrupted by the chime of her cell phone. At first, Skye was afraid to look at the phone. She recognized the ringtone the minute she heard it.

Three weeks had gone by since she had left the state of Washington. Skye hadn't expected to hear Bryan's voice again. She hurriedly hit the TALK button before the ringing stopped.

"Hello."

"Skye, this is Bryan."

"Yeah, I recognized your ringtone."

"How are you doing? Your mother has been calling and is at the end of her rope. Why haven't you called her?"

"I'm fine; I'm glad you cared enough to check up on me."

"Call it what you want. Where are you?"

"I'm in Los Angeles. I'm going to be in the movies."

"Good for you. The one thing I can say is that you're a good actress."

"I'll take that as a compliment."

"Take it any way you like. Look, I'm having our marriage annulled. This will revoke all your privileges as a military spouse to include commissary and medical."

"Whatever. I wasn't using it anyway."

"Now that you're going to be an actress, you'll need to get your own phone for your call backs. I'm cancelling you off of my plan. I'll give you a few days to set it up, but don't wait too long. And please call your mother."

"Do you hate me that much, Bryan?"

"You never loved or cared about me, Skye. You're a user, and you've used me for the last time. You don't have space in that phony heart of yours for no one but yourself. I pity the fool that falls in the next trap you set."

"I trusted you, Bryan. I truly thought our marriage could work… I wanted it to. But I have no room in my life for an adulterous husband, especially one who hasn't taken any responsibility for his actions. I spared you from losing your military career; I owed you that much, but I will never forget how you treated me. So that you're clear on my position, I don't need a man to make my way in this world. I can do it all by myself."

"I'm glad you can. We're done. Please call your mother. You owe her that much."

"Thanks for the phone call. Glad you were concerned. I've got to go so I can finish studying my script for my movie shoot in a couple of days."

"Do what you do best. Bye." The line was dead.

The phone slipped from Skye's hand. There was no way to anticipate how Bryan's call would affect her. She picked up the script but laid it aside, her mood quickly changing from happy to sour. There was nothing to do but show Bryan what she was made of and that she was somebody. She, Skye Culbertson, was going to become an icon whose name would drip from the lips of legends and media giants all across the globe to the little people, including Bryan and his ratchet momma.

Skye picked the phone up from the floor and dialed. It rang and her nerves were on edge.

"Hello," said the voice at the other end.

"Mother, it's me, Skye."

"Skye, my baby, thank the Lord you're all right. You don't know how long I've waited to hear your voice."

"I'm sorry, Mother. You could've called me."

"Child, you had me worried. You were so upset with me, but that wasn't a reason not to call and let me know that you and Bryan made it to your destination okay. Bryan said something about you all not being together. Is that true?"

"Mother, please calm down. I'm fine; I'm living in Los Angeles."

"Los Angeles? Doing what? Why didn't you come home?"

"I'm an actress. I got a part in a movie and I'm going to be on the silver screen."

There was momentary silence.

"Okay, I wish you well. I hope you'll come home someday to see how your old mother is doing."

"Mother, don't be so dramatic. Why can't you be happy for me? Look, I've got to go. I'll call you soon."

"All right, call when you can. Bye." And the line was dead.

The months flew by and Skye was building her resume. She got one bit part after another and hoped it would one day lead to a bigger role and perhaps a lead. She was able to save enough money to move out on her own, in a place that was small but comfortable.

Today was beautiful and Skye took the script she was presently reading and headed out to get something to eat. A small recurring role on a sitcom helped pay the rent and the car note for a used 2010 Toyota Prius she recently purchased.

Skye needed a pick-me-up. She drove to Roscoe's House of Chicken 'n Waffles on West Pico Street and took a table next to a window that looked out onto one of L.A.'s busy streets. The waitress took her order and she sipped on a cup of coffee while perusing the script.

A sudden shadow loomed over her and she looked up into the face of a tall, mocha-colored brother. He had a thin moustache that sat neatly above his lip. A well-lined, close-cropped haircut framed his face. At a glance, he reminded Skye of the actor Leon that she'd had the pleasure of meeting during a brief encounter at a movie shoot. The gentleman was dressed in a crisp pair of Calvin Klein jeans that were creased so well that it looked as if they could cut somebody; a long-sleeved, white, starched dress shirt; and a black linen jacket. If Skye were to guess, the gentleman looked to be in his middle-to-late thirties. And he was handsome. But when he lowered his head to get her attention, not that he already hadn't, it was his cologne that seduced Skye.

"Are you eating alone or should I ask if this seat is free?" The gentleman's smile was inviting.

"One Oscar," the waitress said, placing a plate of three wings, grits, egg, and a fluffy biscuit on the table in front of Skye.

"Well…yes, it's free, although I was studying."

The gentleman sat, not waiting for an official welcome. "What are you studying?"

"A script for a part I recently landed."

"So, you're an actress."

"Yes. I have a small recurring role in a television sitcom and had a part in one of Ice Cube's movies."

The gentleman cocked his head and gave Skye a true once-over. "This may be your lucky day. I've got some connections in Hollywood, and I can hook you up with some major producers—the Tyler Perry/John Singleton type."

"I'm in the process of getting representation from Coast to Coast Talent Group."

"So what you're telling me is that you don't have representation and I, out of the kindness of my heart, presented you with the key to the Oscars."

Skye eyeballed the good-looking gentleman who sat in front of her and was now all ears. She shoved the material she'd been reading back into the portfolio and gave the gentleman her undivided attention. "I'm interested."

The gentleman smiled. "Good. You're a beautiful young woman. In fact, I spotted you first thing when I walked in. I would love to be your manager. By the way, my name is Rico." He extended a hand to Skye. "And you are?"

CHAPTER 16

Rico wined and dined Skye at some of the best restaurants in the city. Flashing his cash as if it grew on trees, Rico generously spared no expense purchasing a new wardrobe for Skye from J. Crew—her store of choice, a cream-colored satchel from Michael Kors, and a wicked suit from Chanel, while they zigzagged through the shops at The Grove and on Rodeo Drive, stopping short of purchasing a beautiful chocolate-diamond ring at Tiffany and Co. Rico introduced her to the *real* club scene in Los Angeles, as well as the ever popular strip joints that dotted the city. Skye loved being chauffeured around in the latest luxury two-door C350 Mercedes-Benz Coupe one day and on another, an IS 250 F Sport Lexus. She wasn't sure what Rico might show up in next.

True to his word, Rico introduced Skye to some prominent people in the industry. Skye was amazed at how connected Rico was in the business. For all of her teenaged years, Skye was enthralled at all of the black actors and actresses there were, especially, with a record number of movies being produced by black directors with black actors such as *Precious* and *The Butler*. Tonight, Rico was taking her to the movie premiere for *The Best Man, Holiday* at Grauman's Chinese Theatre, and she had to call Jaye to get help in purchasing the right dress for the event.

Jaye was gaining notoriety of her own with a big part in an upcoming movie that also featured some big names. Skye picked up her cell phone and called Jaye.

"Hey, Skye, I heard you hit pay dirt. You know Jacob is pissed the hell off about you abandoning him."

"He'll get over it. What are you up to?"

"I'm excited about this new movie role. I'll be going on location soon."

"Location? Where?"

"Brazil. The movie has an exotic backdrop. It'll be my first trip out of the country. I had to get a passport and everything. It looks like I'm on my way, Skye."

"I'm happy for you, Jaye. Right now, I need your help. I'm going to the premiere of Morris Chestnut's new movie."

"For real? Girl, I'm not mad at you, although you could've hooked up a sister who hooked you up when you first arrived on a Greyhound bus." The girls laughed.

"Jaye, I would if I could. I'm trying to play my cards right—trying not to act needy by begging for more stuff than I've already been given. But you'll be with me in spirit."

"So what is it you want of me?"

"I need your expertise. I have to find a fabulous dress for the premiere. I can't do it without you."

"Pick me up and let's hit Rodeo Drive."

"Girl, I don't have Rodeo Drive money…yet."

"That new boyfriend of yours does. However, since you want to play cheap, I'll spring for your outfit and you can pay me back."

"I already owe you."

"You're my girl, although I'm not sure what you're saving your money for."

"Love you, Jaye." Then there was silence.

"What's wrong, Skye? Your excitement evaporated."

"Wow."

"What?"

"I'm so selfish, Jaye. For the first time, I thought about my sister."

"I didn't know you had a sister."

"I have a brother, too. Their names are Whitney and Jermaine."

"Damn, Skye. How long have I known you?"

"It's going on a year."

"I believe in secrets but damn. Did they do something to you? Are they the reason you left home and don't want to return?"

"No," Skye said, almost in a whisper. "I did feel abandoned, though. After my father was killed in Afghanistan, my sister got married and left with her new husband, and my brother went away to college, although the college is in the next town over from where we lived."

"What about your mom?"

"I've talked to her once since I've been here. She still hasn't gotten over my daddy's death. She was a lump of grief that I couldn't stand to be around. I loved my father. I was his favorite, but I do understand how my mother felt—abandoned. I didn't want to admit it at the time."

"Ahh, Skye, do you want to postpone the shopping trip?"

All of sudden, Skye snapped back to herself. "No, no, no, I need to get a dress. I'll be there to pick you up in a few."

"Okay. I'll be ready." The line was dead.

Skye went to her bedroom and picked up her keys and purse off the nightstand. She sat on the edge of the bed and thought about her family. She missed them. Tears began to trickle down her cheeks, but before the tears had an opportunity to assault her face, she stood up and wiped them away with her hand. She grabbed her purse and keys and headed outside. Before the sun went down, she was going to call Whitney.

CHAPTER 17

"You're going to look fabulous at the premiere in this black dress by Julie Brown, Skye. It fits your body perfectly."

"I think I'm hot in it, too. I feel better that we went to one of your boutiques where you had a hook-up. My insides want to throw up when I think about those Rodeo Drive prices."

"When you really start rolling in the dough, you won't give it another thought. It looks like this new boyfriend of yours has got your best interest at heart."

"We've been going out for about a month. We're not exclusive, and believe it or not, we haven't done the do."

"What do you mean you haven't given up the goods? A man like that always wants payback in return. There's nothing free in this town."

"I was surprised, Jaye, that he didn't want to hop in bed with me after our initial meeting and buying me new clothes in the exclusive shops in Beverly Hills and elsewhere. Believe me; I was ready to give him all of it."

"Damn, Skye, there's no need to sell your soul when you don't have to."

"Girl, he's introduced me to some of the big movers and shakers in this industry—black and white. Rico seems to have this elite social card that gets him into every place he goes. If it means the difference between becoming the next Halle Berry or an unknown, I'll sell my soul. Isn't that the Hollywood way?"

"Listen to yourself. You're better than that. You have intellect… in fact; you're ahead of your time in some of your thinking. But this bull crap you're spitting out of your mouth isn't becoming. Now let's pay for this dress and get you made up for your big date. I'm curious about your new man. What's his name again?"

"Rico."

"Does he have a last name?"

"Truth of the matter, I've never asked him."

"Skye, I gave you credit for being an intellectual, but I'm conflicted and may have to reverse my thinking. I'm not getting you lately. You can't trust everybody who has a pretty face and a nice body, especially, if he hasn't asked you to give up anything yet. I'm going to ask Jacob if he's heard of anybody in the business that goes by the name Rico."

"I trusted you when I first met you."

"You didn't have a choice. You were a broken-down, homeless runaway, albeit a runaway from your husband. You were glad for my handout. In fact, you didn't know if I was a hustler trying to take your last dime. You came with me like a kitten to milk." The girls laughed.

"Was I that bad, Jaye?"

"Hell yeah, you were. Desperate was written in all caps across your face."

"I was desperate. I took one look at that Greyhound station and gagged, wondering what in the hell I'd gotten myself into. But I hear you. We expect people to take advantage of vulnerable people, and when they don't take advantage, they're still suspect."

"My mother told me if it's too good to be true, it probably is. How did you meet Rico?"

"I was at Roscoe's minding my own business when he asked to sit down. Nothing suspect about that."

"True, but if I had been a casual observer, I'm sure I would've seen something different."

"Well, you weren't even there so stop trippin' and trying to conjure up some kind of theory that's so far in left field. Let me get this dress and get out of here. You're raining on my good feeling."

"Sorry, friend, I didn't mean to be a Debbie Downer. The dress is my treat and I'll throw in a free makeup makeover."

Skye smiled. "You know how to bring a friend out of a funk. Thanks for being here."

"No problem."

Skye dazzled in her new black dress. A pair of black Giuseppe Zanottis, her first expensive shoe purchase, adorned her feet. Looking into her bathroom mirror, she smiled at the wonderful makeup job Jaye had done on her face. She patted her hair and was pleased at the sight that stared back.

She jerked away at the sound of her cell phone. The ringtone indicated Rico was calling.

"Hey, are you ready? I'm downstairs."

"Yes, I'm coming right out."

Skye clicked the OFF button. She picked up her clutch bag that she'd borrowed from Jaye and headed downstairs. At first, she was leery about letting Rico know where she lived—and in a small apartment off the beaten path—but it was what she could afford. From the moment she met him, she didn't hide; in fact, she had no reason to hide her present station in life. She was a rising star and her goal was to move far beyond where she initially aspired to go as an actress.

Rico stepped out of the off-white Maserati and met her as she came down the stairs. Skye's eyes lit up when she saw what they would be riding in for the evening. *Rico must be drowning in cash*, Skye thought, although she was surprised that he wasn't wearing a tux. But he looked fine in his slate-gray Armani suit. He pecked her on the cheek, and held the door open..

Rico held Skye's hand longer than he planned. "You're the finest woman on the planet, Skye Culbertson. You are rocking this dress. I'm going to have to watch you the whole evening. For sure, the vultures will be circling."

Skye smiled. "I wanted to look my best."

"The best eye candy I've seen in a long time. Let's go." Rico helped her into the car.

Light jazz streamed inside. Skye took occasional glances at Rico as he drove through the streets of L.A. He seemed to be a little preoccupied.

"It's a beautiful night. I'm excited about the movie premiere."

"I am, too. We're going to get a little bite to eat at one of my favorite restaurants on Sunset Boulevard—Gladstones. Maybe a light salad and a glass of wine will keep us until after the premiere."

"Sure, I'd like that."

They rode the rest of the way without uttering a word. Upon arrival at Gladstones, the Maserati was valet parked and the couple went inside. Skye's jaw dropped when she saw the large tank of prime lobsters, begging to be the next victim. A table near a window awaited them.

There was small talk and occasional smiles. They ordered garden salads with raspberry vinaigrette. There was definitely something different about Rico tonight that Skye couldn't put her finger on. She fought against pushing for an answer as her ultimate goal was to get a role that was going to make her an icon in Hollywood. And as soon as she rested the thought, Rico surprised her and almost knocked her out of her shoes.

"Skye, I like you a lot...well, more than a lot. I've watched you for the past month and I like what I see and what I feel when I'm with you. Being 'only friends' doesn't adequately define our relationship. You will be a star, but right now I'd like for you to be my woman."

Skye's mouth flew open. Her green eyes grew large as she stared back at Rico.

"I don't even know your last name," she uttered. "I had no idea you even felt that way about me."

"My name is Rico Tillman and I've fallen in love with you. In fact, I want you to move out of that place you call an apartment and move into one of my upscale condos in Redondo Beach."

Skye's hands flew to her chest. "I...I couldn't...can't afford..."

"Hush. No, say yes." Rico stood and reached over and placed his hands on either side of her face. Without saying a word, he brought her face close to his and planted a tender kiss on her lips. He moved away and sat back down. "Say yes. I want you."

The waiter set a bottle of Pinot Grigio on the table followed by two wineglasses. He poured and promised to be back with their salads shortly.

"So what will it be? You still haven't given me an answer."

Skye picked up her glass of wine and held it out to Rico. Her smile was as wide as the Mississippi River. "Yes," she said as other patrons began to scream and bang on the window.

Skye and Rico looked in the direction the people were barking. Right in front of them, in broad daylight and in living color, a carjacking was taking place. Traffic on the street was packed and no one noticed the woman who was struggling not to be overtaken by what appeared to be an armed gunman who'd finally convinced the woman to get in the car. And then they drove off.

"Oh my God," Skye exclaimed. "Did you see that?"

Rico seemed visibly shaken. "Yes, I did. I hope she'll be all right."

"I got the license plate of the car," someone announced.

"I have the make and model of the car," another added. "It was a navy-blue, late-model Lexus sports coupe."

"Let's get out of here," Rico said suddenly. "If we get caught up in here when the police arrive, we won't make it to the premiere in time." Skye frowned. "I want to showcase my woman tonight. You'll be the prettiest woman there."

Skye offered a smile. "Okay," she whispered. "My heart goes out to that woman. I hope the police find her...alive. Carjackings don't always end well."

"I'm sure they'll find them." Rico summoned for the waiter and explained their need to move on without their salads. They left the restaurant and as soon as the valet brought the car around, they sped off into the night.

CHAPTER 18

The ride to Grauman's Chinese Theatre in Hollywood was met in silence. Rico was completely agitated for some reason. Skye had looked forward to the premiere, but the incident in front of the restaurant had rattled her nerves.

They arrived at the theater and Rico pulled to the curb. A dark, handsome gentleman, dressed in all black with black shades hiding his eyes, reached for the door handle and ushered Skye to the sidewalk. She stood to the side while Rico talked on his cell phone, obviously upset with whomever he was talking to.

Three, four, five minutes passed and Rico was still on the phone. Skye stood off to the side not wanting to invade Rico's privacy. It looked as if the night she'd envisioned wasn't going to go as planned, as the muscles in Rico's face flexed and released until he finally ended the call. He looked up and saw the concerned look on Skye's face and then briefly turned away. She said nothing when he finally approached her side.

Rico sighed. "Let's go in," he said without any explanation.

While they weren't the guests of honor, they walked down the red carpet. Many in the crowd recognized Skye from her role in *Happy but Free* and her secondary role in an Ice Cube movie. She waved as if she owned the crowd who came to see the stars in all their glory.

They sat five rows from the front. Skye couldn't stop gazing at

Sanaa Lathan, Morris Chestnut, Taye Diggs, Monica Calhoun, Nia Long, and of course, Terrence Howard. She was in love with this bad boy.

As the movie rolled, Rico was constantly texting. The light from the phone was annoying each time he pulled it out to respond to the constant barrage of text messages, but Skye refused to say anything. She enjoyed the movie regardless of Rico's distractions, and there was a thunderous round of applause when the film concluded. *It was better than the first movie,* The Best Man, Skye thought.

As she stood up and applauded with the rest of the group and the premiere now over, she was suddenly approached by the director, Malcolm D. Lee. Rico was on the phone.

Malcolm Lee held out his hand. "Aren't you Skye Culbertson?"

Skye was giddy. The director of this wonderful movie was standing in front of her inquiring her identity. "Yes, I am, Mr. Lee. The movie is wonderful and it's going to do great at the box office."

"Thank you; I have a good feeling about it myself. You're a rising talent. I've seen your performance in *Happy but Free.*"

"You're kidding."

"No, I'm not, and you're damn good at what you do."

"Thank you. I'm trying to build my portfolio."

"Why don't you have your manager call me? I think I can help you get to the next level. I'm working on another project, and you might have a good chance to be a part of it."

Skye crossed her heart with her hands. "Thank you, thank you. In fact, my manager is right here." Skye pointed to where Rico was carrying on a conversation.

"What's his name? I don't recognize him."

"Rico Tillman."

Malcolm gave Rico a sideways glance but shook his head. "I don't recognize his name and I know most everyone in the business that's African American." Malcolm pulled out his card from an inside pocket of his jacket. He gave Skye a parting smile. "Have him call me."

"I will. Thanks again."

Skye wasn't sure what had occupied Rico's attention, but she was anxious to share her good news. Nothing that had transpired earlier in the evening could put a damper on how she felt. And then Terrence Howard waved at her; Skye was in seventh heaven.

Rico finally rose from his seat. He noticed that he was still sitting when everyone else was vacating the premises. He looked up at Skye who stood idly by, waiting for him to escort her out of the theater.

"Look, Skye, I'm sorry about tonight. It was business—an emergency. I promise to give you my full attention beginning now."

Skye smiled. "Okay."

"Did I see you talking with Malcolm Lee?"

"Yes, he recognized me from the TV sitcom I'm on."

"Damn, that's dope. Did he say anything about giving you a part on an upcoming movie?"

Skye flicked his card in Rico's direction. "He said to have my manager call him."

"Shut the hell up. You're on your way, girl."

Skye kept to herself the fact that Mr. Lee didn't have any idea who Rico was or that he'd never heard of him. Rico pocketed the business card, but Skye had already committed his number to memory.

CHAPTER 19

*T*he days and months flew by. Skye now lived in one of Rico's luxurious condos in Redondo Beach, although it was farther from Los Angeles than she liked. She kept her apartment in Los Angeles so that on mornings when she had an early morning casting call on the set of the sitcom, she could get there with ease. Having the Prius gave a new meaning to gas efficiency.

She wasn't sure what intervention Rico may have had with her newfound success, but Malcolm Lee came through. In a couple of weeks, she would begin shooting as one of the supporting cast members in his upcoming movie that presently had only a working title. Who cared? She was realizing her worth and succeeding at the one thing she really aspired to do.

It was a shame that she wouldn't have family support. She never called her sister and she hadn't spoken to her mother since the one time she'd called her after arriving in Los Angeles. Almost two years had passed since she'd left Junction City, Kansas.

Her living arrangements were wonderful but puzzling. Although she was Rico's woman, they didn't live together. He was private about many aspects of his life, but he wined, dined and made love to her the moment she moved into the condo, as if there was no one else left on earth.

As her manager, Rico set up and controlled her bank accounts—to keep an eye on things in the wake of so many accountants and managers taking advantage of celebrity incomes, or so he'd said. He only had Skye's best interest at heart and her earnings had moved from five figures to six.

There wasn't a casting call today, and tonight Skye promised to fix Rico a wonderful meal that included rotisserie chicken, garlic mashed potatoes, asparagus, a Mediterranean salad with mixed salad leaves, blue cheese, pecans, mandarin oranges, bits of red onion and a Mediterranean sauce. The one thing she'd learned was that Rico didn't eat red meat or pork. It was fish or fowl.

Skye looked at the clock. It was close to six-thirty. Rico was punctual and would be there any minute. She'd already taken her bath and soaked her skin in her favorite body lotion and sprayed herself with a mist of her favorite perfume, Pleasures Delight by Estee Lauder. It made her feel so sensual.

Like clockwork and on the dot, Rico let himself in. He took off his jacket and gave Skye an appreciative smile.

"It smells good in here." He sniffed. "Smells like you've got my favorites on the menu."

"That I do." Skye walked around the black and brown granite countertop and into Rico's awaiting arms. They kissed passionately—their tongues searching and their lips keeping it all together.

"I've got something for you."

Skye pulled back as Rico went to his jacket and pulled out a pretty blue box from Tiffany and Co. "For me?" She took the box without waiting for Rico to respond. Inside was a beautiful sterling silver cuff bracelet.

"Look at the inside."

Skye held the bracelet at an angle. There was an inscription which read, *My Hollywood Skye*. Rico's initials weren't inscribed. "It's beautiful. You shouldn't have done it."

"You deserve it. You're making your way, baby. I'm calling you Hollywood Skye. Watch, they'll have a street named after you."

Skye hit Rico on his shoulder with the soft side of her fist. Droplets of water fell from her eyes. She was overcome at the gift she'd been given. "I love you, Rico. I've never been given a gift like this before."

"Baby, there will be many more."

"Have you thought about us living together? It's time that we become one. I want to be with you all the time…not only when the moment presents itself. It's not that I don't appreciate living in this beautiful condo, but sometimes it gets lonely."

Rico flinched but recovered quickly. "It will be soon; I promise. I use my home for my operations, and I don't want to mix business with pleasure."

"You make me wonder if you don't have a family that you're hiding out. I really don't know that much about you."

"Okay, let's not get into a discussion about my life. I don't want to ruin the mood. In time, I'll share my life story with you. It's not so pleasant and I'm not ready to relive it out loud."

"All right, although I'm not sure what that has to do with us living together. But I'll drop it. I've made all your favorites."

Rico was quiet and sauntered down the hall to the bathroom. After closing the door behind him, he balled up his fist and went to strike the wall. He pulled back before he did any damage. He turned the water on in the sink and let it run for a second, finally slipping his hands under it and splashing his face. He towel-dried his face and resurfaced.

"Wow, everything looks delicious." He looked around. "You look so at home here."

The interior of the house was completely white. From the furniture in the living area, the bedrooms, to the dining room area, white was the color. Rico had it furnished for Skye by an interior decorator friend he'd met during his early years as a two-bit hustler, hustling leftover carpet that he confiscated from the carpet company where he worked, often offering to lay it down for a nominal fee. He became known as the carpet man and his blacklist grew into a clientele that included some famous names. After being discovered by the owner of the carpet company that he was keeping a lot of their residual, which sometimes amounted to a large footage of carpet, he was immediately released. This was a minor setback and Rico resolved to become something more.

Having been to more homes than he could count during his days of laying carpet, Rico realized real estate was the way to go. He studied, passed the exams, and became a licensed broker. And he made lots of money.

"The house is cozy. I'm not sure that I would've decorated it in all white, but I'm fitting into it well. Now sit down so we can eat."

They ate and drank, oblivious to all else around. They made small talk and Skye pushed the earlier conversation to the back of her mind. She'd put on her bracelet and gazed at it every five minutes, smiling at how thoughtful Rico had been. *He loved her,* she thought.

"That was delicious, Skye. What's for dessert?"

"You mean besides me?"

"Girl, that's already on the dish. I'm going to lap you up like butterscotch sauce."

"We can skip the lemon pound cake I made especially for you."

"No, girl. I love your lemon pound cake. Is that your mother's recipe?"

Skye wiped the side of her face and looked straight at Rico.

"Did I say something wrong?"

"No…well, you reminded me of what a selfish daughter I've been. I've spoken to my mother once in two years. Can you believe that I had the nerve to make my mother's cake but haven't had the decency to pick up the phone and call her? And here I am living the life that I so wanted for myself, not giving a thought to how my mother is doing or if she needs anything."

"It sounds to me that you need to stop right now and call her."

"You're right, but I'd like to do so during my private time. I'll call her."

"If you say so. Now let me have a piece of pound cake so I can love up on you like I'm getting ready to do to that cake."

"One piece coming up."

CHAPTER 20

*T*heir lovemaking reached new heights unimaginable only months ago. They were so into each other that the lines were blurred between lust and love. Najee's "Anticipation" played softly in the background.

Rico lathered Skye's body with kisses from head to toe, his mouth a suction cup for all in its path. He teased her nipples between his tantalizing lips; she begged for more until she couldn't endure any longer. He explored the sensual part of her—her crown jewels that welcomed him openly—until her excitement became his excitement.

Skye obliged him, smothering his maleness with her experienced hands. Unable to resist the stimulation of her erotic hands, Rico quickly pulled a raincoat over his erect manhood and gave Skye the ride of her life.

Sweat poured from their bodies as they lay consumed from the fire that was still smoldering. Heavy breathing and Najee's "Trip to the Moon" was all that could be heard in an otherwise silent condo.

"You were so good," Rico said, still breathing hard as he opened his eyes, searching Skye's fluttering ones.

Eyes now open, Skye smiled broadly at Rico. "Divine."

"Baby, I need you to do something for me."

"Anything for you, baby. Right now, I'm ready to do this all again."

"We will."

Skye drew a circle around one of Rico's nipples with her finger. "What do you want me to do?"

"Tomorrow, I need you to drive my Mercedes to a customer's business address and park it in the parking garage next door."

"Sure, no problem. What time? I'm on set for most of the morning."

"What time will you break for lunch?"

"Not sure. I more than likely will be finished with my shoot by three. How will I get the car?"

"It's parked in the garage. Drive it to work. When you get off, drive it to the address I'm going to leave with you."

Skye raised her head, using her arm as a brace. She seemed puzzled. "How will you get home? You've never spent the night."

"I'm going to take your car tonight."

"I'm confused. So why am I taking the Mercedes and leaving it?"

"I've sold it, and I promised to get it to the buyer tomorrow. The problem is that I won't be able to get away at all, and I need this big favor."

"Okay, but how will I get home?"

Rico sighed. "If you don't mind, catch a cab to your apartment and I'll bring your car to you."

Skye absorbed all that Rico said but was not satisfied with the itinerary he set before her. Slowly rising up, Rico gently grabbed her shoulder.

"Baby, let me make love to you again. I want to make you cum like it was your last day on earth."

"I'm not sure I'm ready for the experience."

"You said only a moment ago that you were ready for round two. I only want to please and give you that satisfaction."

"Rico," Skye whispered, searching his eyes. "Do you really love me?"

"I'm offended."

"I wasn't trying to offend you. I feel some kind of way and I don't like it."

"Lie down," Rico whispered in her ear. "Lie down and let daddy take you to the moon."

Skye obliged, although her heart wasn't completely in it. She lay back on the bed and let Rico take complete control, while she did her best to re-create the moment before that took them to ecstasy.

CHAPTER 21

*T*otally rested and ready to plunge into character, Skye drove to the Warner Bros. studio to begin her day on the set of *Happy but Free*. Still baffled by Rico's round-the-way explanation about driving one of his prized cars, she chose to put it aside for now. She smiled while gripping the wheel of the Mercedes that rolled down the 405 like it was on a cloud. It didn't hurt that the smooth jazz flowing from the Sirius XM Satellite Radio mellowed her all the way out.

Skye's morning went smoothly. If all the takes went as well as they had gone earlier, she'd be out of the studio a little before three. She and the cast had become a family of sorts, and she looked forward to their daily pow-wows.

Her shoots done for the day, Skye left her trailer and headed for the car. Once inside, she pulled the handwritten address out of her purse that Rico had given her to make the delivery. She placed the information in the GPS and drove off the studio lot.

Although it was another sunny and rather hot day in L.A., Skye opted to keep the sunroof closed. She turned on the air conditioner, waved to the attendant as she passed him upon exiting the lot, and turned south as the navigator instructed. She checked her phone for a call from Rico but decided to call him instead.

The phone rang once. "I'm on my way."

"Good," Rico said. The line was dead.

Skye looked at the phone and was disgusted. "He must think I'm some damn slave. I could've gotten a warmer reception than that," she said out loud. "No 'thank you' or anything."

Fuming, Skye continued to drive. A couple of times she looked in the rearview mirror and noticed that the same black car had been following her almost since she'd left the studio. If it weren't for the fact that she had no idea where she was going and was at the mercy of the GPS navigator, she might have taken a side street to be sure.

She drove on. All of a sudden the car that had been a couple of cars behind earlier made a move. When she looked again, it was right behind her. She was on the edge of Hollywood and only two-point-five miles from her destination, according to the nav. The car behind was kissing her bumper, and before she could speed up or move over, blue flashing lights appeared out of nowhere.

Skye took a right at the next intersection and pulled over at the first available spot. Before she was able to get the window down, two officers were at her side with weapons drawn, asking her to get out of the car.

Surprise and alarm registered on Skye's face. "Don't you want to see my driver's license? What did I do?"

"Get your license, slowly," the first officer said, still holding the gun steady.

Skye looked down the barrel of the gun and slowly went into her purse.

"Don't try anything," the second officer said, playing the tough cop.

"Here's my license." Skye passed it through the window.

"Now get out of the car, slowly," the first officer said again, taking control of the action. The second officer went back to the patrol car and got on the radio.

Skye stepped out. "What did I do, officer? I wasn't speeding."

"Shut up and put your hands on the car. Where is the registration?"

"I guess it's in the car. The car belongs to my boyfriend. I was dropping it off for him."

"Where were you dropping the car?"

"At an address he gave me. It's on the GPS. What's this all about?"

"You're in a stolen vehicle, ma'am."

"It couldn't be. I can call my boyfriend. He'll tell you that this is his car."

The second officer stepped out of the patrol car and headed back in their direction. As soon as he reached the car, he nodded to the first officer. Within five to seven minutes, sirens rang out and four cruisers joined the group.

"Keep your hands up, ma'am. I'm going to read you your Miranda rights. You do know what that means."

"Yes, but I haven't done anything wrong. Let me call my boyfriend."

"Oh, you'll get a chance to call him down at the station."

Skye listened as the police officer garbled a bunch of words together, making her aware of her rights as a United States citizen. The last thing she heard was something about *if you can't afford an attorney* and blanked out the rest when she felt and heard the metal cuffs being placed around her wrists snap in place.

Anger replaced surprise. The anger wasn't so much for the police as it was for Rico. Her mind kept slipping back to the previous evening and how he'd so subtly slipped the task of driving the Mercedes upon her. He was different, uttering things to her about love in a way he hadn't before. But now that she was riding in the back of a police cruiser separated by a metal partition, her concern and uneasiness about why Rico wanted her to drive the Mercedes was beginning to make some sense.

Skye rode along in silence, ignoring the chatter of the two arresting officers. Once at the police station, she was ushered into an interrogation room where a number of officers and federal agents had assembled. She was made to sit in a chair that sat under a four-by-two table.

After the group decided who would do the interrogating and the others departed the room, Skye looked at the two detectives—one white, the other black. "I want to make my one phone call."

The two detectives looked at each other and nodded their approval.

"I need my phone."

"Sure," the black detective said, as he went to the door and retrieved it from someone who brought it to the room.

Skye took the phone from the detective and then looked down at the phone without saying a word. She put the phone on the table, pulled up the phone icon, and selected the number for Rico. "My boyfriend will tell you that I was doing him a favor." She put it on speaker.

The detectives gave her a half smile.

The phone rang. And then the operator's voice belted out a message. "The number you have dialed is no longer in service."

"What?" Skye picked up the phone and screamed. "No, this can't be."

"Miss, you need to calm down. Is there someone else you'd like to call?"

Skye looked at the smug black detective with the big ears and round, out-of-date glasses. "No."

"I'm Detective Simmons," the black detective said.

"And I'm Detective Roper," the white detective said. "Ms. Culbertson, we need for you to tell us everything you know."

"The sad thing is," Skye began, "I don't know a damn thing. I'm an actress on a wonderful TV sitcom. I did someone a favor and here I am."

"Sounds convenient," Detective Simmons said without any feeling. "You looked comfortable driving that nice car, almost as if you've driven it countless times before."

Skye looked at him with contempt. Her smile was upside down, and she wasn't in the mood for this dick-head, wannabe Dick Tracy. "That was the first and only time I drove the car. I own a Toyota Prius."

"Where is the Prius now?"

"My boyfriend has it."

"What's your boyfriend's name, Ms. Culbertson?" Detective Roper asked.

Skye looked at him with the same contempt as she did Simmons. "His name is Rico Tillman. He's also my manager."

"Do you have an address for this Tillman?" Roper continued.

Skye looked thoughtfully at him. She had nothing to lose; it was she that had been humiliated on the streets of Los Angeles with Rico nowhere to be found. "Yes, I'll give you the one I know." Skye wrote down Rico's name and an address he'd given her and gave it to Roper.

Before another word was uttered, an officer was at the door to pick up the note Skye had written.

"Being in possession of a stolen vehicle is a federal crime," Simmons began.

"But I didn't steal it. I was only asked to drive it to an address that was given to me. I wasn't aware that the car was stolen."

Simmons pushed his glasses up on his nose and took a good look at Skye. "The car tag was stolen from another vehicle and the Mercedes you were driving had been repainted.

"We've been well aware that a group of professional carjackers have been operating in the area for some time. We received a break almost a year ago when a car was jacked on Sunset Boulevard. Thanks to the quick action of some of the patrons at the restaurant where the carjacking took place, we were able to recover the car and the woman to whom it belonged. Unfortunately, the suspect got away."

Skye arched her eyebrows. She remembered a similar incident when she and Rico were dining at a restaurant on Sunset Boulevard. He became agitated and was out of sync the rest of the evening. Could it be one in the same?

"We do have a person of interest we've been watching. He's probably not high up in this organization. We received an anonymous tip today that there was to be a shipment of hot cars. But we never expected to find one of Hollywood's up-and-coming actresses tied to this car theft ring."

"So does that mean you believe me?"

"Tell us about Rico Tillman."

"I met him at a restaurant purely by accident," Skye said with a scowl on her face. "I was studying a script and he appeared out of nowhere and asked to sit down."

"What did he say?"

"It was casual conversation. He seemed nice and all. When he realized I was an actress, he offered to help me by exposing me to some of his connections in the industry."

"It must have gone well."

"I'm not making a million dollars a movie, but I did score a great role in an upcoming movie."

Detective Roper nodded his head at Detective Simmons who batted his eyes. "Sit tight, Ms. Culbertson. We're going to step out for a minute. We'll be back shortly."

Folding her hands together, Skye sat without uttering a word. She watched as the two detectives marched out of the room and out of sight. With her elbows on the table, Skye let her head fall into her hands.

And then she noticed the bracelet on her arm that Rico had given her last night with the inscription, *My Hollywood Skye*. Love had nothing to do with it; it was a peace offering for the hell she was now experiencing.

CHAPTER 22

Rico stomped the floor after he hung up from talking to Benny, his right-hand man. Benny had been several cars behind Skye when she was suddenly pulled over by the police, he explained. After circling the block twice, Benny confirmed that not only was Skye being arrested, but the Mercedes was headed for the impound lot.

"Damn, double damn." Rico took his hand and knocked the paperwork off his desk. Quickly coming to his senses, he went into defense mode to cover his tracks.

Without wasting another second, he disconnected his telephone service that was connected to Skye and had someone rearrange the rental properties he owned. The furniture was completely removed, replaced, and set up for the decoy at the condo in Redondo Beach. Next, Rico jumped in the Prius and headed for Bank of America and closed down the dummy accounts he'd set up under Skye's name with him being the joint administrator. He made sure he wore light gloves so as not to leave any fingerprints by which he could be traced. Last, he shredded the driver's license, credit cards, and social security card that bore the name Rico Tillman. He didn't need it any longer. Besides, it wasn't his real name.

CHAPTER 23

After twelve grueling hours, Skye was finally released to go on her way without any further explanation. She wasn't to leave the city under any circumstances.

It was early in the morning and Skye was without a car. It was cold, even for Los Angeles in the fall. There wasn't a visible taxi in sight and without giving any thought to what time it was, Skye called Jaylin.

"Damn, Skye, this better be good. Do you know what time it is? I've got an early morning shoot."

"Sorry, Jaye."

"You're always sorry about something."

"Never mind."

"I'm awake now. What is it?"

Skye ran down the last twelve hours of her life at the LAPD and how she had ended up there.

"I told you there was something not right about Rico. I've got the L.A. vibe, and I wasn't feeling that brother from day one."

"Well, he never showed me any other hand. How was I to know that he was involved in a car-theft ring?"

"Where's your car?"

"He has it. I probably won't see it again."

"Damn, Skye, that asshole made sure his ass was covered. He probably had some inkling that something was amiss and used innocent Ms. Skye to do his dirty work in the event something went down."

"Am I that naïve?"

"Girl, this is Los Angeles...not Junction City. This place is full of all kinds of people—good and bad. This city takes advantage of folks. Anyone coming to Los Angeles looking for a big break is vulnerable."

"Would you please come downtown and get me? I need my friend."

"When was I appointed to be the one to rescue you every time you get in a bind? I should've left your ass on the bench at the bus station. My life would be less stressful." They laughed. "I've finished preaching. Give me a few minutes to put some clothes on and I'll be right down."

"Thanks, Jaye, for being my guardian angel. I'm going back inside to wait for you. Call me when you're close."

"I will."

Skye went back inside the police station and waited. Tears flowed from her face as she hugged one of the walls to keep herself upright. She didn't understand why she kept making one bad mistake after another. First there was Bryan, now Rico, if that was his real name. She brought it on herself, and things had to change.

CHAPTER 24

Before long, Jaylin arrived and scooped Skye up from hell. Skye wasted no time in jumping into the car, and Jaylin sailed off into the early morning darkness.

"Skye, I've been thinking about your situation. Make sure everything that connected you to Rico is safe and secure."

"Like what?"

"Girl, do I have to spell everything out for you? Didn't you tell me that he handled your financial accounts? God, I wished you'd told me you were going to let him be in charge of your life. I tried to warn you, though, to not be so trusting of him."

Skye sighed. "I'll go to the bank first thing this morning to check my bank accounts. If Rico messed with my money, I'm going to kill him."

"You'll have to find him first. Has he called you yet?"

"No," Skye said flatly. "The only telephone number I had for him is disconnected. He hasn't even inquired as to whether I delivered the car or not. If he is tied up in this car-theft ring, he's not going to call."

"He ain't nothing but a piece of dog do-do." Jaylin gripped the steering wheel. "I have a cousin who's a private detective who can sniff out Rico's ass and bust him down to the white meat if you want me to ask him."

"No, I don't want any blood on my hands. I've got to move forward."

"You're a better person than I would be. Well, we're almost at your apartment."

"Whoa," Skye said, as they turned the corner and saw her car sitting on the street. "I wonder what this means?"

"Look, I'm going inside with you to make sure he's not hiding out in your crib."

"I doubt it if Rico believes the police may be looking for him."

"It's better to be safe than sorry. Let's go."

The ladies got out of the car, walked up the steps, and down the walkway to Skye's apartment. Nerves had seized every inch of Skye's body as she moved forward and put the key in the lock. She turned the key slowly and opened the door.

Following close behind was Jaye. "Flip the light on. Quick."

Although nothing appeared out of place, the ladies walked from room to room until they were satisfied that Rico wasn't lurking anywhere.

"Don't leave, Jaye. My nerves are getting the best of me."

"I figured you'd say that. I brought a change of clothes. I've got to be up in an hour anyway."

"What's that noise?" Skye asked, grabbing Jaylin's arm.

"My cell phone. It beeps each time I get a text, tweet, or an email."

"That's annoying."

"I usually have it on vibrate. Let me see who's up texting or tweeting at this time."

"Do you want some hot tea?"

"It won't hurt."

Skye went to the kitchen to put water in the kettle.

"Skye, you've got to see this."

"What is it? I'll be right there after I put the water on."

"Skye, you better come now. TMZ has already scooped up your story and is rolling with it on Twitter. It's going to be in all of the tabloids by morning."

Skye flew into the living room where she found Jaye with her hand covering her mouth. "What are they saying?"

"Girl, it's not nice. Basically, they said that you," Jaye sighed and patted her chest with her hand, "were working with a car-theft ring and was arrested transporting a stolen vehicle with stolen license plates. An anonymous tip to police led to your arrest. You can read it for yourself." Jaylin handed Skye her cell phone. "That was about it, except that your picture is on the link they sent out."

"Oh my God."

"Be glad it was your promo picture instead of one with your hands handcuffed behind your back."

Skye slid down on the seat next to Jaylin. "My career is over."

"The police let you go; that should mean something."

"But what if the producers think that my association with Rico makes me off-limits?"

"I wouldn't worry about it. You're not guilty and everyone has to know that."

CHAPTER 25

Skye rushed to the bank and was the first person standing in line. She prayed that Rico hadn't compromised her well-being by tampering with her accounts.

The bank teller motioned for her to come to the window. She walked briskly to the counter and let out a sigh.

"I'd like to check the balance on my checking and savings account, please." Skye passed the teller a piece of paper with the account numbers on it, along with her driver's license.

The teller punched out the numbers on the computer and frowned. She looked at Skye and then back at the screen. She punched in some more numbers and then cocked her head as the same reaction was registered.

"What's wrong?" Skye asked, concerned.

"My records show that both of these accounts were closed yesterday and a cashier's check was issued for the balances."

"I didn't close any of my accounts; in fact, I haven't even stepped inside the bank for months. How can this be? Can you tell me whose name was on the cashier's check and for what amount?"

"Ma'am, let me get my supervisor."

"For what? Can't you tell me who accessed my accounts?"

"Just a minute." The teller left the counter and went into a back room. A minute later, she was followed by an older woman, who wore heavy makeup and her hair ratted up into a beehive.

"Ma'am, I understand you're inquiring about your accounts."

Skye stared at them both. "Yes," she said in a gruff tone of voice. "Your teller has told me that my accounts were closed yesterday, but I didn't close them nor did I authorize it. I'd like to know who closed them and how much the cashier's check was written for."

The older lady stood in front of the teller and looked at Skye. She let out several sighs. "Ms. Culbertson, a Mr. Rico Tillman came in yesterday near closing time and closed the accounts. As administrator of the accounts, he was perfectly within his right to do so."

"But it was my money...my accounts."

"Mr. Tillman had the accounts set up so that he was the main account holder and you were secondary. Have you not spoken with Mr. Tillman?"

The silence was almost audible. Skye looked at the two ladies who stared back at her like they didn't have any sense. There were no smiles, no apologies, and definitely not an ounce of compassion. "No."

"Well, Ms. Culbertson," the older woman said, "we can't help you. You'll have to speak with Mr. Tillman."

"How much money was withdrawn from my accounts? I do have the right to ask, am I correct?"

The older woman sighed, looked back at the teller, and whispered something. She left the teller to answer the question as she exited the cubicle.

"Ma'am," the teller said without batting an eyelash, "the total amount was ninety thousand, five hundred and fifty-six dollars and thirty cents. The gentleman said he was moving it into another account."

Skye stared without saying a word. Where did the money come from? In the two accounts together, she thought she may have had a sum total of thirty-five thousand dollars. She pushed back the tears, turned, and walked out of the bank. Not only was all of her money gone, but Rico Tillman was gone with it.

She rushed to her car and got in. There was no calling Jaylin since she was in the middle of a shoot. She needed someone to talk to.

Skye shook her head from side to side and let the tears roll. Another man had disappointed her and left her with nothing.

CHAPTER 26

*S*kye left the bank and headed for Warner Bros., grateful that she didn't have to be on set until ten. She drove onto the studio lot, parked, and headed for her trailer. When she approached it, a note was taped to the door. She pulled it off, went inside, and sat down on the leather couch. Toying with the envelope, she finally opened it.

It read: *Your services are no longer needed, effective immediately. We will send your final payment to your account. We wish you much success in your future endeavors.*

Skye stared at the words. Her hands began to tremble and she cursed out loud. "Damn you, Rico. Damn you to hell, you sorry son-of-a-bitch."

She balled up the piece of paper with the studio logo on it and threw it in the trash. Skye no longer had a manager to call, but she had to talk to someone about getting her final payment in check form.

As Skye sat contemplating her next step, there was a knock on the trailer door. She jerked her head, took a deep breath, and stared at the door. There was another knock.

"Is anyone in there?"

Skye recognized the voice of the production supervisor, Jan. "Yes, come in."

The blonde-haired executive opened the door and waltzed in, scanning the interior. In her hand was a brown clipboard with a piece of paper tucked under the clamp. "I gather that you've received and read the notice that was attached to your trailer."

Skye fumbled with the empty envelope that sat next to her. She raised her head and looked at Jan. Lips tight, Skye looked away without saying a word.

"Look, we didn't want to do it. But riding around in a stolen vehicle, Skye? It's bad publicity for the network. We had no other recourse."

Fidgeting, Skye rolled her eyes and tried to suppress tears that threatened to run down her face. She opened her mouth, but words didn't find their way to her tongue. Exasperated, she sighed and shook her head.

"Okay. There's nothing else I can say, except that you must vacate the premises—like in the next twenty minutes."

There was no warmth in Skye's voice. "Jan, if that's what you stopped by to say, you could've saved all the formality and this charade would've been over. You don't give a damn about me anyway."

"Suit yourself, Skye." Jan held out the clipboard. "I'll need you to sign this waiver which releases you from the four remaining episodes that were left on your contract. And oh, please leave your key at the gate." Jan held out a pen.

Snatching the pen from Jan's hand, Skye scribbled her name on the line where indicated without reading the document. She got up from the couch, collected her purse, and took out the key to the trailer. She threw it at the executive, walked out, and slammed the door behind her.

Tears burned her face as Skye raced to the car. The humiliation hurt worse than losing her job. It wasn't even her fault. Four more episodes and she would've been done. But her performance on the show received Emmy nods, and she felt that she would've been a definite shoo-in for the next season.

CHAPTER 27

Without a job and the loss of her hard-earned money, Skye wandered around the streets of Los Angeles in a daze. An hour passed before she decided to drive home after looking at the needle on the car's dashboard. She had less than a quarter tank of gas. A hundred and fifty dollars was all Skye had in her purse, but she had no plans to buy gas with it.

Then it hit her. She had a stash of cash, approximately five-thousand dollars, hidden in one of the dresser drawers at the condo in Redondo Beach. In fact, some of her belongings, including a recently purchased designer dress and a mink coat that had been given to her by Rico, were still there.

Quickly, she turned her car around and headed to a gas station. An idea formulated in her mind. Skye still had the key to the condo; she would go there and pick up her stuff. For the first time today, a smile lit her face.

Skye pulled out a credit card, purchased gas, and pumped away. The money in the condo would hold her over until her next gig. She was due to start her next movie in a couple of weeks.

With the car filled up, Skye hopped in and headed for Redondo Beach. She switched on the radio and Babyface and Toni Braxton were singing their newly released song, "Hurt You." Skye sang along, but she also ingested the words and thought about how life had treated her. Had her ex-husband, Bryan, and Rico *meant* to hurt her? It sure felt that way.

As she drove, Nona Taylor appeared as an apparition. Skye shook her head and blinked her eyes, as she kept her hands steady on the steering wheel. Nona's face was still there, shaking a warning finger in her face. And then as suddenly as it had appeared, the apparition was gone.

Skye sucked in hard. It must've been a sign; she was sure of it. With pedal to the metal, she drove as fast as the speed limit allowed, eager to get to her possessions.

It was mid-morning, and the freeway was crowded. It was the one thing Skye hated about living in Los Angeles. In Kansas, there was one main highway that went from east to west, and there were hardly any stop and crawls except in the larger cities like Topeka and Kansas City.

She wasn't far now. If only the traffic would move. The sooner she picked up her things from the condo, the sooner she could rid herself of Rico's existence in her life.

Finally, she was off the freeway. Skye breathed a sigh of relief. She barreled down the street, praying that Rico wouldn't be on the premises, although, it was inevitable that a coming-to-Jesus meeting was in order. And she wanted the money he had stolen from her.

The condo in sight, Skye pulled to the curb and turned off the ignition. She sat for a moment, glancing around to make sure there weren't any signs of life. Blowing air through her lips, she glanced once more at the condo, opened the car door, and hoisted herself out.

Walking briskly, Skye headed to the front door, her key already in hand. Not wanting to waste one second, Skye tried to insert the key in the lock, but it didn't fit. "Damn." Again, Skye tried to force the key, but to no avail. She stood there and stared at the door, her anger apparent.

Without caring if anyone was looking, Skye began to bang on the door. She pounded on it with her fist, but there was no answer.

With the key still in hand, she took it and scraped it across the wooden door. And then the door opened; she almost fell in from leaning on it so hard.

Startled, Skye rocked back on her feet. A brunette with the figure of a model, who looked to be in her late twenties or early thirties, stared at her.

"Who in the hell are you?" Skye shouted.

"I was wondering the same thing," the woman said, giving Skye a once-over and then noticing the scratch on the door. She folded her arms across her breasts. "I'll have to sue you for destroying my property."

"Your property? I live here and someone has tampered with the lock. I've come to pick up my things."

The woman's eyes widened and she dropped both hands to her hips. "Well, you don't live here anymore. I do."

"Move out of my damn way." Skye reached out to push the woman.

The woman moved back. "Put your hands on me and you'll regret the day you blackened my doorway."

"Was that supposed to be some kind of racial slur...bitch? Don't let me have to kick your boney, white ass."

"Bitch, you interpret it any way you like. I've told you as nicely as I could that I live here now. You need to turn around and get off my property."

With a scowl on her face and her hands balled into fists, Skye tried to move forward. The woman blocked the entrance with her body, but Skye pushed full steam ahead. The woman moved out of the way and kicked Skye to the floor as she flew by.

"If you don't want any more, I'd suggest you take your raggedy ass out of here now." The woman stood over Skye, her arms folded again across her chest.

Skye slowly got up off of the floor, scanning the room as she did. Her eyes bulged from their sockets when she noticed that the furniture that was there only two nights earlier had been replaced with a whole new set. It was no longer all white; the furniture was now French Provincial-antique in gaudy brown tones. There was a tall, porcelain vase that stood in the foyer on a round, white antique table, full of colorful hydrangeas. In fact, nothing about the house was the same except for the address.

Turning around to face her foe, Skye looked dead into the woman's eyes. "Where is Rico?"

"Rico who?"

"Don't play me for a fool. This was his home too, although the furniture has conveniently been changed. I had some expensive personal items in here, and I want them."

"Look, I don't know what you're talking about. Nothing in here belongs to you. Maybe you went to the wrong house."

"I didn't go to the wrong house; you and I both know that I'm telling the truth." Skye moved in front of the woman, close enough that she could feel her breath on her face. She pointed her finger. "I don't care what you say, I'm going to my room to get my things."

"Suit yourself," the woman said, finally giving Skye access to move further into the house.

Skye huffed and then scoffed off down the hallway to her bedroom. Within seconds, she returned with tears forming in the corners of her eyes. She balled up her fists and screamed. "You tell Rico Tillman that I want my money and I better get it soon."

"Well, honey, like I asked before, who is Rico? I can't give a message to someone I don't know."

Skye's fingers were within inches of the woman's eyes. "Pass my message on, bitch." And then Skye walked to where the porcelain vase stood and knocked it off the table. The vase broke into a thousand pieces. "Sue me." And she walked out of the house as fast as her feet would carry her.

CHAPTER 28

*I*f hell was any hotter than how Skye felt now, there was no way in the world she wanted to go there. But she was madder than an uppity diva whose Louboutin shoes were stuck in a crack on a Beverly Hills sidewalk.

If she had a gun, she'd search for Rico's sorry ass all over the city until she found him. And when she found him, she wouldn't give him a minute to offer up an explanation for what he'd done to her. With gun in hand, she would steady it and shoot him point blank between the eyes without giving it a second thought. That's how mad she was.

She didn't have a gun and she felt defeated. Tears streamed down her face as she sat in bottleneck traffic, waiting to get from Redondo Beach to the safety of her apartment.

Skye's immediate distress took a temporary backseat when her cell phone began to ring. She reached into her purse, pulled out her cell phone, and mustered a half-smile. Director Malcolm Lee was calling, no doubt wanting to discuss the shoot for the new movie.

"Hello, Mr. Lee," Skye said, trying to sound upbeat.

"Hello, Skye."

"You don't sound like yourself. Is something wrong?"

"Well, I've got some bad news."

Skye's body stiffened. The stalled traffic in front of her became a blur. Her upbeat tone took on a sour note.

"What is it?" Skye felt in her gut what was coming next.

"We'll have to replace you in the new movie. I'm sorry about the abrupt notice."

"Why, Malcolm? Why are you doing this to me?"

"There's been a lot of publicity about your arrest for driving around in a stolen vehicle and your association with Rico Tillman."

"I had no idea what Rico was up to, let alone that I was driving a stolen vehicle. I've fully cooperated with the police, and they've let me go. Malcolm, please don't do this to me. I haven't done anything. What about innocent until proven guilty?"

"Are you guilty?"

Skye wanted to end the call—hang up on his trifling ass for asking her such a ridiculous question. "No, I'm not guilty. Rico asked me to drive the car, and now I can't find him anywhere."

"Look, I'm sorry, Skye. If I was financing this movie alone, I'd probably make a concession, however, that isn't the case. I have some major investors, and in order for them to continue to back the project, I have to let you go. There's no reason to taint the movie before we begin the first shoot. I hope you understand, and if everything should clear up as far as you're concerned, maybe we'll consider another project with you in mind."

"Thanks." Skye ended the call without waiting for Malcolm's last words. Forget the movie; she was already tainted and Rico was the cause.

She inched her way on the freeway for the next hour. When she finally got off, she navigated the streets of Los Angeles with its palm trees waving as she drove by and stopped at a liquor store. Opening the door of the car, she got out and walked in with a purpose. She picked up a bottle of rum and a case of Coke and headed back to her car.

After she arrived home, Skye put her purchases on the kitchen counter. She paused to mull over her morning—her hatred for Rico escalating even more.

Sighing, she reached in her purse and pulled out her cell. She stared at it for a few moments and then pushed in a couple of buttons and waited. Her fingers trembled when she heard the voice on the other end and abruptly ended the call.

"It was good to hear your voice, Mother," Skye said out loud, staring into space.

Still standing at the kitchen counter and coming out of her cloud, Skye took the bottle of rum out of the brown bag. There were no *drinking* glasses in her apartment, so she grabbed a regular water glass from her kitchen cabinet. Upon opening the bottle of rum, she poured it into her glass until it was half full, adding some Coke to give her the extra caffeine. Alcohol had never entered her body until she became a slave to the Los Angeles way of life.

Skye drank four glasses of rum and Coke, fell asleep, and didn't wake up until several hours later when her cell phone rang.

CHAPTER 29

*Y*awning, Skye sat up and wiped her eyes. She realized she hadn't been dreaming when the phone rang, which had temporarily stopped, and was again belting out a tune that announced Jaylin was calling. Lazily, she reached for the phone that was still in her purse and hit the ON button before it stopped.

"Hey, Jaye."

"Where are you, Skye, and why do you sound like that?"

"Sound like what?"

"Are you drunk?"

"No, but I may have had too much to drink. I think I've been sleep for the past three hours."

"Get yourself together, girl. What did you find out at the bank?"

Now somewhat alert, Skye sat up on the couch where she had fallen asleep and sighed. "Please don't tell me you told me so, but that asshole closed out my accounts and took every penny I had in them. The strange thing, there was more money in the accounts than I put there."

"Do you think he was funneling money from what appears to be his illegal business dealings through your bank account?"

"It sort of looks that way. I can't ask him since he's vanished into thin air and disconnected his cell phone. But this you won't believe."

"Your stories aren't fiction by any stretch of the imagination."

"After I left the bank this morning, I was distraught. But then I remembered I had money stashed out at the condo. I guess I felt it would be safe out there."

"How much are you talking about, Skye?"

"Five-thousand dollars."

"In cash?"

"Stupid, idiot, fool that I am; I trusted a man that saw my fool ass coming. The money is history, Jaye! All my damn money is gone."

Jaylin sighed. "You're the poster child for dumb and dumber at its best. You are a prime example of a country girl not having a clue about what goes on in a big city."

"Jaye, I'm not a country girl and I'm not stupid. I'm a woman who made a mistake."

"Listen to yourself, contradicting every word you say each time you open your mouth."

"Whatever. I went out to the condo and the lock was changed. I banged on the door and this brunette-haired woman comes to the door."

"What the hell?"

"She said she lived there."

"You ought to know where you live."

"I told her that it was my place that I shared with Rico; however, she was adamant about it being her place and that I should leave. She claimed she didn't know Rico."

"I'm sure you knew she was lying, although she may have been telling the truth."

"Of course she was telling a lie, Jaye. And then the devil in me pushed past her and she kicked me in my behind."

Jaylin snickered. "With her foot?"

"Yeah."

"Skye, you didn't let the woman kick your ass?" Jaye tried not to laugh. "Well, what did you do?"

"I fell on the floor. But when I got up, I noticed that all of the furniture had been changed. I even went to my bedroom, and the furniture, along with my money and clothes, weren't there. Rico Tillman is a straight-up dog. If I get my hands on..."

"I've already told you that my cousin can hunt his ass down. Real talk."

"Let's do it, Jaye."

"He better hope the police get him before Marcus."

"Marcus?"

"My cousin, silly. His name is Marcus."

"Oh."

"Cheer up, girl. Consider this a lesson learned. In a couple of weeks, you'll be shooting that new movie with Malcolm Lee. You can start over again."

There was silence. "You all right, Skye?"

"Jaye, I was nixed from the movie. The publicity about my arrest scared the investors."

"I'll be over when I get done here. You need a friend."

CHAPTER 30

Several months had passed since Skye's scrape with the law. She hadn't worked since then, and while the money she'd collected from her last gig and the little she received from unemployment had kept her alive, she was now close to being evicted from her apartment. She didn't know what she was going to do.

Jaylin's cousin, Marcus, still hadn't found Rico and neither had the police. Police accounts said that the chop shop Rico was said to have been operating from was stripped of any evidence that it had existed, and the car thieves were long gone.

Revenge was in Skye's brain. The hate was so strong that she could taste it. But until such time that she was able to confront Rico, she had to get a job. The rent would be due again, and she didn't have twenty-six hundred dollars to give the apartment manager for the past month and what was due on the first of the month. If nothing else was taken care of, she made certain that her car note was paid.

Skye climbed out of bed and retrieved her iPad from the entertainment center. Underneath the iPad lay the script for the movie she was supposed to appear in. It might have been her breakout role, but she'd never know. She hadn't been given a chance, even in light of the fact that she was never charged for the theft of the stolen car. Her association with Rico put her on the blacklist before her career got a chance to get started.

Hunger was calling her name. Skye laid the iPad back down on the entertainment center. She went to the bathroom and took a quick shower. All dried off, she put on a pair of skinny jeans and a short, pink, loose-fitting top. She grabbed her purse and headed outside.

She walked the three blocks to the mom-and-pop diner in her neighborhood and entered. It was dark inside—the sun's rays not yet penetrating the side of the building where the four small windows afforded some kind of view to the outside world. Several four-by-four tables surrounded by two red chairs on either side filled the interior. Ten bar stools, the seats made of red vinyl, stretched the length of the counter.

As predicted, an earlier patron had left the day's newspaper on a table. Skye politely took a seat at the table, retrieved the paper, and opened it up. When the waitress arrived, she ordered toast and coffee.

The want ads were full of stuff for which Skye was unskilled, however, she lacked the initiative to get up and see if she could. Skye was intelligent and bright, but now that acting was in her blood, that's all she wanted to do.

She sat up straight when her eyes came across the ad for exotic dancers. Starting pay with the possibility of earning more in an evening was attractive. Skye wasn't a good dancer, but after watching the women at the few strip clubs Rico had taken her to, she was sure she could fake it and make it.

Skye took a bite of her toast and slurped down a mouthful of her black coffee. Not caring who was looking, she folded up the paper and put it under her arm. She left a five-dollar bill on the table that took care of her meal and a dollar tip. For the first time in a month, Skye felt hopeful.

With an extra bounce in her step, Skye walked briskly to her apartment ready to reclaim her life the best way she could. As soon as she entered the door, she hurried to her desk and perused the exotic dancer want ads again.

After circling the ads that were most appealing to her, she picked up her iPad from the entertainment center and opened it. She conducted a search of the locations she'd picked out to make sure they weren't seedy out-of-the-way joints. And then she went on a Google search and pulled up what Los Angeles considered to be the top ten strip joints, so that she had options. Skye made a few calls and in another minute, she was walking out of the door with keys in hand.

She'd never tell Jaylin about her new job prospect. She would only be condescending and try to talk her out of it. Furthermore, Jaylin hadn't extended an offer for her to come and stay until she got on her feet. If dancing was going to keep a roof over her head, then that's what she was going to do. What other option did she have?

CHAPTER 31

With a renewed sense of spirit, Skye drove to several of the clubs and lounges she'd circled in the newspaper to size up the location and its appearance—from the outside. She was disappointed that most of them had not yet opened, but she should've known that it was too early in the day. Early afternoon was when things started to jump off, but it didn't hurt her resolve to find employment that was going to take care of her immediate needs.

The bulk of the clubs she'd researched were in Canoga Park, West L.A., North Hollywood, and the Valley. Unable to go inside any of them at the time of her arrival, she was still in the dark about what to expect, although in truth, she was somewhat leery about the profession as a whole. Would she have to go topless? Bottomless? She hadn't given it any real thought until now, although when she went online to do her research, customer reviews indicated what they wanted and what was going on at a specific club. Desperation kept her on course.

Skye sighed and started to head toward home. She turned on the radio; Toni Braxton and Babyface were singing "Hurt Me" again.

With one swift turn of the steering wheel, Skye headed for the 405. The scene that played out at Redondo Beach months ago resurfaced. Skye wasn't sure what she would find, but she was going to confront the devil once again and maybe put a pitchfork in its heart. She needed answers. Where in the hell was Rico?

The traffic on the 405 ran smoothly, in fact, too smooth. Maybe that was a good sign. She tossed the thought out of the window and stayed on course.

Inside of forty minutes, she was near her turnoff. She exited the freeway and drove the short stint to the condo. Everything seemed quiet as she rolled down the street. And then Skye put on brakes, spotting Rico and the woman she'd seen when she visited the condo. They stood on the sidewalk conversing and then traded a small peck on the lips.

Fire coursed through Skye's body. Without giving it any thought, she put her foot on the gas and ran up on the sidewalk, missing the couple as Rico pushed the woman out of the way. Skye maneuvered her car, turned it around, and gunned it again. And then she saw it.

The barrel of a gun was pointed in her direction. And there was Rico, running toward her.

Skye hurriedly put the car in reverse and drove backward as fast as the Prius would go. Daring to take a look in front of her, she saw Rico running after the car and still pointing the gun. And then she heard the shot. Skye pushed the car to the end of the street until she was able to make a quick turn on the intersecting one and head out of the neighborhood.

Catching her breath, Skye drove like a bat out of hell, still pushing the car as fast as it would go. That was a close call. A sigh of relief escaped her mouth when she entered the freeway with no one following behind.

She'd never expected to see Rico. As far as she knew, he was on the other side of the world. He probably had been in L.A. all of this time, getting away with his crime. That said something about the Los Angeles Police Department. They were either short-staffed and had more high priority cases to handle or they didn't know what the hell they were doing. How could Rico roam around town undetected? Now she was afraid…afraid to go home.

"Blurred Lines" now played on the airways. Abruptly, Skye turned the radio off, agitated at the sound of the thumping noise that made Robin Thicke's song a favorite among music lovers. Should she report seeing Rico to the police? There was no way she could go back to the apartment, but the last thing she wanted to do was impose herself on Jaylin.

She wanted to call Jaylin, but California had strict laws about using your phone while driving, although she had a Bluetooth. It was best that she waited until she was off the freeway.

Her nerves made her jump as her cell phone began to ring. Skye reached in her purse and pulled out her cell, but she didn't recognize the number. She touched the Bluetooth to accept the call, but as soon as she did, a chill went down her back.

"Bitch, I should've blown your ass away. If you know what's good for you, it's in your best interest to never return to Redondo Beach. And if you go to the police, you better have your insurance premium paid up and someone to administer last rites. Do you understand?"

"You sorry son-of-a-bitch! You played me; you used me. Where's my money, Rico? I want the damn money you stole from me."

"Bitch, I don't have anything that belongs to you. The money in the bank belonged to me. Manager's fee for all I did for you."

"You didn't do a damn thing for me except make my life a living hell."

"Well, we're even. Heed my warning."

Without saying another word, Skye disconnected the call. "I've got your bitch, sucker," she said out loud. "You're going to pay; you're going to pay every cent you owe me."

CHAPTER 32

Skye drove to her apartment and flew up the stairs. Once inside, she gathered her clothes and stuffed them into two suitcases. She collected her iPad and whatever other possessions she could feasibly fit into the trunk of her car. She'd have someone else, maybe Jaylin's cousin, come back and clean out the rest of her belongings. Right now, her mission was to get as far away from the place as soon as possible.

After packing her trunk with the few belongings, she headed down the street. The thought of uprooting again boggled her mind. For a fleeting moment, she thought about her mother, sister, and brother whom she hadn't seen since she'd left Kansas. In an odd sort of way, she missed them. They represented peace at a simple time in her life.

Pulling into a store parking lot, Skye pulled out her cell and called Jaylin. There was no answer at the other end, only the constant ringing of the phone. Skye hung up. She'd try again later.

Time had flown by. It was already one-thirty in the afternoon and she still hadn't found a job. Most of the clubs were open by two, others later. Calling ahead, Skye was able to secure an on-the-spot interview. She steered her car in the direction of North Hollywood.

The club was dimly lit and eerily quiet when Skye stepped in. She looked to her left and then to her right, casing the joint like a Secret Service agent making sure that the elements were free of harm.

Out of the shadows, a tall, sinewy figure appeared. He wore a white, silky turtleneck shirt, black slacks, topped with a black-and-white tweed, lightweight wool jacket. The man appeared to be in his late forties or early fifties. He ogled all over Skye's body and seemed pleased with what he saw. The man smiled and extended his hand.

"You must be Skye," the gentleman said, removing his hand when she didn't immediately shake it.

Looking around the room again, Skye turned and faced the gentleman. She extended her hand, and he shook it. "Yes, I'm Skye Culbertson. And I need a job."

The gentleman nodded his head up and down. "Glad to meet you, Skye. I'm Rudy Nixon, but my close friends and associates call me Junebug. I'm from the country...the Dirty South."

For the first time since entering the building, Skye smiled. She recalled the time when her ex-husband had used the phrase, the "Dirty South." This time, she wasn't naïve to what it meant, and there was something about Southern folks who migrated west that put her at ease. She didn't know why; they just did.

Junebug took another good look at Skye. He smiled and rocked his head up and down in approval. Skye hated when men stared at her the way Junebug was doing now, but she needed a job...she needed the money to keep off the streets.

"Have you danced before?"

"Yes," Skye lied.

"Where?"

"Back east. That's where I'm from."

"How long have you been in L.A.?"

Although Skye hated his line of questioning, she was grateful that Junebug hadn't recognized her name.

"Almost a year," she lied again. "I've been doing odd jobs here and there."

"So why did you choose today to pay us a visit?"

Skye set her purse down on one of the plush, red-velvet chairs. "You don't mind if I sit down, do you?"

"Excuse my manners," Junebug said, seeming to be somewhat apologetic.

Skye picked up her purse and sat down with Junebug taking the opposite seat.

"You don't mind me calling you Junebug?"

Junebug smiled. "No, I rather like the sound of my nickname coming from your lips. It has a pleasant and sensual sound to it."

Skye breathed in and out. The last thing she wanted to do was throw off any sexual innuendos. She needed a fast-paying job and sex had nothing to do with it, at least that's what she tried to tell herself.

"Junebug, I've been scraping the bottom ever since I arrived in Los Angeles looking for a promise of a better life. I need some help to jump-start my career."

"So, are you in L.A. to become an actress?"

The question startled Skye. Had he known all along that she was Skye Culbertson, the actress who was caught driving a stolen vehicle that belonged to her boyfriend? Or was this a simple question made on the assumption that a lot of young women her age came to Hollywood to become famous?

"I'm from a small town back east," Skye heard herself say. "My life was boring and I was always under my mother's thumb. I had to get away…find myself. I was naïve when I first came here, but I had to grow up fast."

"How old are you? "

"I turned twenty-two a few months ago. "

Junebug's hands were perched beneath his chin, seemingly tied to every word Skye said. "Thank you for sharing that with me. Many young women and men come out here looking for instant gratification, but all the glitz and glamour is not within everyone's reach.

"It's quite obvious you need a job. You look older than twenty-two, and that works. I like you and I'm going to give you a chance. A night's pay can be good. It depends upon the amount of work you're willing to invest to get that payday."

"What does that mean?"

Junebug wrinkled his nose and twisted his lips. "We have a dancing platform, complete with three poles and several VIP booths that we use for bachelor parties and the like. And we also have private dance areas that can be somewhat lucrative, if you know what I mean. And, this is a topless club. Los Angeles prohibits serving alcohol if it's a fully nude establishment. We don't allow men to get sloppy drunk and take advantage of or abuse the dancers."

"When can I start?" Skye asked, not batting an eyelash.

"That was presumptuous of you since I haven't offered you the job yet."

Skye stared at Junebug and then offered a smile. "I'm sorry to have gotten ahead of myself. I guess I had already imagined myself on stage."

Junebug let out a full grin. "I like you, Skye, and you've got the job. You can start tonight." He looked at her again thoughtfully. "Your stage name will be Hollywood Skye."

Skye shook where she stood, her raised eyebrows signaling an alarm. The last time she heard "Hollywood Skye," Rico had called her that. In fact, it was inscribed on the bracelet she was wearing.

"Why Hollywood Skye?" she asked, trying to quiet her nerves.

"It has a certain ring to it. We're in Hollywood and the two names seem to flow together. Don't you think so?"

Skye wasn't sure if it did or not. All she could think about was

Rico. Junebug seemed to be on the up and up and didn't appear to recognize her from her short stint on television. "Thank you, Junebug. I look forward to being on stage."

Junebug got up from his seat. "Let's take care of a little paperwork and instructions on what you're to wear. I think you'll work out fine and raise the bar. Be here at five-fifteen."

Skye got up and followed Junebug into a small office. After getting instructions and completing necessary paperwork, she exited the building with a new lease on life.

CHAPTER 33

Skye drove from North Hollywood toward Inglewood. Beyoncé was singing her explosive new hit, "Drunk in Love," on the radio. The song made no sense to Skye, since she wasn't head over heels in love with a man. Instead, it crystallized the hatred she had for Rico.

Continuing to listen to the song aggravated her. Quickly, she selected another radio station and settled for some light jazz. Nearing Crenshaw Boulevard, she looked in her rearview mirror as she prepared to stop. The car behind her had been following for several miles.

When the light turned green, she moved ahead and then sped across two lanes of traffic and pulled into the parking lot of a McDonald's restaurant. She saw the car slow down and try and make its way over to the outer lane. Was the driver one of Rico's people?

Skye quickly turned around and exited the McDonald's and drove in the opposite direction. She retrieved her cell phone from her purse and called Jaylin.

Breathing a sigh of relief when she heard Jaylin's voice, Skye let go and emptied all that had happened hours before on Jaylin's lap.

"Slow down, Skye. Did you say that you saw Rico and he pointed a gun at you?"

"I did. Yes, and he's probably been in L.A. the whole time. I'm afraid, Jaye. I picked up some things from my apartment. I need a place to stay."

Jaylin was quiet longer than Skye would've liked. "I promise I won't stay long. I found a part-time job on the other side of town, and I start tonight. Please help me."

"All right. It looks like you're in my life to stay."

"I really do appreciate this, Jaye. I don't want to be a burden; I have nowhere else to go."

"Skye, I'm here for you. As I've said before, I'm not sure why God appointed me your guardian angel, but I accept the job."

"Thank you, thank you, and thank you. I owe you big."

"You don't owe me a thing. I'm almost home. I should be there in fifteen minutes."

"I'm right around the corner. I'll wait."

Skye didn't want to tell Jaylin about the car she saw following her. If she had, Jaylin might've been reluctant to let her stay, guardian angel or no guardian angel. She had to put her car on ice—get a cheap used car or a rental that didn't cost too much. In her heart, she felt that Rico was on a mission to destroy her...eliminate her, but her will to live was much greater.

Rounding the corner was Jaye's blue RAV4. Skye hadn't been so happy in all of her life to see a familiar anything. When she saw Jaylin exit her car, she got out and retrieved the two suitcases from the trunk.

"Wow," Jaylin said, as she walked to where Skye was pulling stuff out of her trunk. She gave her an air kiss and smiled. "You meant business."

"I'm scared, Jaye. I think Rico is coming after me."

"Why don't we go inside and get off the street in case he attempts a drive-by. I'm kidding."

"That makes sense, though." Skye shook her head. "I can't believe that my once uncomplicated life has come to this."

"I'm going to call Marcus as soon as we get inside." Jaylin turned and looked Skye straight in the eyes. "Sometimes we bring it on ourselves, Skye. Hopefully, there will be a lesson that can be learned from this."

"Trust no man. Trust no woman."

"You haven't learned the lesson yet."

"What are you talking about, Jaye?"

"You called me. You put your trust in me. I could be a detractor."

"God led me here, silly." Skye smiled.

Jaye smiled back. "He did, and I'm here for you."

Jaylin picked up one of the suitcases and headed to her apartment with Skye at her heels. Skye looked up toward the heavens and blew God a kiss and mouthed, *Thank you.*

CHAPTER 34

S kye felt much better now that she was away from her apartment and had updated Marcus on all that had transpired earlier in the day. He took her key and promised to get the rest of her things out of the house and put them in storage.

Unceremoniously, Skye picked up her cell and checked the time. It was going on four o'clock and she had yet to ask Jaylin if she could use her car. There was no way she'd put herself in harm's way by driving her car, exposing herself to the criminal element that she happened to believe was Rico's henchmen. She drew a breath and pushed the words out of her mouth.

"Jaylin, ah…"

"What is it, Skye?" Jaylin asked, turning around in her small kitchen to peer at Skye who was sitting on the couch in the living room.

"I…I need a favor. I need to borrow your car to go to work."

Jaylin frowned. "Why do you need to borrow my car when you have a perfectly good one parked out front?"

Skye looked down and breathed in, then exhaled. Jaylin turned the stove off and came and sat next to Skye.

"There's something I didn't tell you this afternoon."

Jaylin frowned in disgust. "I've opened my home to you. At least I deserve the truth."

"You're right. I believe someone was following me today. I was able to shake them when I realized the person behind me had been following me for some time. My gut says Rico is involved. I need this job, but I don't want to put myself in any danger if I can help it, especially not knowing for sure if my suspicions are correct."

"Did you call the police?"

"I told you why I can't call the police. Rico will kill me."

"If you're right, he may attempt to kill you whether you call the police or not."

"I hope that Marcus can find him soon."

"But until that time…"

"I know, I know." Skye sighed. "I'll be careful and will have your car back before you have to go to work."

"Why don't I take you to work?"

"I'll be getting off late and I wouldn't want to disturb you."

Jaylin looked thoughtfully at Skye. "Tell me the truth. Look into my eyes and tell me the damn truth, Skye. What kind of job is this you're going to?"

Skye turned her head to the side and exhaled.

"Don't lie to me, Skye. I've put myself at risk helping you out. I care about you, I do. I love you like a sister, but don't make me regret the day I met you."

Skye bunched up her lips. She tapped Jaylin lightly on the knee. "It's a strip club."

"Have you lost your freakin' mind? Do you know what happens up in those joints? You're jumping out of the chicken flour straight into the hot grease."

"For real, Jaye?"

"Don't try to sideswipe the question and play dumb. You absolutely know what I'm talking about."

"I need the money."

"There are other ways of getting money." Jaylin jumped up off the couch. "Do you have any idea the kind of people who frequent those places?"

"All kinds of people. Rich people, not so rich people. Ordinary people…people like us. I went to a strip club once with Rico."

"Girl, don't play stupid with me. Did you get a clue? I was born and raised in L.A. I'm not some transplant from some town you can barely find on the map that arrived on a Greyhound bus yesterday and think they know what the city is all about. South Central was like my second home. I know firsthand about gang violence. I had friends who were caught up in gangs and have died at the hands of the dope dealer. I might have been young, but I remember the riots that almost demolished a community after Valley cops were exonerated in the Rodney King beatings. Don't come to me with your flippant, nonchalant attitude. Skye, sometimes you make me want to smack some sense into you."

"I only asked to use your car."

"Do you know what happens in those clubs, especially the private dance areas?"

"You dance?"

Jaylin stared at Skye and shook her head. "You're still drinking tittie milk, my friend. I don't know firsthand, but I hear that a lot of those women have sex with some of the patrons, and they don't even know where their stuff has been."

"I'm sure if that was going on, the men would use protection."

"Sister girl, sister girl, you're so naïve. But if you want to work there and want to use my car, I'm going to drive you. Take it or leave it."

A slow sigh filtered through Skye's mouth. Jaylin had been her savior ever since the day she'd landed in the heart of L.A. She'd been there for her every time she needed a true friend, but it was getting hard to listen to all of her verbal abuse when all she was trying to do was stay alive. Why couldn't Jaylin understand that?

"Well, what's it going to be?" Jaylin asked, obviously agitated and impatient with Skye.

"I'll accept the ride. I will have to make a stop."

"What kind of stop?"

"I've got to get something to wear."

"All you'll need is a matching bra and panty set. You're going to be taking it off anyway."

"Jaylin, I heard everything you said, but please cut me some slack. Right now, I need a way to pay the bills."

"You can stay with me for free."

"I have a car note."

"Can't do anything about that." There was a pause. "Okay, but when you get on your feet, I want you to quit this job and do something else."

"I was on my way when Rico pulled the rug out from under me."

CHAPTER 35

S ilence ensued on the ride to the strip club. Skye looked straight ahead, as Jaylin stayed on course. Every now and then, Skye could hear Jaylin's heavy breathing—a vocal sign of her disgust.

When they arrived, Jaylin cut off the engine and turned to look at Skye.

"You don't have to do this, Skye. As long as you need to stay at my house, you're welcome to it. Marcus has gathered some of his cop friends to aggressively look for Rico, and when they find him, you'll be safe again."

"Thanks. I appreciate everything you've done for me, even though I don't deserve it. A burden is the last thing I want to be."

Jaylin cupped her hand over Skye's. "You're not a burden. Remember when we first met and I took you home? I said I would be moving soon, but I'm still in the same rickety apartment. It takes time, Skye. I decided to save my money and purchase a home instead. Whether I get a great part in a box-office smash or I'm still doing hair, I'm going to get mine, even if it takes my whole life. I'm going to be comfortable, get something that's affordable, and still be fabulous without being in a lot of debt.

"True, you can make some fast money at some of these strip clubs, but why do you have to sell your soul to get it? This place is a dump. Look at it; it needs a coat of paint and a paved parking lot. I'd have felt a lot better if you'd come to me and ask which strip joint had better clientele and was better suited for you."

"If it was that easy, you'd still give me the third degree…"

"But I would have felt better."

Skye managed a smile. "Thank you for the talk; I appreciate that you're looking out for my best interest. I better go in now before I get fired before I even get started."

"Okay. Think about what I said. I'll have Marcus come and pick you up. By the way, he has some friends who're in the used car business. I'll talk to him and see what he can do to hook you up."

Skye reached over and gave Jaylin a hug. "Thank you, sis."

Skye got out of the car and walked the few feet to the entrance of the club. Turning around to look back toward where Jaylin was sitting in her car, Skye waved and then disappeared inside.

Disco music flowed throughout the club. The warmly lit interior helped to calm Skye's nerves. Other women were coming on duty and gave her a half-hearted smile when they realized that she was their competition.

Walking further into the club, Skye spotted Junebug, wearing the same clothes he had on when she'd first met him. He was leaning against the bar caught up in an animated conversation with the bartender—his head twisting from side to side while his free hand made exaggerated circles in the air every few seconds. He nursed a drink in the other hand, hugging and holding it so tight against the bar that it looked as if he were keeping it down against its will. It was Skye's imagination running rampant, but it was comical to her.

When Skye stepped forward, Junebug turned away from the bartender, possibly feeling her presence, and looked in her direction.

Recognition set in and he smiled. Junebug took a sip of his beer, set it on the counter and waited for Skye to come closer.

"Well, you were serious. I wasn't sure that you were coming back," Junebug said.

"You did give me the job."

The bartender snickered and then turned around to finish opening a jar of maraschino cherries.

"You're right…"

"Skye."

"That's right. Henderson," Junebug called to the bartender, "this is our new dancer, Hollywood Skye."

Henderson nodded. "She's prettier than most."

Skye glanced at the bartender for the first time, taking a good look at him. He was close to six feet and muscular, probably from lifting weights. His caramel-mocha skin and rugged good looks made him a shoo-in for eye candy, if she was looking for someone old enough to be her daddy. Skye turned back to Junebug.

"Give me another beer," Junebug said, pushing his glass toward Henderson. "Skye, I'm going to escort you to the dressing room and introduce you to the other ladies. My assistant, Jenny, will give you the lowdown on what you're to do. Be yourself and you'll do fine."

Skye batted her eyes. "I'm ready to get started."

CHAPTER 36

S kye followed Junebug, with beer in hand, to the back of the club, down a flight of stairs, and through a short corridor, stopping abruptly in front of a closed wooden door. Without knocking, Junebug opened the door and went right in, beckoning her to follow.

Women were in various stages of dress—breasts exposed with only a G-string covering their private parts, some fully clothed and in the process of changing, while others were completely buck naked. The ladies dismissed Junebug like he was a gnat, irritating but posing no real threat.

The room wasn't dim but not brightly lit either. Each girl had a station where they changed and put their belongings. Skye counted the women; there were fifteen in total.

As Skye followed Junebug to the area where his assistant, Jenny, was assisting one of the girls, she took casual glances at the other girls. She was surprised to find that several of them had an extra bulge around the tummy with stretch marks that looked like a road map to nowhere and oversized booties that looked as if they'd been shot with five pounds of silicone. Even more than that, a large majority of the girls weren't even pretty; in fact, there were two that put the *ug* in ugly. She wasn't a beauty queen, but for sure she was a nine-and-a-half in somebody's book.

Jenny gave Junebug a warm smile. She was pleasingly plump

with large breasts, a tiny waist, and a large, flat behind. Draping her body was an ill-fitted Lycra dress that hit midway on her thighs and had to be two sizes too small. Junebug introduced them and he was off, slurping down the last bit of his beer.

"So, you've danced before," Jenny stated rather than asking the question. She gave Skye a once-over. "You're not sassy enough to have been a dancer. But what do I know?"

Skye was amazed that Jenny was able to assess her real character that quickly. Although Jenny was telling the truth, Skye needed the job, and she was going to use her body to make sure she received a steady paycheck.

"Hollywood Skye," Jenny continued after Skye didn't respond. "Is that what they called you on the other stages you've danced on?"

"No, in fact, Junebug gave me the stage name right after he hired me."

Jenny frowned and rolled her eyes upward, but Skye didn't take offense to it. "So what stage names have you used before?" Jenny asked with sarcasm dripping from her mouth.

"Ah, ah…"

"Just as I thought. You've never danced before, have you?" This time Jenny had a malicious grin on her face.

"Ms. Jenny, I need this job in the worst kind of way. Please don't tell Junebug that I lied."

"I may not have to. Your performance will tell the story."

Skye sighed and fought back tears. She wasn't going to cry in front of this woman. However, if getting on her knees to beg for the job was her next course of action, she'd drop to the floor in a New York second.

"Look, I won't tell Junebug. You go out there and dance your heart out; give them what they're paying for. As long as you can make the crowd happy, Junebug won't give a damn." Jenny chuckled.

"I know. I make him happy all the time and I don't dance at all."

The pressure in her head felt as if it was about to blow. *Stress relief*, Skye thought, as the pain subsided. Although she'd only seen the few strippers at the club Rico had taken her to as a reference, she'd seen enough to get by. She was going to dance as if her life depended on it.

CHAPTER 37

Feeling more comfortable about her lot, Skye quickly changed into her stage clothes that consisted of a hot-pink, two-piece swimming suit that had drops of gold glitter scattered on its surface. The top tied around the neck and the back and the sides of the bikini bottoms were held together by gold-plated, plastic rings. However, she noticed that all the other girls wore thongs. Tomorrow, she'd wear a more appropriate outfit if she planned to stay in the game.

Three girls were on stage at a time, while others walked around and gave lap dances to those who requested them. And then the girls rotated—those on the stage offered lap dances and the others took to the stage. Occasionally, a patron might request a more private session in one of the private rooms, she was told. If at all possible, Skye was going to try and avoid them.

Skye's adrenaline began to flow as she and the other two dancers approached the stage. The music had a disco beat and she was surprised how easy dancing on the stage was for the other two.

The stage was in the middle of the club with three poles attached to it—ceiling to floor. Both men and women were seated around the perimeter of the stage, waiting to be seduced into some kind of fantasy. The men, young and old, looked like vultures stalking their prey. Their eyes seemed to be trained on the dancers' breasts and the upside-down V between their legs.

The two girls who accompanied Skye began gyrating as soon as they hit the stage, going down to the floor and twirling their bodies around like they were made out of elastic. She could hear the crowd egg them on with their roars of satisfaction—the dollar-bills hitting the floor in their direction. And then the awful boos and the empty floor around her told another story.

"Do sumpthin' or get off the stage," one man hollered. "I didn't come here for this crap."

"Yeah, shake that pretty ass of yours or move out the way and let somebody else work it."

Skye caught Junebug's frame in her peripheral. He had a severe frown on his face and a glass in his hand. He began shouting out something and pointing his free hand at her. She couldn't hear a thing he said, but was sure he was mad as hell. Junebug set his glass down and started for the stage when Skye saw Ms. Jenny approach, grab his arm, and gently pat his chest.

Junebug seemed to quiet down. And in the next instant, Skye closed her eyes and began to move her body. She stood in front of the pole...in front of the crowd, threw her arms backward, and began a sensual movement of her hips and thighs. Even with her eyes closed, she could hear the screams of enjoyment, when only moments ago, the screams were loud boos.

Slowly, Skye opened her eyes and batted them seductively. She moved around the pole, lifting her body onto it like she was a pro. After wrapping her body around the pole, she slithered down it, caressing it as if it were her lover. When her feet hit the floor, she extended her buttocks in the air. She waved them at her new adoring fans in slow motion and the money flew from the patrons' hands.

Feeling the moment, Skye turned around and dropped her body close to the floor. With her legs spread wide apart, she made suggestive movements with her body, all while balancing on the strength of her legs. She wiggled her way up slowly and waved her buttocks again. And without warning before an attentive crowd, Skye untied the string from around her neck and the bikini top came off. And her perky, healthy breasts were exposed for all to see.

"Damn!" someone yelled.

"Yes, that's more like it," another called out.

"Rock it for me, baby," another said. The dollar bills continued to flow.

Skye shook her wares and her inhibitions to the wind.

At the end of their set, Skye and the other two women scampered off the stage. Skye needed a towel to wipe the sweat away. She didn't recall ever dancing like that in her life, but it was exhilarating, especially hearing the howls of the folks who seemed to enjoy it.

She sniffed herself. At least her deodorant was still working. Slipping off into a side bathroom, she pulled paper towels from the dispenser and disappeared into one of the stalls. Quickly, she mopped up the sweat from her body, put her top back on, and was about to come out of the stall when she heard her stage name being called.

"Hollywood Skye, are you in here?"

It was Jenny. Damn, was the establishment watching her every move?

"Yes, Skye said from behind the stall. "I'm coming out."

When Skye opened the stall door, Jenny stood next to one of two sinks with an arm on her hip.

"You've got to get back out there and get those lap dances. You're hot and you don't want those men's fantasies to go to waste."

"Water was pouring down my body."

"That's okay. It's part of the illusion."

"That's nasty. I wouldn't want anybody dripping their sweat all over me."

"Listen up, girl. I went to bat for you and you didn't prove me wrong. But I won't tolerate an insubordinate employee. Now get your ass out there."

Surprised at Ms. Jenny's reprimand, Skye sauntered past, throwing the soiled paper towel in the wastebasket. Skye was pissed, but she was going to show her that she was a money-maker.

CHAPTER 38

"So, how did it go?" Jaylin asked after Skye climbed into the car.

There was a smile on Skye's face. She reached into her purse and pulled out a number of twenties. "This is my first night's cut. I didn't do too badly."

Jaylin examined Skye's face, turned on the car's ignition, and proceeded to drive away. "You seem pleased at your accomplishment."

"Jaye, I'm not going to be dancing forever. This is only a means to an end. I've got to act happy so I can keep the job in order to pay the bills. In fact, I'm going to pay rent. Since I'm working, I'll pull my fair share."

"You don't have to."

"I do."

"So what was it like…for you, having to dance in front of all those ravenous men that want nothing but your body?"

"To be honest, it was an adrenaline rush. Once I was able to get into it, I lost myself in another world. I became someone else, someone I didn't even know. But it felt good to know that the crowd appreciated me helping them get to their fantasies."

"For real, Skye? Those men are nothing but lecherous, booty-hungry imbeciles."

"The women were going crazy too."

"I have never understood why a woman would want to see another woman's naked ass turned up in their face."

"Even if I made a grand doing it?"

"I'm sure the club owner took most of it."

"Jaye, it may not be the most honorable profession, but it's paying someone's college tuition, pampers for someone's baby, a car note, and food for the six hungry children at home who aren't mad that momma's kickin' it up so they won't starve."

"Okay, I'll stop riding you about it, so long as you promise to give it up when you land on your feet."

"Deal."

"So tell me what happened when you gave one of those lap dances?"

"You're a hypocrite, Jaye. How is that you have the nerve to ask me about my night after I had to sit through five minutes of your ridicule?"

"You can't wait to tell me. I'm letting your butt off the hook." They laughed.

"I was afraid to go up and get in somebody's face at first, but when they started calling me by my stage name, Hollywood Skye, I was in the moment."

"Hollywood Skye? Isn't that the name you told me Rico gave you?"

"Yeah."

"Aren't you a least bit concerned that someone at the club may have ties to Rico or that he may accidently hear the name and come hunt your dancing ass down?"

"I had reservations at first, but Junebug…"

"Jesus. What kind of name is Junebug?"

"He's harmless. I'll admit the place isn't first class and I may be the prettiest girl in the joint, but Junebug seems to be on the up and up."

"Damn, Skye, I don't know what I'm going to do with you."

"Love me. That's what Jennifer Hudson said in *Dreamgirls*."
The ladies laughed.

"Well, we're home now and you're safe. Hopefully, Marcus will have found you a little putt-putt so you can ride in peace. I hope they find Rico soon."

"Me, too. Thanks, Jaye, for all you've done for me."

"What are friends for? But I still want to hear about those lap dances."

They exited the car and went inside.

CHAPTER 39

*D*ays turned into weeks, and weeks turned into months. The money Skye earned at the strip club panned out to be more than enough to embark on a brand-new start. Every time the club was open, she was dancing. She even had regulars who'd come only to see her dance.

Christmas was in a couple of weeks. Junebug said that this was one of their peak seasons, along with February when the Grammys were held or when a big-named entertainer was in the city for a concert. The club always seemed busy to Skye, but if Christmastime meant more dollars in her wallet, she was ready to punch the clock.

It was coming up on three years since Skye had been in Los Angeles, and she'd yet to go home and see her mother. Her family had been on her mind a lot lately, especially since receiving a call from her sister, Whitney, about her mother's health. As soon as the New Year rolled around, she planned to take a trip home.

As usual, the place was jumping and Skye was anxious to begin her night. She'd purchased several new outfits to dazzle her customers. She'd even brought a change for each night. Contrary to what Ms. Jenny had said, she didn't like dancing all night in the same sweaty clothes.

Junebug was in his usual place at the bar when she entered and talking to Henderson. Skye thought that Henderson was cute, but he was much older than she liked. One night before they'd gone home and he was getting his coat to leave, he stopped to tell her how beautiful she was.

Skye recalled having been flattered at Henderson's compliment. And then she lightly kissed him on the lips; it was innocent enough, but she knew he wanted more.

Now he stared at her as she neared the bar on her way to the dressing room, dressed in a pair of tight, skinny jeans and an off-white, crocheted blouse that exposed a little of her midriff.

"Hey there, Hollywood Skye," Junebug said, raising his half-filled glass to her and giving her the once-over. "Henderson, this girl is my Power Ball. Everyone in the county is coming this way to see Ms. Hollywood Skye. After she worked the kinks out of her first performance, people come in asking for her by name."

Henderson turned away and rinsed off a glass that he'd washed. He dried it, but didn't comment on what Junebug said.

"Don't you think she's pretty, Henderson?"

Skye held her head down, somewhat embarrassed.

"Yeah," Henderson said in response. "In fact, she's the prettiest girl in the club. I've told you that before."

Junebug downed the rest of his drink and asked Henderson for another. Henderson obliged, all the while taking glances at Skye as she moved away and out of sight.

"I've seen the way you watch her, Henderson. You want some of that, don't you?"

"I don't let my hormones dictate to me, Junebug. I respect these ladies and what they do. Some of them have fallen on hard times, and this is the only work they can get."

"What about Ms. Skye? She's beautiful; she could've worked in Hollywood."

"Well, she doesn't work in Hollywood; she's here dancing her ass off in your club."

"You seem to be a little overprotective, my friend. You don't want to mess with a girl like her. She'd end up breaking your heart."

"Don't worry about my heart. Jenny is whom you should be worried about. She's been so supportive of you. She has your back night and day, yet I've watched you screw half of these women right up under her nose."

Junebug slammed his glass down on the bar. "Let me worry about Jenny. She's none of your concern."

"Stay out of mine," Henderson whispered.

The night marched on. Skye danced and gave more lap dances than she'd ever given in one night. She aroused the men and let them pretend to live out their fantasies as long as they didn't touch the merchandise.

In the middle of a lap dance, Skye opened her eyes and saw Henderson looking in her direction. He abruptly turned away when he noticed that she spotted him. There was jealousy in his eyes; there was no mistaking what she saw. On purpose, she closed her eyes again and pretended to give her client the thrill of his life. When she opened her eyes, Henderson walked out to get some air, leaving an assistant to attend the bar.

It was a good night, and Skye collected her take. She sponged off her body with some moist towels she had in her overnight kit before changing back into her street clothes.

Ms. Jenny was in her office writing in a ledger when she passed by.

"Good night, Ms. Jenny." Skye waved and Jenny waved back.

More than half the girls had already left the club. Skye wished she had brought her jacket inside. It was three in the morning, and it had gotten colder than usual. Even though it was a hop-skip-and-a-jump to the car, Skye wasn't ready for the arctic blast that hit her as soon as she opened the door.

"Brrr," she mumbled, as she grabbed her chest to brace herself against the elements. Skye hadn't noticed that Henderson was right behind her.

"Take my coat; you can give it back to me tomorrow."

"No, Henderson, you take it. I have a jacket in the car."

"Why don't I wrap my jacket around you and walk you to your car?"

"You don't have to do that."

"I insist."

Skye looked into Henderson's eyes. "Okay, if you insist."

"I do." Henderson put his jacket around Skye's shoulders and escorted her to the car.

"Thank you, and here's your coat."

Henderson took his jacket and watched as Skye tried to start her car.

Irritated, Skye tried to start the car again. It was a loaner that Marcus had gotten for her. She was still afraid to drive her car around town, not sure that Rico wasn't a threat. It had been a long day, and all she wanted to do was go home.

Henderson trotted back to her car when he noticed that it wouldn't start. He pounded on the driver's window, startling Skye.

"Do you need a jump?"

"It looks as if my battery might be dead. I hate to bother you, but I'd appreciate it."

"I have a better idea. Why don't you come home with me and I'll fix you some hot tea…maybe talk awhile."

Skye threw up her hands. "Henderson, while I appreciate your thoughtfulness, it would be in my best interest to get that jump and go on home."

Disappointed, Henderson nodded in agreement. He went and got his car and placed the jumper cables from his battery to hers. It still didn't work.

"It might be your alternator. Your car will have to go into the shop for that. I've got AAA, and I can have it towed for you."

"Why are you doing this for me?"

"Don't you need help? I'd offer my services if it was someone else."

Skye smiled. "Thank you, Henderson. By the way, what is your first name?"

"You're not going to laugh, are you?"

"Why would I do that?"

"It's not the most exotic name you've ever heard."

"Try me."

"Corlis. Corlis Henderson."

Skye began to laugh. "I'm not laughing at your name. I'm laughing at you for making me laugh about your name when there's no reason to laugh about it."

Henderson laughed with Skye.

"Corlis sounds professional…Wall Street, almost aristocratic."

"Now, you're making fun of my name."

"It's a nice name."

"Come on; get in my car. It's cold out here. I'll have AAA pick your car up tomorrow morning and see about getting it fixed. So, your place or mine?"

Skye didn't answer but followed Henderson to his car. He drove an older-model Lexus, but it still looked good in the little light that she had. She walked around to the passenger side and got in and he closed her door. *A gentleman*, she thought.

Henderson got in the car and turned on the ignition, letting the car idle until it warmed up. He looked toward Skye and smiled. "Your place or mine?" he repeated.

Skye stared at him. "Your place…but only for tea and small talk."

"Okay, fair enough."

CHAPTER 40

*T*hey rode in silence to Henderson's house. He lived farther out of town than Skye had anticipated. From her vantage point and it being dark, Henderson lived in an Art Deco type of house that looked like walls of concrete on all four sides overlooking a lake. Skye looked from Henderson to the house, wondering how a bartender was able to afford such a place.

After all she'd gone through with Rico, Skye was suddenly hesitant about being there. Henderson was a complete gentleman, but so had Rico been.

"I hope you don't mind if I ask a silly question," Skye said, fidgety and unable to move forward after they'd entered his home, still standing in the foyer.

"What is it, Skye? No question is silly to me."

She blew air from her mouth and then proceeded to ask her question. "If you're only a bartender, how can you afford to live here?"

Henderson chuckled. "Whew, I thought you might be having second thoughts about being here."

"Well, that's part of it."

"I was in the NFL for eleven years. I even have two championship rings to show for it. I wasn't a Jerry Rice or Emmitt Smith."

"Who are they?"

"You know nothing about football, I see. I made a good living playing pro ball; in fact, I was inducted into the Pro Football Hall of Fame last year. I was one of the fortunate ones who didn't squander all of their money away. I've made some good investments, and I'm living a comfortable life. Junebug is my cousin, and I bartend to give me something else to do away from my other businesses. And my cousin pays me, too."

"Let's Google your name. I need to know that you're legit."

"Somebody's been hurt by love, but I don't have a problem verifying who I am. First, let me show you my football room with all of my trophies."

Reluctantly, Skye followed Henderson into the house and then to one of the rooms at the back side of the house on a lower level. Her eyes widened at the glass case full of trophies and accommodations. There were framed pictures of him in uniform and framed newspaper clippings of his prowess on the field during his college days, as well as during his professional career. Henderson stopped in front of a picture that hid a wall safe, opened it, and produced two championship rings.

Skye's mouth flew open. "Oh my goodness, you are for real."

"But to prove to you that I have nothing to hide, let me get my iPad and look me up."

There in black and white was Corlis Henderson's name, his picture, suited up in a uniform of the once L.A. Raiders. He still looked the same, maybe a couple of extra lines in his face and a hint of gray in his hair, but Skye was convinced that he was the real deal.

"Satisfied? Do I need to get my birth certificate?"

"No, no, I believe you."

"But I don't blame you, Skye. This world is full of pretenders and predators, and I admire you for going the extra mile to find out if I was a fraud or not."

"But I still made myself vulnerable by coming out to your house early in the morning."

"Do you have to check in with someone?"

Skye noted the curious look on Henderson's face. "I'm staying with my girlfriend right now. I'm planning on moving out soon. But let's get back to the issue at hand. You could be using someone else's name."

"Please, I have no reason to."

"So, Mr. Corlis Henderson, do you have a girlfriend?"

"No, I'm single. I've been married before and have two teen children—both boys. They live with their mother back east. I see them occasionally. The oldest is getting ready to go off to college."

"How old are you?"

"You don't leave any stone unturned. But since you ask, I'm thirty-seven. I know that you're twenty-two; Junebug told me." Skye looked surprised. "So, I guess you're saying that I'm too old for you."

"I didn't say that, although I may have thought it when I kissed you a few weeks ago."

"So, Ms. Hollywood Skye, why did you agree to come to my place in the wee hours of the morning? I could've taken you home."

"All right, Henderson. Let's cut the crap. Don't deny that you were sending me signals. You wanted me to come home with you—for tea and a little talk, so you said."

"I meant precisely that, although I would be lying if I said I didn't have an ulterior motive."

"And what might that ulterior motive be?"

"To get to know the real Hollywood Skye."

Henderson moved to where Skye was standing and drew her to him. He cupped her chin with his hand before placing his mouth over hers. He wrapped his free arm around her back and gingerly kissed her lips, teasing her with his tongue. His teasing became passionate and they kissed as if passion had wings.

Holding her close, Henderson planted kisses down her neck and back up to her mouth. She felt so good under his touch. Amazed that she seemed a willing vessel, Henderson took a small liberty and ran his hands down the length of her back, moving further down to the plump roundness of her buttocks. He squeezed and she moaned.

He could feel his manhood harden, resting next to the crevice between her legs. He squeezed her buttocks again and she moaned with pleasure as she pushed her body into his.

Henderson didn't want the moment to end, but he didn't want to give the appearance that he wanted to take advantage of her— to rip the clothes from her body and stroke her passion until they exploded. He did, but he couldn't.

There was something about this woman that was far beyond fire and desire. She was someone who he believed could fill his longing for true love. He'd watched her many nights dance in front of many men, even topless, but she wasn't slutty by any means, unlike many of the other girls who worked there. She kept it professional and always went straight home after the club closed, or so he believed.

She felt him tense up and drew her lips away to look at him. Skye looked at Henderson with a different set of eyes as he unmasked who he was. The feel of his hands on her back and buttocks was magic, and she didn't want him to stop. His lips were velvety and made for kissing. She'd never felt so good kissing a man.

"Is something wrong?" Skye asked, fluttering her eyelashes as she came out of her stupor.

"No, nothing is wrong," Henderson replied.

Skye searched for the words. "I'm not sure how to say this, Henderson, but this feels so right. In fact, I'll have to admit that I don't want it to end."

Henderson smiled. "I feel the same way, Skye. I love saying your name. I understand why Junebug gave you the name Hollywood Skye."

"My name is Skye Culbertson. So, why did you stop kissing me?"

Henderson continued to hold her but moved his head back so that he could get a good look at her. "Skye Culbertson, I'm feeling some kind of way about you. I'm probably putting myself in jeopardy, but I have to say this. Night after night, I've watched you dance. There is something, I can't explain, that draws me to you. Although we haven't said hardly a paragraph to each other, I think I'm falling for you...in love with you."

Skye pushed away. "Falling for me? You don't know anything about me. You see me push my body in front of those lecherous men night after night for the almighty dollar bill, and you say that you're falling in love with me? That doesn't sound real."

"I see you differently. You're doing a job out there. You're professional in every way. I'm sure that's why I care what happens to you while under my watchful eyes.

"I'll be one-hundred with you. Tonight, this morning or whatever it is, I wanted to take you home and make love to you. I wanted to see what the end result of all the foreplay was all about. Yes, I've watched you thrust your breasts in other men's faces and gyrate your body to give them their ultimate fantasy, but when I look at you, I see someone I could love...make love to...maybe have children with...live my life with for the rest of ours."

Skye was stunned into stone-cold silence. Then she raised her eyes and looked at Henderson. "That was the most beautiful thing anyone has ever said to me. Wow, I'm speechless."

"Say you won't run away. I was blunt in telling you the truth, but that's how I feel."

She looked into Henderson's eyes. "No, I'm not going to do that." She looked away and pursed her lips. "Do you care about me that much?"

"Like I said, I believe I've fallen in love with you already."

"I didn't expect this conversation at three-thirty in the morning. What about that cup of tea you promised?"

"Let's go to the kitchen and I'll get you some tea. I hope that I proved to you that I'm on the up-and-up. I'm the real deal."

"That means that I need to come clean with who I am, if it means not having secrets with someone I'm attracted to."

"Why don't you tell me all about it over that cup of tea I'm making you?"

"Deal."

CHAPTER 41

S kye watched as Henderson put the tea kettle on the stove. Sitting in the kitchen at the round, glass table in front of the bay windows that looked out at the lake behind the property, she thought about what she'd tell Henderson about her life. She wasn't sure that she wanted to divulge her whole, sad story, but she wanted to come correct, as there was something about the man who professed to loving her or growing to love her. He was meek, mild and seemingly full of understanding. Honestly, her life had been perfect up until the day her daddy died.

"A penny for your thoughts," Henderson said, smiling at her in a way no man had since she'd left home, including her ex-husband, Bryan, whom she hadn't thought much about.

Her chin sat on top of her interlocked fingers, her elbows on the table. Skye looked in his direction at the sound of his voice. "I was thinking about how wonderful this feels. No pretense. And there's something about the moon sitting in the sky in the early morning."

Henderson continued to smile. He sat down at the opposite end of the table and folded his hands. "I meant every word I said to you earlier. I could…no, I want to be with you, Skye. Forever."

Tears sprung from Skye's eyes and rolled down her face.

"Did I say something wrong?"

Skye reached across the table and placed her hand on top of Henderson's. "No, it's all good."

The steam from the tea kettle began to whistle and Henderson got up. He retrieved two cups and saucers from a kitchen cabinet and placed them on the kitchen counter next to the stove. He opened a tin can and pulled out two tea bags. "I hope you like Orange Pekoe."

"Sounds delicious."

Henderson gently placed the tea bags, one each in the two cups, poured steaming hot water over them, and brought them to the kitchen table.

"Sugar?"

"Yes, please."

"You don't have to be formal with me, Skye."

"I'm sorry; you caught me off guard by all of this."

Henderson brought the sugar bowl to the table and placed two teaspoons of sugar in her tea and sat down. Skye smiled.

"Now that you have your tea, I'd like to hear all about you."

Before she could answer, her cell phone began to ring. "I'd better get this. I'm sure it's my girlfriend checking on me since I didn't come home and she's worried."

Henderson nodded.

"Hey, Jaye," Skye said, in a cheerful mood.

"Where in the hell are you?" Jaye asked. "It's almost four in the morning and you aren't home."

"I took a detour."

"A detour hell," Jaylin screamed into the phone. "If you're going to take detours, you need to have the decency to call me and let me know you're not coming home. Got me all worried about your ass. Skye, I can't live like this."

Skye smiled at Henderson as she tried to put Jaylin at peace. "I'm sorry, sweetie. The car wouldn't start and one of my co-workers gave me a ride to their house. We got to talking."

"You weren't able to get a jump?"

"The battery wouldn't charge. It might be the alternator."

"Where's the car?"

"At the club. I'll get it towed away later today."

"No, don't bother. I'll call Marcus and have him pick it up."

"Are you sure?"

"Yes. It was an old hooptie anyway. I'll probably have to give you a ride for a few days unless you feel safe driving your car again."

"I don't know; we'll talk about it when I see you tomorrow morning."

"Okay, I'm glad you're all right. Wouldn't want anything to happen to my girl."

"Thanks, Jaye."

"Tell your friend thanks for having your back."

"I will."

Skye ended the call and put her cell phone back in her purse. She took a sip of tea and began her long, drawn-out story that ended with the day Rico pointed the gun at her.

Henderson stared at Skye and was silent for more than a few moments. She breathed in, then out, and he was still staring at her.

"I'll be here to protect you, if you let me."

That wasn't what Skye expected to hear. Didn't Henderson hear everything she'd said? She was tainted…blacklisted as an actress in the Tinsel town city. Her picture and name had been headline news, splashed in the newspapers and on all the television news shows. But it didn't seem to faze Henderson, as she laid the truth out before him, not leaving out a single episode of her life since her departure from Kansas.

"You want to protect me, someone you hardly know? I'm poison for whoever gets near me." Skye wiped her eyes as the tears continued to fall. "I had to resort to dancing since I don't have the necessary skills to do anything else. Why would you want to complicate your life with someone who has a whole lot of baggage?"

"As I said earlier, I felt there was something special about you, and I still feel that way. You've only confirmed my suspicions. I'm here for you, Skye, despite the disruptions that have become a part of your life. I have no ulterior motive but to get to know you better, love you, and be all that you need me to be."

"You can't be real," Skye said, her tears flowing even faster.

Henderson got out of his seat and held out his hand. Skye got up and went to him and melted in his arms.

"You're safe with me." Henderson pulled her chin up and turned her face to meet his gaze. "I do love you and I'm going to take care of you." And then he leaned down and kissed her.

Skye kissed him back and held him as tight as he held her. She didn't want to ever let go. Who would've thought that her knight in shining armor would be holed up in a strip joint, waiting for her arrival?

She kissed him with passion and then pushed slightly away so that she could see his face. "I want you to make love to me, Corlis. I want to feel what it's like for a man to make love to a woman."

"Skye, you don't have to do this. I'm willing to wait until you are ready."

"I'm ready."

She followed him into his bedroom. He'd seen her naked on more than one occasion. At the club, it was work—a job; in the comfort of his bedroom, it was his love for her being manifested.

Skye seemed enthralled at the size of his bedroom. It was massive—the décor was in colors of browns, blacks and beige. A king-size bed stood in the middle of the room with its back against a wall. A large bay window, overlooking the same lake that could be seen from the kitchen and set off by two masculine chairs, almost took up one side of the room. On the front wall was a built-in fireplace that extended into the next room—an enormous closet that housed all of his suits, coats, shirts, sweaters, slacks, you name it, as if it was on display at an upscale clothing store. But also suspended from the wall in front of the bed was a retractable, sixty-four-inch flat-screen where he could watch television, movies or whatever his preference in the comfort of his bedroom.

Bringing Skye back to the moment, Henderson slid the top she wore over her head and released her firm, voluptuous breasts from their holster. He stopped and kissed her on the lips.

With his lips still playfully tasting hers, Henderson let his hands roam to her breasts. He cupped them in his hands and squeezed them like he was testing for a ripe piece of fruit. He closed his eyes and squeezed them some more, appreciating the fullness and firmness of the twin beings. His appetite whet, he closed his mouth over an extended nipple and caressed them gingerly until she moaned with pleasure…he moaned with pleasure, repeating the cycle with the other.

Not wanting to give up the precious fruit, he slowly lifted his head and smiled. "Let's take a shower together, and then I want to make passionate love to you."

"Yes," Skye said without hesitation. She bent down to remove her pants and panties, but he moved her hand out of the way.

"Let me do that for you," Henderson said.

He kissed her lips and slid his hands down to the waistline of her pants. He found the zipper that held the pants in place and unzipped them. His fingers tingled as he touched her body moving the pants over her lacy bikini-cut panties, feeling the skin of her buttocks as he pushed the material down. Without wasting any time, he slid her panties from around her waist, purposely touching the fruit of her loin. He wasn't sure that he could wait to enter her, his manhood throbbing at the bit, begging to be released.

Hurriedly, he undressed. Henderson led Skye to the shower, turning it on to let the water get warm. He pulled two sets of clean towels from the linen closet inside the bathroom and handed a set to Skye.

The water now ready, they entered. The fast streaming water hit their skin, and the warmth of it made the heat that was already searing inside of them even hotter. Henderson lifted a bottle of body wash from one of the built-in shelves and poured a handful of the liquid onto his cloth.

He let the water fall on the cloth to allow the liquid to lather. He poured some on Skye's cloth and she did the same. Without hesitation, Henderson took his cloth and began to wash Skye's body, gently stroking her breasts and all the other parts of her body.

Skye followed suit, exploring his body as much as he was hers. She was delighted at the strength in his muscles, especially the one that begged for more than the casual few strokes the sudsy water and cloth evoked.

They dropped their washcloths almost simultaneously and molded their bodies together. They kissed again, the water splashing their bodies and fanning the heat of their desires. And then he lifted her and inserted his throbbing manhood into her secret garden. And Henderson made love to her like no man had ever done before.

CHAPTER 42

*S*kye sat up as the sun's rays brightened the room. She was unaware of what time it was, but she hadn't slept like that in ages. Skye turned to her side and saw the rumpled sheets were Henderson had lain. And then she smiled as she recalled the wonderful morning she'd had, making love to her new lover over and over again.

Most of all, Skye remembered Henderson's endearing words of love, respect, and how he valued her as a woman. What she was afraid to admit was that she was falling hard for him. It wasn't all about the sex, although it was a vital point that made her attraction to this man even more real.

She pulled the covers tight around her, not ready to separate from the heavenly bliss. And then she thought about the car she'd left at the club and what she needed to do to get it off the lot.

Reaching for her purse that was on the side of the bed, she jumped when Henderson entered the room carrying a tray bearing two slices of toast with jelly and a cup of tea.

"I wasn't sure what you wanted, but I figured I'd start with this." He placed the tray on Skye's lap.

"Perfect. I had a wonderful time last night…this morning. It was like a fairytale come true."

"A fairytale it wasn't. Skye, I could make love to you morning, noon, and night. Your body was so willing and you gave so easily of yourself."

"I hope I didn't disappoint you…that I made you feel as wonderful as you made me feel."

"Oh, you did, my Hollywood Skye. You did, and I'm going to have another round before we go in to work today."

"I've got to check on my car. Let me call Jaye to see if she was able to take care of it for me."

Finally pulling her cell phone from her purse, she saw a text from Jaylin.

Marcus has already removed the car. We'll talk about what ur going to do when I see u in the morn. Luv J.

Thanks J. Luv u back.

"Is all okay?" Henderson asked, bending down to plant a kiss on Skye's lips.

"Everything is great. I want you. I want you to make love to me again. I can't begin to make you understand how I feel."

"I believe I know; I feel the same way, too."

"What will this mean when you see me working tonight?"

"I won't like it, but it's too early to say what I'd like."

"What is it you want to say?" Skye begged.

"I don't want you to dance anymore."

CHAPTER 43

*I*t was a beautiful December afternoon in the City of Angels. The sun was high in the sky with the temperature already soaring to seventy degrees. It was hard to tell that Christmas was almost descending upon them with the weather warm enough to go surfing. But all the talk about Christmas parties at various venues and Christmas pageants at various churches put people in the mood to celebrate the season.

Henderson dropped Skye off at a small strip mall two blocks from the club. She didn't want anyone to observe them entering the place at the same time. Usually, Henderson was there early, setting up the bar for the night. This wasn't the time for slip-ups. Regardless of how Henderson might be thinking, she was still on her own and she needed the job.

An hour passed before Skye ventured toward the club. She felt her cell phone vibrate and she pulled it from her purse. There was a text message from Henderson that said, *I luv u. CH*

Skye smiled and texted back. *Luv u 2. On my way. HS*

There was pep in her step as Skye walked the couple of blocks to the club. The music was already jumping when she came in, and that made her feel good inside.

Skye walked and moved past the bar, which was her usual route... only route to the dressing room. She said hi to Junebug, who was chug-a-lugging his liquor down as usual, but she didn't pause to acknowledge Henderson. From the corner of her eye, she could feel his gaze, but she moved on past, afraid that all the feelings she had for him would spill out in front of Junebug and give her away.

Grateful to finally hit the dressing room, she exhaled, went to her bench, and sat down a moment to breathe. She nearly fell off when Ms. Jenny rounded a corner and spoke.

"Hey, Skye, why are you all out of breath? Oh, by the way, this towing company came and towed your car away this morning. What happened to your car?"

"It wouldn't start last night."

"How'd you get home?"

"A friend of mind gave me a lift."

"I'm sorry you were left alone. Junebug and I were anxious to get to this barbecue joint before it closed for the morning. It stays open after hours, but we had only a few minutes to get there."

"It's all right, Ms. Jenny. My girlfriend will pick me up for a few days, and I hope to be rolling again real soon."

"Well, if you need me, I'm here. We can't have our star dancer stranded."

Skye pretended to laugh. Ms. Jenny and Junebug would probably have had a fit if they knew Henderson had escorted her…to his house.

She closed her eyes, reliving in her mind how Henderson had made love to her, how he made her feel. He was so gentle, loving, and so accommodating. It was as if she was in elementary school and he was the teacher giving her, the pupil, basic fundamentals and tools to succeed, making sure she grasped every detail.

There were so many tender moments—from kissing every inch of her body to the time he entered her and gave new meaning to pleasure in the first degree. Skye always had trouble spelling "ecstasy," but for the first time in her life she knew what it was, whether she could spell it or not.

Snap, snap.

Skye jumped as the fingers of one of her dance mates popped loud in her ears.

"Where were you at?" Pleasure P asked, one hand on a hip while she twirled the other in the air. "Are you in love or sumptin'? You sure are actin' like it."

"No, Pleasure, I was thinking about my family back home," she lied. But in that instant, she did think about them. She wanted to see her mother, sister, and brother in the worst kind of way. Not sure what had prompted it, but there would no longer be lip service. Tomorrow morning, she was going to purchase a ticket to Kansas. Maybe Henderson would like to take the trip with her.

"T'aight. It's time for us to dance, sister. Make dat money like only you know how to do, Hollywood Skye." Pleasure P tapped Skye playfully on the shoulder.

"Pleasure, you're a better dancer than I am."

"Yeah, true dat, but dem dudes be hollerin' your name—Holly-wood Skye, Hollywood Skye. For sho', some nights it do be making me and Juicy jealous, but when I stop and think about how Junebug be saying we a team, I stop being mad 'cause as a team, we be raking in the dough. You get more on dem lap dances, tho." Pleasure P twerked her body until Skye couldn't look at her.

"That's nasty, Pleasure. And I don't do that."

"Uhm-hmm. That's not what dem dudes be saying, dat you get all hot and bothered. But we loves you, Hollywood, 'cause me and Juicy takes care of dem in the private room since you don't want none of dat money. Mo for us."

"See, I think about you sisters. Now let's go dance. Where's Juicy?"

"She's already out there talking to Junebug," Pleasure P whispered. "Can't let Ms. Jenny hear me. Juicy got it hot for Junebug and she tryna give him a private dance tonight—free of charge."

Skye and Pleasure P left the dressing room and walked down the hallway that would take them to the main room.

"Have you ever been in love, Hollywood?"

"Why you ask?"

"You always seem so sad, dat is until today. Sumptin' perked you up, Hollywood. I've been in love. Got me two babies by my man."

"That's great, Pleasure. I'm happy for you."

"Don't be too happy for me. Dey shot him dead. In cold blood. Dey shot Mad Dog in da head, Hollywood. All 'cause he didn't want to sell anymo dope."

Skye turned around and hugged Pleasure. "It's going to be all right."

"Yeah, it already is. It happened five years ago. Today is Mad Dog's anniversary—the day he got shot and all. I remembers it and I don't forget."

"It's going to be all right."

"Okay, let's dance."

Hollywood Skye, Pleasure P, and Juicy rocked the house. It was Thursday night and the eagle had flown in advance for some, while others waited for the eagle to land tomorrow. It was almost a packed house, and the brothers came with dollar bills ready to sling to the floor.

It was time for the ladies to switch and do lap dances. This is where they made the bulk of their money. The girls were able to keep most of it, as Junebug made money off the bar and the fifteen-dollar admission fee that included one drink.

"Hey, Henderson, did you notice that Hollywood Skye was a little off tonight—not bringing it as she usually does? Nobody has complained, but she doesn't seem to be in it."

"Naw," Henderson said, taking a peek at Skye, wishing she wasn't fanning what he'd made love to over a perverted, horny man. He'd noticed that she'd tamed her usual number somewhat, and he was appreciative.

"Watch her for me. I don't want to have to remind her about how bad she said she needed this job."

"Hollywood Skye may be feeling a little off tonight, but for the sake of the job, she didn't call in sick. Your girl came in and did what she had to do. She's a firecracker."

"I didn't figure that angle; it makes sense. One day I'm going to ride that train, Henderson. She's fine as hell and can make that booty sing."

Henderson dumped a dirty glass in the sudsy water, rinsed it, and put it on the small metal rack to dry. He could feel his muscles tense, as Junebug talked about Skye like she was a piece of meat. This wasn't the time to come to her defense, but if Junebug even remotely tried to take a liberty with Skye, cousin or no cousin, he'd beat Junebug dead into the ground. Yes, she might be dancing now, but Skye had been groomed for bigger and better things.

CHAPTER 44

Another night over, Skye called Jaylin to pick her up. She wished she'd called earlier so she could leave the club as soon as she got off. Now she had to wait the thirty-five minutes or so until Jaylin arrived.

It was close to three in the morning. Everyone was straggling out of the place, ready to take their weary selves home. Skye waited in a seat near the entrance of the club, checking her cell phone for messages, both Facebook and Twitter.

"Hey, Hollywood Skye," Jenny said, walking up behind her with hands intertwined with Junebug. "Are you waiting for a ride?"

"Yes, Ms. Jenny. My girlfriend should be here in a few. I waited too late to call her, but I'll be okay."

"We can stay with you if you need us to," Jenny offered. Junebug looked at Skye with contempt in his eyes.

"Hollywood, you were off tonight," Junebug said. He gave Skye the evil eye. "Whatever bug done bit you, shake it off by tomorrow night. I need to hear all them boys screaming your name."

"Leave her alone, Junebug," Jenny said, dragging him by the arm.

"Yes, sir," was Skye's reply. She loathed Junebug, especially the way he took special liberties with many of the ladies there, even though many of them asked for it. It was downright disrespectful to Ms. Jenny who seemed to love his crooked ass. She'd never get in bed with him, even if it meant losing her job.

"I'll be here a couple more minutes," Henderson offered, sweeping up a bit of trash that was in the bar.

"Thanks, Henderson. I owe you one."

"No problem, Junebug."

There was a deathly silence after Junebug and Jenny cleared the door. Henderson set about putting the final touch on his area so that it would be ready to go when he came in on Friday. He was neat and tidy, and he appealed even more to Skye.

Henderson got his coat and scarf and proceeded to where Skye was sitting. "Long day."

A smile crossed Skye's face. "Yeah." She looked down and away. "I had a hard time dancing tonight in front of those people." She looked up at Henderson, now a small frown on her face. "I was convicted, but I'm not sure what it all means."

It was Henderson's turn to smile. "You're feeling what I'm feeling."

"What are you feeling?"

"Skye, I'm in love with you. It was hard as hell for me to watch you out there tonight. True, if you hadn't come in here, I probably wouldn't have ever met you. I had to mentally block what you were doing and dwell on the reason you were doing it. But I didn't like it one bit." Henderson lifted her chin and kissed her gently on the lips.

"In truth, I was thinking about you the whole time I was out there dancing."

Henderson's smile was deep.

"It had nothing to do with the dancing or the shaking. I couldn't shake the whole experience—everything you said to me and the fact that you feel more for me than a booty call."

"Please don't say that again, Skye. You'll never be a booty call to me. What I did was love you the way you deserved to be loved. Junebug noticed that you weren't on your game tonight."

"So I heard."

"He said you weren't giving it your all. I smiled behind his back, but that's when I knew for sure that you were feeling something for me too."

"I do, baby…I mean, Henderson."

"You can call me baby anytime. You're my baby, Skye. What are we going to do from here?"

"My mind has been racing. Can love happen like this? I've watched *The Bachelor/The Bachelorette* on TV and swear there's no way a guy or girl can come on that show and fall in love in two months, especially after they've kissed twenty men or women, sometimes on the same day in the name of looking for love."

Henderson began to laugh. "You're so comical when you express yourself."

"I do want to be with you."

"I want you to be with me, too. If you like, you can move in with me. Tonight or tomorrow, whichever you prefer."

"Maybe we're moving too fast…too soon. I don't want to rush into something that I'm not totally sure about. Questions keep swirling in my head. Was it lust or love? I love that you made love to me last night, but I wouldn't want you to get tired of me after I've lived with you for a minute and then be put out to pasture."

"Skye, do you really believe that's what I'm asking? That would be a booty call. I'm talking about something different, possibly for a lifetime. What I feel about you started long before you pecked me on the lips. In fact, from the first day I saw you…noticed you, you worked my heart strings."

"I didn't get the message back then. It's only now that I'm realizing my heart is in turmoil…in a good way. Henderson, you're a breath of fresh air, and although you're much older than me, I get you…I feel you. I feel a lot for you. My head is telling me you're right, but my heart doesn't want to be broken again."

"I understand about heartbreak, but I'm not offering these words to you to break yours. What I feel for you is deep…real. Making love to you wasn't the determinate factor. My soul was already tuned into your spirit."

"Whew, baby. You've got to stop talking like that to me. I already feel on top of the world and don't want to come down."

"Why? For fear it is real and that someone truly loves you? Fear of the unknown?"

Skye smiled at Henderson and touched his nose with her finger. "I know it's real. But what about work? It won't be right for us to come in together. I don't want the world to know that we're one, at least not right away."

"We'll work through it. Why don't I follow you to your girlfriend's house, pick up your stuff, and you go home with me?"

"Jaye isn't going to take this well. First, I lied, well, told a half-truth about where I was this morning. And I guess I'll have to move my car."

"I see a pair of headlights, now. Let's go outside and tell your friend that I'll be following you. It would be best if you rode with her. That way, some of the thunder will be out of her roar by the time we reach her house."

They kissed each other passionately before walking out of the building. They were both in another place and time.

"Hey, Jaye," Skye said, as she opened the car door.

Jaylin jumped out, noticing the man standing next to Skye. "Hey, Skye, are you all right?"

"Yeah, fine." Skye pointed to Henderson. "Jaye, this is Corlis Henderson. He's the bartender here. He stayed behind to make sure that I would be all right."

"Thank you for taking care of my friend," Jaylin said. "Corlis Henderson...weren't you a professional football player? I don't remember the team, but my dad always talked about a Corlis Henderson he went to college with before he went into the Army that played professional ball."

"I'm the one and only Corlis Henderson. What's your dad's name?"

"Bernard Scott."

"Bernie is here in L.A.? I lost touch with him once he went into the military."

"Oh my goodness. My dad is going to go crazy. Imagine, Skye, if you hadn't gone to work here and this situation hadn't happened with your car, I may have never met one of my dad's good friends."

Skye hesitated and then got up the nerve to say what she had to say. "Jaye, I've got something to tell you."

"What is it, Skye? Can't you see I'm talking with one of the greatest ballers of all time? I remember now. He made it happen for the L.A. Raiders."

"That's well and good."

"What's wrong with you? I'm sorry, Mr. Henderson. My friend has been like a little lost puppy ever since I found her at the bus station."

Ignoring Jaylin, Skye put it all out there. "I'm going to live with Henderson."

"You're going to do what?" Jaylin's eyes roved from Skye to Henderson.

"Henderson and I are going to live together. I'm in love with him." At least she felt she was on the fast track to doing so.

"Skye, I know you. What in the hell are you talking about? You haven't even been with a man in God knows how long. Mr. Henderson, did she tell you that her ex, a crazy car thief, let her go to jail and left her cold when she was caught in his stolen vehicle? Did she tell you he stole all of her money out of the bank and threatened to kill her? She has a perfectly good car sitting in front of my house but can't drive it, as she's in fear of her life."

"Yes, she told me all about it, Jaye. And I appreciate that she did."

"Damn. My girl works fast. She usually tells me everything, but I had no idea."

"I'll tell you all about it later, Jaye. Let's get in the car and go to your house. I'm going to pick up my things." She paused. "And then I'm going to follow Corlis home in my own car."

"Cut me off at the quick until you need me again. Get in the car. Hold up. Mr. Henderson, do you realize that Skye is much younger than you?"

"Yes."

Jaye turned to Skye. "You slept with him last night, didn't you?"

"Excuse my friend, Corlis. She's overprotective and sometimes rude."

"Get in the car, Skye. I've got a lot to say on the ride home. It was nice meeting you, Mr. Henderson. I'll tell my dad that I met you, although under extreme circumstances."

"I'd like to see him again. We can exchange numbers later."

"Whatever. Right now I need to talk some sense into my friend's head."

"I'll be right behind you."

CHAPTER 45

*T*he ride to Jaylin's house was tense and somewhat brutal for three in the morning. Jaylin pushed Skye's last nerve and Skye tried to push back. There was no other way to explain to Jaye how she felt about Henderson but to come correct, tell her the truth as it was, but Jaye refused to believe and Skye somewhat understood.

After a ten-minute silence, Jaye turned to Skye.

"Skye, I'm not trying to be the big sister and dictate your life. You walked into mine at my invitation. I accepted the challenge, but I tell you, it's been a roller-coaster ride. I've come to love you as a sister, been there for you as a friend should, and have been supportive of you through all of your mishaps that were, for the most part, self-inflicted. I've given you a place to stay—not once but twice. I got my cousin to provide you with transportation so that you would be out of harm's way, and now you have the audacity to approach me in the middle of the freaking damn morning to tell me you're moving out—not next week or at the end of the month—but right now…with an older man that you barely know."

"Jaye…"

"Uhh…be quiet and let me finish. If you walk out of here tonight, I'm done with your ass. Don't bother to dial my number, text or social media me the next time you need a damn favor. I'm not your 'it girl' every time you get in trouble. And for someone who wants to change the course of their life, you don't have it in you to stay the hell away from trouble. You're like an obese person who swears out they're going to change their eating habits tomorrow since they know if they don't, it's going to kill them, but in the next minute, they're on their way to Dunkin' Donuts to buy two-dozen assorted, glazed, and cream-filled donuts."

"Damn, Jaye, you don't have to be so mean."

"There's no other way to talk to you, Skye. Nothing penetrates that thick skull of yours. I try and try again to help your ass, but all you do is take, take, take and never give back. Walk and I'm through. We're home. The rest is up to you."

Skye sat without saying a word. Jaylin's words had hit to the core. As much as she wanted to go to Jaye, hug her, say that she was sorry and that she was staying, not even her good sense would let her do it. "I'm going inside and get my things. I love you, Jaye. If I never see you again, know that I appreciate everything you've done for me. You will always have a special place in my heart and will always be my BFF."

Jaylin began to cry. Her head bobbed up and down, while a steady stream of tears flowed down her face. Skye had never seen Jaylin break down like that before. Jaylin was always the strong-willed, level-headed woman who was bad all by herself. She reached out to touch her arm, but Jaylin shook it off.

"Leave me alone, Skye. I don't ever want to see you again. Now get the hell out of my car."

Skye stepped out of the car and used her own key to enter Jaylin's apartment. Henderson's car was parked behind them. She hurriedly gathered her things together and threw them in the two suitcases she had carried to Jaylin's house. Taking a moment to look around, she remembered this was the first safe haven when she'd arrived in Los Angeles. Skye took Jaylin's house key off of her key ring and laid it on the coffee table. And then she picked up her suitcases and whatever else she could hold in her arms and carried it to the car.

Henderson got out of his car and assisted by pulling the tarp from over her car. Skye prayed to God that it would start. She hadn't driven it in awhile, although once or twice a week, Jaylin's cousin, Marcus, had cranked it up.

Hurt by Jaylin's words, she turned her head away when she saw her get out of her car, then walk away without waving goodbye. Silent tears stained Skye's face.

In luck, the car started right away, and in the next few minutes, she was following Henderson, headed for a new home with promises of forever.

CHAPTER 46

After arriving at Henderson's home, Skye requested to sleep alone. She didn't feel like being made love to. She'd hurt someone badly, someone she loved dearly. Her heart ached. Henderson understood. He made no protests or any attempts to console. Skye needed to be alone to deal with the heartache. In fact, it made him recall his own heartache when his wife that he once loved left him, taking their two sons far away and out of arm's reach.

Sitting at the kitchen table, Henderson couldn't get the scene of the two friends out of his mind. If truth be told, he was the one being selfish. He should've told Skye to wait and let the idea of her moving out settle with Jaye. But he wanted Skye near him, afraid that she'd blow away like a dandelion, if he didn't hold on tight.

A cup of Orange Pekoe tea would mellow him out. He got up and put fresh water in the kettle and set it on the stove. He sat back down and waited for the water to boil. Even in the darkness, he could see the edges of the lake when he peered out the window. It was calming.

The whistle on the kettle began to blow and scared Henderson out of his daydream. He jumped up from his seat to quiet the noise and stopped dead in his tracks when he saw Skye walk into the kitchen.

Henderson quickly turned off the kettle and moved it to another burner. He turned toward Skye, trying to assess her emotions. He held his hands out to her in the event she wanted comfort. And before he could blink an eye, she walked to him and fell into his open arms. Henderson swallowed her whole.

"Oh, Skye, I hate to see you hurting like this. I should've insisted that you stay with Jaye a little while longer instead of ejecting you from that place of comfort and warmth to satisfy my ego and wants."

She held him tight and wouldn't let go. "I made a choice. Don't get me wrong. Jaye is my girl and I'll love her until the day I die. She's been nothing but the best friend to me and I owe her, even if she never speaks to me again."

"Why don't I get you a cup of tea?"

"Thanks."

Henderson watched as she left his side and went and sat at the table. She'd been crying, and every now and then, she used the backside of her hand to wipe her face. Without uttering a word, she turned her head and peered out of the window, seemingly lost in her thoughts.

"You won't regret your decision, Skye."

"I believe you."

Henderson fixed their tea and brought the two cups to the table like he'd done the previous morning. He kissed her on the forehead and went and sat down as Skye continued to look out of the window.

"A half moon; I hadn't noticed it earlier," Henderson said, after taking a sip of his tea.

"It's amazing how God has the planets revolving around each other—the sun in the morning and the moon in the evening, each with a purpose of its own."

"I couldn't have said it better. It's remarkable how we don't always notice the moon in the sky, but when night comes and we're in the dark, the first thing we'd ask is where is the moon, and the same for the sun during the day."

Skye took a sip of her tea. "I don't want to dance anymore."

A slight smile formed on Henderson's face. "Are you sure? I don't want you to, but it has to be your choice. I've listened to every word you've said to me, Skye, and I want to support you in your decisions and hopefully offer suggestions when necessary."

Skye looked at Henderson thoughtfully and smiled. "I'm going to continue through the holidays since Christmas is right around the corner. I want to take a break and go home to see my mother and siblings.

"I don't know why, but I've been thinking a lot about them lately, Henderson. I need to ask them for forgiveness. I've done a lot of growing up in the three years I've been away from home. I've come to realize that the God who put the sun, moon, and stars in the sky has taken care of me all this time, and I'm sure it's that my mother was praying for me."

"God works in mysterious ways."

"He does."

"Skye, it may be presumptuous of me to say this, but I'd like to go home with you. I'd like to meet your family—get to know them."

Skye's eyes widened. She stared at Henderson like he didn't have good sense. "Are you sure?" Skye pointed at herself. "You want to go home with me?"

"Yes." Henderson took a sip of tea, then another.

The momentary silence was broken with a bout of laughter. Skye leaped from her seat and went and sat on Henderson's lap, almost knocking over the remainder of his tea.

"Baby, I love you. To say that you want to go home with me means so much. It tells me that there is more to our newly formed friendship...relationship. Am I right?"

"Skye, I haven't stuttered once about my feelings for you. I want it to be a whole lot more. I want our friendship to blossom into a love that goes beyond anyone else's expectations or understanding. I know it may not seem real, but my love for you is real. Maybe it was God who aligned the moon and the stars to bring us to this moment."

"Okay, babe, you're stretching the truth a little bit."

Henderson laughed. "Maybe so, but there's a reason you're in my life…at this time. I wasn't looking, per se, but I'll go on record by saying out loud that the day you walked into that club, my spirit recognized you were for me."

"I feel like I'm on reality television."

"That's bull. This is real. Reality television is set up by producers who thrust their cast members into ridiculous, stupid situations where they end up making an ass out of themselves."

"You're right about that." Skye placed her arms around Henderson's neck and kissed him passionately.

He held her around the waist and kissed her ferociously, giving her all he had. He was puzzled too about how it all had happened… so fast and in such a nontraditional way. Henderson thanked the Lord above for sending this woman to him.

Skye pulled away first. "First thing when we get up, I've got to talk to Jaye. I have to make her understand that I've truly fallen in love with you and that it isn't a replay of what my former life has been. I've got to reconcile this thing between us. But now, I want to take back what I said when we first got home."

"What was that?"

"I don't want to sleep alone. I want my man to make love to me. You know what?"

"What is it, baby?"

"I'm going to call in sick tomorrow. Junebug is going to be some kinda pissed, but I'm taking a day off. I'm going to fix my man a nice meal before he goes to work and I'll be waiting for him when he returns."

"You don't have to ever go back there, if you don't want to. Junebug will be mad as hell, but he'll get over it. Go ahead and make that last bit of money, though. I don't know how I'll be able to stand it, but at the end of the day, the prize is in knowing that I'm the one you're giving your private dances to."

"You're right about that, baby." Skye cupped her hands around Henderson's face and kissed him again. "This is so right."

"Enough of this foreplay, baby. Get up. Let me take care of you."

"Umm, umm, umm."

CHAPTER 47

For the first time in a long time, Skye was truly happy. Her new-found love with Henderson was magical, so totally different from the relationship she had with Rico. She and Henderson were one. They talked about everything under the sun. They listened to what each other had to say, whether they agreed or disagreed.

Henderson might have been older, but he was wiser and an excellent lover. Skye had to admit that she was a little naïve about the art of love-making and what sex was really all about. She'd gone through the motions with Bryan and Rico, but it was Henderson who taught her the real art of seduction and how to please not only her man but herself. And she had fun learning.

One Monday, she and Henderson rode down the coast to Malibu for a casual lunch and great conversation. With swimsuits underneath their garments, they stripped down at a cabana and headed to the beach. They put their toes in the sand and enjoyed the ocean. They were a couple in love.

Now only a few days before Christmas, Skye raked in the money. She'd saved up a nice little sum for herself and didn't make the mistake of pooling her money with anyone else. She was single and she handled all of her affairs like the sole person responsible for her livelihood should. It made her think of Jaylin, though, who refused to take any of her calls or respond to the many text messages she sent.

Henderson had to make an early run and Skye was thankful for the alone time. Her plan was to run to Beverly Hills and purchase her man a Christmas gift. She also wanted to get something for her mother who she'd be seeing soon. Henderson had already purchased their airline tickets for New Year's Eve, so that they could ring in New Year with her mother.

"Happy, happy, happy," Skye sang, as she applied lipstick to her lips. Her reflection in the bathroom mirror told the story she sang.

All set to do her Christmas shopping, Skye grabbed her purse and headed for the garage. Never in a million years would she have believed that she'd be living in a $4 million house. She got in her car and strapped her seatbelt. God had truly been good to her.

Now that she was living with Henderson, she drove her own car to work. Privacy was their number one priority, other than loving up on each other. Finally, she was able to relax, as there hadn't been any sightings of Rico or his boys.

Overcast skies didn't hinder Skye's mood. She was in a world of her own, thinking about life, as she sailed through Baldwin Hills on the way to her shopping excursion. She hadn't been this excited about Christmas in a long time. A simple gift is what she wanted to give Henderson, and she headed to Cartier to purchase a watch that she'd seen him eyeballing. He'd given her a small allowance and a credit card, which helped to make up her mind about what to get him.

With a boat load of confidence, Skye walked into Cartier and asked the sales associate for the Tank watch her man had been eyeing. She paid no mind as the sales associate kept staring at her, possibly wondering how she could afford to purchase a gift that nice.

"Yes, thank you," Skye said with assurance. "It's a Christmas gift for my man."

Skye was irritated as the sales associate continued to stare while ringing up the sale. And then the sales clerk startled her.

"Aren't you the actress that played in *Happy but Free?*"

Skye was speechless. "Yes, yes, I am. My character had a recurring role but was eventually written out of the script."

"Too soon."

"I'm sorry?"

"They wrote you out of the script too soon," the sales associate said. "I thought you added that pizazz the show needed. You were becoming the star of the show and they must've gotten jealous."

Skye smiled. Nothing could ruin her day after this. Now she understood why the sales associate was staring so hard. "No, that wasn't the reason, but I appreciate your feedback."

The sales associate completed the transaction and wrapped Skye's purchase for her. "He's a lucky man."

"No, I'm a lucky woman."

"I hope to see you on another sitcom soon. Your character, Tracey, reminded me so much of myself."

Skye let go of a smile. It was so heartwarming to hear the praise from this woman. Maybe her acting days weren't over. "Thank you and I'm sure you'll be seeing me again soon."

She took her package and headed to Neiman Marcus. She was going to buy her mother a fabulous dress so they could celebrate when she returned home.

CHAPTER 48

The club was bustling with early partygoers. Skye slipped through the lobby and past Henderson without being detected. This was the night she planned to give Junebug her resignation notice. She was in a good place, and this afternoon's acknowledgment by the sales associate of her acting abilities only strengthened her resolve to make something better of her life. If acting was it, she was ready for the challenge and the drive to reenter the arena when the time was right.

"Hey dere, Ms. Hollywood."

"What's up, Pleasure P?"

"It's gonna be jumpin' and poppin' up in here tonight, girlfriend. I'm ready to make dat cash. Me and mines are going to Vegas for Christmas."

"Good for you, Pleasure. But make sure that new man of yours spends some of his money on you."

"Hollywood, don't take me for no fool. I may act like I ain't got no sense, but I ain't goin' let no man take vantage of me."

"Way to go. Let's find Juicy and get this show on the road."

Pleasure P got close to Skye and whispered in her ear. "You missed the sho-down. Juicy was up at the bar rubbing on Junebug's leg when Ms. Jenny come from outta the bathroom and caught dem. Ms. Jenny got up in Juicy's face. Juicy played all big and bad, pointing her finger in Ms. Jenny's face."

"No wonder I didn't see anybody when I came in."

"They was probably behind closed doors tryna hash it out. Ms. Jenny want Juicy gone, but Junebug come to her defense like normal. Junebug be likin' wat Juicy be puttin' down."

"No one has the right to mess with someone else's man."

"Hmph, I know wat you talkin' 'bout. Let's go on up befo' they send someone to get us. Don't want no trouble; I only want to make dat cash for me and mine."

"Have you ever thought about doing some stand-up comedy?"

"You think I'm good, Hollywood?"

"Pleasure, you keep me in stitches."

"I must have some magic cuz you been happy every day for over a week."

"I am happy. My life has come full circle, and I've decided to go and see my family that I haven't seen in a long while."

"Good for you! I'aight, let's go sling some booty."

The music grew louder as they neared the entrance to the main room—the heartbeat of the club. Skye peeked in and saw that the crowd was growing. She tried to sneak a peek at Henderson, but he was out of eye view. If things had gotten heated between Junebug and Juicy, there wasn't a hint of it in the air—except Juicy was nowhere to be seen.

Skye and Pleasure P moved forward, waiting for the other girls to exit.

"I'm not playin'," Pleasure P started in. "Juicy better bring her ass on over here. We used to dancin' in threes."

"Here comes Junebug," Skye remarked. "And he doesn't look too happy, either."

"Aww, hell. He's gonna ruin my good feelin'."

Junebug stopped in front of the duo ranting and raving, twirling his hands in the air, as if he was a maestro conducting an orchestra.

"Juicy isn't dancing tonight. The two of you will have to work hard to bring in those extra dollars she would've made. I don't want any slacking, Hollywood. That also means you're doing private dances tonight."

"Why can't some of the other girls do it?" Skye asked, trying to remain calm and control the volume in her voice.

"Because I said so, if you're going to work in this club."

"Is she sick?" Pleasure inquired.

"No, she's not sick," Junebug hollered back.

"Well, I saw her…"

"Listen up, Pleasure, your job is to go out there, dance and rake in the money. Let me worry about personnel issues."

"Pleasure was only concerned," Skye interjected.

"You don't have to take up for me, Hollywood. My daddy isn't here, and Junebug know betta than to raise up on me."

"Listen here, Pleasure," Junebug began, "I can send you packing like we did Juicy."

"You fired her? Of all the low-down dirty crap you be doing, you had the nerve to fire Juicy? Damn."

"I'm warning you, Pleasure. You're standing on thin ice and my one last nerve. You aren't even as good as Juicy and you ain't that pretty. Now shut the hell up and get out there and do what I pay you to do."

A nasty scowl enveloped Pleasure's entire face. If looks could kill, Junebug would be dead. Her fingers flexed before balling them up into a fist.

"He's not worth it," Skye whispered in Pleasure's ear. "Payback is a dog, and he'll get his."

Pleasure looked at Skye and released the frown slowly. "Thanks,

Hollywood. If I didn't need da money, I woulda hauled off on that monkey's ass." She sighed. "Let's dance."

The girls moved forward when it was their time to go on. Junebug watched them like a hawk ready to snatch its prey. Hollywood Skye and Pleasure P rocked it, and the dollar bills seemed to rain from the sky.

Skye knew Henderson was watching. She tried to tame her act, but every time she glanced at Junebug, he would make funny facial gestures…his attempt to get her to bring it up a notch.

Whenever she found the right time, she was going to tell Junebug that it was a week from it being her last day on the job. She looked forward to leaving this part of her life behind; it had satisfied its purpose—the need to survive. She was ready to move on. Move on with Henderson.

When she caught sight of Henderson looking at her, he gave her a brief smile that she didn't reciprocate—not that she didn't want to. If she had her way, she'd walk off the stage right then and there, grab her man, go home and make love to him. But she couldn't and so she kept on dancing.

The crowd was a little more rowdy than usual. The festive mood of the holidays had more people out and about. And they seemed to have a lot of disposable cash.

Skye hated lap dancing, but tonight would be no different than any other. She'd perfected the illusion she gave those beer-breath-drinking parasites, and the money came easy out of their pockets.

Finishing up her second lap dance, she headed to the restroom to wipe the sweat from her brow. As she moved through the crowd, someone caught her hand. The gentleman wore a maroon-colored suit with a tieless, black, dress shirt underneath. A black, suede fedora lay low on his head, blocking his eyes.

"I want a private dance," the gentleman said, keeping his eyes hidden and still holding Skye's hand.

Without seeing his face, she recognized the voice. It had been a minute, but there was no forgetting the voice of the enemy.

Skye tried to snatch her hand away, but he tightened his around her wrist.

"There's no need to put up a fight. I came in here to get what every other patron came here for—to be tantalized by the star of the show, Hollywood Skye. Isn't that the name I gave you? Couldn't get me out of your system, could you?"

"I don't do private dances," Skye said through gritted teeth. "Now take your damn hands off me, Rico. Your ass should be in jail."

Rico tightened his grip around Skye's wrist. Before Rico could say another word, Junebug was front and center.

"What's going on here, Hollywood?" Junebug asked with hands on his hips.

"I want a private dance," Rico offered. "This beautiful lady said she doesn't give private dances."

"Oh the hell she does," Junebug roared. "Get your ass on over to the private rooms and do what I pay you to do."

With a severe frown on her face, Skye pointed her finger at Junebug. "I don't do private dances."

"Tonight you will and I don't want to hear another word."

Rico smiled, amused at Junebug's theatrics.

"I guess I'll get that private dance after all." Rico stared at Skye with dreamy eyes. "And I'll pay well."

"Go on, Hollywood, you heard the gentleman. He said he pays well."

Not wanting to make a scene, Skye headed for one of the private rooms followed by Rico. She saw Junebug run to the bar, no doubt to tell Henderson what had gone down. She loathed Junebug; she despised the ground he walked on. But it made her decision easy.

Tonight would be her last night dancing in anybody's strip joint.

The door closed and Rico eased back onto the purple velvet chair. "Dance for me, Skye. And I want you to put it on me like you used to."

Hands on her hips, Skye stared at him. "Where is my money, Rico? I want to see all the money you owe me before I make one move with my body. I want every red cent, down to the last penny."

Rico sat back, arrogant as they came. "I don't owe you a damn thing. Don't make me have to call my boys in here and rough you up."

"You should be in jail. I don't understand how the LAPD has allowed a simple-minded criminal like you to walk around the streets of L.A. without getting caught."

"It's called staying under the radar. Besides, more than half the cops on the force are crooked—on the take. I'm small potatoes as compared to the criminals they're really trying to catch…or not catch. Now, shut up and get to dancing."

Skye didn't move. Her defiance was getting the best of Rico.

"I want you to dance and not over there by the door. Is it money you want?" He reached into his pocket and took out a wad of bills. He pulled off five twenties and threw them on the floor. "That's all you have left. Now dance for me, bitch, before I slap the make-up off of your face. By the way, it looks crappy on you. Makes you look cheap."

Skye studied Rico for a moment and walked over to where he sat.

"That's my Hollywood Skye." Rico took off his jacket and un-buttoned his shirt. "Now move on command. I want you to put it in my face."

Her face was void of expression. She moved in close, her torso right at his face.

"Take off your top and move that ass."

Skye began to gyrate her lower torso and pretended to take off the covering over her breasts. Before Rico knew what was happening, Skye balled her hand into a fist, drew it back, and punched him full force in the face.

Rico tried to jump up, but Skye took the heel of her stiletto and kicked him in the groin. A blood-curdling scream erupted from his mouth. However, with one swift motion, he grabbed one of Skye's legs and pulled her to the floor.

"You stupid-ass bitch," he yelled as he took his fists and continuously pounded Skye in the face. Then he took his shoe and kicked her in the ribs and stomped her in the abdomen several times.

Blood oozed from Skye's mouth and she lay on the floor helpless and not moving. The door was pushed open in the next instant, and Henderson, Junebug, and two of Rico's boys flew in. No doubt, they had heard Rico's screams.

"Skye, are you all right?" Henderson asked, dropping to where she lay motionless. Her face was bruised and swollen with blood oozing from her mouth. He felt her pulse. It was faint.

Scrambling to get up with the help of his boys, Rico rushed to speak. "That bitch hit me in the face. I'm going to sue your ass and have this rinky-dinky piece of a hole-in-the-wall shut down."

Junebug started to say something, but Henderson jumped up and pushed him back. He took one look at Rico and rammed his face with his fist. And then Henderson felt a blow to his, as one of Rico's boys tried to lay him out, but Henderson was too strong for the man. The other man came toward Henderson, and he knocked him on the floor, reminding him of his former days on the gridiron where he knocked many opponents down.

"What are you doing, Henderson?" Junebug asked in a frightened voice. "He said he's going to sue."

Henderson continued to hit Rico in the face until he lay there bleeding. "Make yourself useful, Junebug. Call the ambulance. NOW! And call the cops, too."

Junebug nearly ran from the room, anxious to get out of harm's way. At the same time, Rico's boys hoisted him in the air and fled the room.

Henderson went over to Skye and held her head up. He checked her pulse and put his ear to her face. Skye's breathing was shallow. "Hold on, babe. We're going to get you to a hospital."

CHAPTER 49

The LAPD and ambulance arrived one behind the other. In his colorful way, Junebug described the ordeal to the police, his arms flailing this way and that in an attempt to demonstrate the sequence of events. Henderson also gave his account of things at the point he entered the room. The EMS personnel hurriedly went to Skye who was still lying on the floor. Her pulse was weak, and the EMS team quickly scooped her up.

"We need to start her on IV meds right away," one of the attendants said to Henderson who was lingering so close to Skye, the paramedics were hardly able to maneuver around him.

"Where's the perp?" one of the officers asked as he took notes. A technician took pictures while the other collected items that were in the room.

"He had two bodyguards. I hit them hard, but I couldn't hold them down. I got in a couple of good punches, but his bodyguards lifted him up and ran out of the room."

The officer wrote something down on his pad. "I'll need a description."

"Riiiico," Skye said in an almost inaudible voice. "Riiico," she repeated.

"Rico?" the officer asked, moving close to her while writing feverishly on his notepad as the EMS team moved Skye from the private room and through the club.

Skye nodded her head. "Riiiico Tilllman…wanted by the police."

"Rico Tillman is an alias," the other officer stated. "His real name is Tyrone Rogers. He's on the LAPD radar. He's part of a car-theft ring that was operating in the city."

There were gasps from partygoers as Skye was wheeled through the club.

"That's a shame," a female observer said, her hand spread broadly across her heart.

"She was the best dancer in the house," a male observer added, as the gurney finally exited the building.

Henderson felt helpless. He turned to Junebug. "I'm going to the hospital to see about Skye."

"Somebody has to bartend, and I don't want that assistant of yours, who can't do anything without your assistance, to stand in your place. And why do you care what happens to her? She's nothing but trouble. I can't stand a subordinate wench."

"You don't care about anybody but yourself, Junebug. Skye was mugged in your club."

"Well, she must've brought it on herself. Good riddance."

"She was probably going to quit anyway."

"How do you know? Did she tell you that…that sneaky wannabe diva?"

"No," Henderson lied. "She didn't tell me, but I sensed it."

"Whatever. I need you to bartend. I'll have Jenny check on her."

"I'm going, Junebug." Henderson took off the apron from around his waist and threw it at Junebug.

"How can you leave me stranded, Henderson? We're flesh and blood."

"That lady who was taken out on a gurney and beaten within an inch of her life in your club needs someone to champion for her."

"You're all battered and bruised yourself. How are you going to help somebody?"

"I'll be fine. While I'm at the hospital, I'll get it attended to."

"Go on. It doesn't matter to me. She's a whore who dances."

Henderson turned around and grabbed Junebug by the collar. There was pain in his face. "Don't ever let me hear you say that again about Skye. You're mad because you couldn't manipulate her like you do these other women. You need to worry about whether or not she's going to sue you. After all, this happened at your club. And from what I hear, she adamantly told you that she didn't do private dances."

"What's up with you, Henderson? You act as if you're in love with the girl."

"He is," Jenny said, coming up behind Junebug. "It's been written on his face for some time. I wish I had someone who loved me half as much."

CHAPTER 50

"I want that bitch dead," Tyrone Rogers, alias Rico Tillman, declared. His lower abdomen was painful from the blow he'd received from Skye's high-heeled shoe. "She's going to pay for this."

He continued to hold his groin as he waited for a nurse to come and examine him at the residence of a distant cousin who lived in Riverside—approximately an hour drive from Los Angeles. He'd been hiding out there for months on end, moving between there and several properties he owned, while hiding his operation in the bowels of the city. He might have to move again since Skye's amateur kung-fu move had brought attention to him. Thank God for his bodyguards who quickly picked him up and escorted him to safety.

"Benny, I need you to find out what hospital Skye is in."

"Okay, boss, but I hope you aren't going to do anything stupid… you know… that'll jeopardize what we're doing."

"I don't pay you to think, Benny. Get the name of that hospital, now."

"Yeah." Benny exited the room and made phone calls to several hospitals in Los Angeles. No one would give him any information, but he knew someone he could call that might be able to get it for him.

Big Sarge, Rico's other bodyguard, walked into the room where Benny was placing calls. "What's up, Benny?"

"Trying to locate the girl."

"You mean Tyrone's ex-girlfriend?"

"Yeah. I'm sure she was taken to the hospital after seeing that ambulance whiz by us."

"Why is he looking for her? If he left well enough alone, we wouldn't be in this mess. We can't keep running from the law forever."

"You're right, man. After fleeing L.A. and coming here, I thought it was a bit too close for comfort, but we've been able to manage. I don't understand his fascination with his ex. He had me tail her one day when we spotted her cruising through L.A., but we lost her. She's a slick chick. However, ever since one of his other homeboys went to the strip club and told him about this dancer named Hollywood Skye, he's been obsessed with finding her."

"Benny, this is the kind of crap that gets your ass locked up. I ain't going out like that, especially since we came so close the last time. If I have to cut my losses, I will."

"Big Sarge, don't let Tyrone hear you talking like that. He has the mean streak on him today. I'm afraid that he's going to ask one of us to go to the hospital and kill her."

Big Sarge's muscles flexed. "Damn, Benny. I'll strong-arm anybody who tries to get at him. I'll help him move these cars he's been stealing, but kill an innocent somebody? I didn't sign up for that."

"Oh, you did, my friend. Dah…does the word 'bodyguard' tell you what's in the job description?"

"I'm not making sense; I realize that. But his obsession with the girl is his doing and he's only making matters worse by pursuing her."

"Big Sarge, don't go and get soft on me. We're all in this thing together. Tyrone's ex can finger him. He scraped clean any and all identifiable connections to the last name he used before, although the LAPD may already know that Rico Tillman is an alias. That's all the girl knows, too. She still doesn't have a clue as to who Rico/

Tyrone really is or where he lives. I did forget to tell you that she saw him at the condo some months back."

"Damn, Benny. Tyrone makes too many slip-ups."

"He had no idea that the ex was going to show up there."

Big Sarge sighed. "Well, we're all going to be in the pen with numbers painted on our jumpsuits."

"That's why I believe he will want us to kill his ex—to keep her quiet."

"Whatever, man. This is some messed-up crap. Call me when the nurse arrives. I've got to make a run."

"Don't go too far, Sarge. I have a feelin' stuff is going to jump off real soon."

"Okay."

CHAPTER 51

Skye was clinging to life. She had trauma to the head that included a broken nose. She sustained several cracked ribs and there were bruises all over her body from where Rico Tillman tried to stomp her to death. Her face was so swollen that she didn't look anything like herself. The paramedics were able to control the bleeding, but fear of brain damage was a real possibility.

Henderson stayed close, vowing not to leave Skye's side until the doctors whisked her into the ER. He silently prayed for the new love of his life—that she'd come out of this ordeal with a minimal amount of suffering.

Realizing he was the only support Skye had, Henderson got up and walked around. He needed to call someone to let them know what had happened to Skye. He had no idea how to get in touch with Jaylin, although she hadn't responded to any of Skye's messages. And there was her mother and siblings. Surely, they needed to be notified.

All of Skye's belongings were probably in her locker at the club. Henderson pulled out his cell phone and immediately called Jenny.

"Jenny," Henderson said, not giving her an opportunity to say hello.

"Henderson, is Skye all right? I've been worried sick about that child ever since they took her out of here. That dude beat her up some kind of awful."

"Yeah, it's bad, Jenny. Right now I need you to do me a favor."

"Anything, Henderson. Shoot."

"I need you to get into Skye's locker and retrieve her belongings, especially her cell phone. I've got to call someone who's close to her to let them know what's going on."

"Yeah, yeah, yeah, you're right. I'll do that right away. Look, I've got to ask you something."

"What is it?"

"Are you in love with her, Henderson? I've seen the way you look at her when she's dancing and when she's not dancing."

"Jenny, this is between you and me. I love Skye. I haven't felt this way about anyone in a long time."

"But you hardly know her. She's a dancer at your cousin's club. No telling what kind of crazy life she's been leading beyond our four walls."

"You're right to make that assumption, however, I'm well aware of whom Hollywood Skye really is, and I'm still discovering."

"What are you trying to say?"

"I've already told you enough. All you need to know is that I'm in love with her."

"Does she know that? She comes in here, does her job, and leaves. I've not once seen her give you a sideways glance nor is she all up in my man's face like these other hussies."

"It doesn't matter. Now, I'd appreciate it if you'd get Skye's stuff and bring it to Cedars-Sinai."

"Cedars-Sinai?"

"I wanted her at the best hospital."

"Hmph, there's more to this than you're telling. Okay, I'll get her things."

"Call me when you arrive and I'll come and meet you."

"All right. You know Junebug is going to be mad that I'm leaving."

"He'll get over it. Tell him I'm making the request."

"Okay, I'll see you as soon as I can."

Henderson ended the call and waited.

From out of nowhere, photographers, cameramen, reporters with all types of camera and video equipment, notepads, and microphones flooded the waiting room where Henderson sat alone. How in the world did they find out?

"Excuse me, sir," said a medium-height brunette who wore a pair of khakis and a plain white blouse, flashing her credentials. "I'm Presley Eubanks, reporter with KABC-TV. Were you with Ms. Skye Culbertson when she was brought into Emergency this evening?"

At first, Henderson was reluctant. He had been away from the limelight a long time and preferred the quiet, non-invasive life he had acquired.

"Yes, I was." He barely remembered Skye's last name. She'd only mentioned it once that he recalled.

"Aren't you Corlis Henderson, former linebacker for the L.A. Raiders?" the videographer asked, dropping his equipment to his side.

Henderson smiled. He stood up and gave the videographer a fist bump. "I'm one and the same, brother."

"Damn, this is real. Presley, get Todd to take a picture of me and the greatest linebacker to play in the NFL."

"We're trying to do a story, Darnell," Presley said, not too happy with the interruption. "Todd, please take Darnell's picture so we can get on with it."

Picture taken, Henderson and Darnell took the opportunity to bump fists again. Darnell picked up his video equipment and it was back to business as usual.

"Can you tell me what happened to Ms. Culbertson and how

you became involved," Presley rambled, her immediate concern…
getting the hot news headline story.

"She was assaulted by a man named Rico Tillman at a club this
evening. I'm the bartender at the club and I came to the hospital
to be with Ms. Culbertson since there was no one else to accompany
her at the time."

"Did you witness the beating?"

Henderson sighed. "I didn't see the actual altercation, but Skye
didn't walk into the room the way we found her."

"Did anyone else see what happened?"

"No, however the circumstances surrounding how it happened
points directly to this guy, Rico Tillman."

"What were the circumstances and how do you know Rico Tillman?"

"Ma'am, Ms. Culbertson was giving Mr. Tillman a private dance."
Henderson looked away. He sighed. "The club is a strip club. Ms.
Culbertson was in a private room with Mr. Tillman when we heard
screams coming from inside the room. Several of us went in and
we found Skye lying on the floor and Mr. Tillman off to the side
looking crazed."

"Who else went into the room with you?" Presley pressed.

"The owner of the club, Rudy Nixon, who goes by the name of
Junebug, and two men who had accompanied Mr. Tillman."

"How do you know Mr. Tillman? Is he a regular at the club?"

"No, I can't say that I've seen Mr. Tillman before. In fact, I'm
not sure that Mr. Tillman is his name. After the police arrived,
Skye…Ms. Culbertson, tried to speak and uttered Rico Tillman's
name. One of the police officers recognized his name."

"Do you have any idea why Ms. Culbertson was beaten?"

"None whatsoever."

"What about this Mr. Tillman, if that's his real name?"

"What about him?"

"Was he hurt? Did the police arrest him?"

"Ms...."

"Ms. Eubanks."

"Ms. Eubanks, it all happened so fast. My concern was for our employee. I did hit the man the police called Tillman, but before I knew it, his companions took him out of there before the police and ambulance arrived."

"Thanks. You've been quite helpful, Mister…"

"Henderson, Corlis Henderson."

"That's right, the greatest linebacker to play in the NFL."

Henderson didn't smile.

"One more question. What about Ms. Culbertson's family?" Presley asked.

"No one has been contacted as yet. Ms. Culbertson was a loner for the most part. We don't know much about her."

Presley put her notepad away. "We've got what we came for. Let's get this into the station." She and her crew packed up and left. Henderson gave the same answers to the other news media, but it was a TMZ reporter that got his attention.

"Ms. Culbertson was a rising star when the unfortunate incident about her driving a stolen vehicle abruptly ended her career."

Henderson wasn't going to acknowledge that Skye had shared that bit of her life with him. Even though it sounded like a fairytale when she was telling the story, the reporter's comment made it all too real. He offered no comment to the reporter.

The cell phone in his pants began to vibrate. Pulling the phone from his pocket, Henderson quickly checked to see who had texted him. It was Jenny, and she was downstairs. He was grateful that Jenny hadn't come a moment earlier.

CHAPTER 52

*H*enderson hugged Jenny when he saw her; she hugged him back. And before he could ask, Jenny was handing him Skye's belongings.

"I feel like I'm trespassing," Henderson said, as he opened up Skye's purse to search for her cell phone. "Got it."

"Great. She needs her family's support."

Henderson tapped on the phone and swiped his finger across it. "Damn, it's locked."

"You've got to be kidding me."

"No, Jenny, it's locked and without a password there's no way I can get the answers I'm looking for." Henderson threw his hands up in the air in disgust.

"I'm sorry, Henderson. Technology is wonderful, but sometimes we defeat ourselves with ourselves."

"I couldn't have said it better. May I ask you a question?"

Jenny frowned. She put one hand on her hip and bent her leg slightly, like she was getting in ready mode to do a karate film. "What's on your mind, Henderson?"

"This may be none of my business, but I care about you."

Jenny smirked. "If you're thinking it's not any of your business, you're probably one-hundred percent right that it isn't."

Henderson smiled. "You are so feisty when you want to be." Jenny smiled. "Look, you and Junebug have been together a long time.

I don't know what his intentions are for you and what you would like to see happen in your relationship."

"You're two seconds from getting your feelings hurt. First of all, I thought this rendezvous was about Skye. How did my personal life become a topic of discussion?"

"Let me put it like this. I care about you, Jenny, and I hate how Junebug treats you. How you put up with him and his disrespect of you by doing what he does with other women right under your nose, I'm not able to comprehend. You deserve so much more than that."

Jenny took her hand off of her hip and tried to catch a tear that dripped from her eyes and down her face. She caught her breath and fought back more tears that threatened to fall. Henderson reached for her, but she brought both hands up like a wall of protection to ward him off.

"You're right, Henderson; it's none of your business."

"But, Jenny…"

"Let me finish, Henderson. I appreciate your concern, I really do, but Junebug is my concern. I don't like what he's doing with those whores…"

"So why in God's name are you putting up with his crap? Love is one thing, but abuse is another. The two don't go together. What it leads to in the end is domestic squabbling, and I don't want to pick up a newspaper one morning and read a domestic violence story with a sad ending with you and Junebug as the main characters."

Jenny looked at Henderson for a long while without speaking. "You're serious, aren't you?" she finally said.

"Yes, sweetie, I am. Who knows what these women have that Junebug has been fornicating with. STDs, HIV…that stuff is real. He says he uses protection, but Junebug lies all the time. If he really loved you, he wouldn't touch any of them. I do realize that some of these girls are only doing it for the extra money, but they know you are Junebug's woman."

Jenny threw her hand up for a second time. "I get it, Henderson. On the real, I'm not happy about Junebug and his disrespect, as you call it. On more than one occasion, I've thought about leaving him, but every time I think my mind is made up to walk out of the relationship, my heart gets weak. I love him, and if I have to take him as he is, I'll have to accept the lifestyle he's chosen."

Henderson shook his head and let out a deep sigh. "Jenny, you should hear yourself. You are a beautiful woman, and you act as if Junebug is the only one who could love you."

"He is."

"Stop, stop it right now. True, I can't decide for you what you should do with your life, but I feel that as your friend, I can be truthful and honest with you. As I said before, you deserve so much more and I wouldn't put up with Junebug and his disrespectful ways."

"What about Skye? She's a dancer like the rest. Who's to say that down the road she wouldn't be Junebug's piece of meat?"

A severe frown crossed Henderson's face. It was apparent that he wasn't too happy about Jenny's choice of words.

"Did I say something wrong? Don't tell me you think Ms. Hollywood Skye is above board."

"Skye is above board. That's why what happened to her tonight occurred. She isn't going to sell her soul to the devil. The only reason she's dancing is to keep from being homeless."

"I can't understand what she's done to make you go to bat for her. You've become her protective shield and won't let anyone say anything about her. Don't get me wrong, I like Skye, but how is she different from any of the rest of the girls who dance at the club?"

"I happen to know that she's different."

"Well, you have her cell phone. I'm leaving."

"Thanks, Jenny."

Henderson watched as Jenny walked away. Her large frame cast a mocking shadow on the seasick blue hallway carpet. She looked as if she was moving in slow motion, her thighs rubbing together. Jenny may have gone fifty or one-hundred yards, but she abruptly turned around.

"Thank you, Henderson. Thank you for caring."

Henderson blew her a kiss and Jenny strolled out of sight.

CHAPTER 53

*D*aylight streamed into the small window. Skye had been placed in a private room at the request of Henderson. Her bruised, swollen face resembled kneaded dough after it had set for a time to rise. Her upper torso was bandaged tight in an effort to bond the cracked ribs she had suffered from Rico's blows. The drugs had kept her drowsy through the better part of the day.

Still asleep, Henderson sat next to her bed, holding and caressing her limp hand. Aside from the bruises and the puffy face, she looked angelic in every way. Henderson dropped his head and said a prayer—a prayer that the new love in his life would be okay.

Needing a distraction, Henderson turned on the small, flat-screen television that was attached to a metal arm that jetted from a side wall. KABC-TV News was on the air with the newscaster announcing the top news stories for the day. And then they broke away to the top story of the day, and there in living color was Presley Eubanks with microphone in hand, standing in front of Cedars-Sinai Medical Center.

Henderson's eyes were glued to the television set, bracing himself for Eubanks's report about Skye. He jerked his head when he heard Skye Culbertson's name and listened to her account of the story.

"Actress Skye Culbertson, turned exotic dancer, was beaten to within an inch of her life last night by a former boyfriend, Rico Tillman, who is on the FBI's Most Wanted List, according to the

Los Angeles Police Department. Rico Tillman's name is believed to be an alias.

"Ms. Culbertson was in the midst of giving Mr. Tillman a private dance at a strip club in North Hollywood. As there were no eye-witnesses to the actual beating, people in the club heard screams. The club's manager, bartender, and two unknown persons rushed through the door of the private room and found Ms. Culbertson beaten and bloodied on the floor. An eyewitness stated that the man believed to be Mr. Tillman was sitting off to the side, catching his breath but was whisked away by the two unknown men who eye-witnesses stated accompanied Mr. Tillman into the club.

"Mr. Tillman is being sought by police and the FBI for stealing luxury vehicles and reselling them across the U.S. and overseas. Police reports claim that Mr. Tillman operated a chop shop in the heart of Los Angeles, but nothing was found at the location given to them by a tip that was called into the police hotline. Ms. Culbertson was arrested about a year ago driving a stolen vehicle that was given to her to drive by Mr. Tillman, but she was later released when police discovered that she didn't have knowledge of Mr. Tillman's activities. However, in the aftermath, although she was exonerated, Ms. Skye Culbertson's blossoming career as an actress in Hollywood was cut short, and the entertainment world forgot her name.

"We will provide updates as they become available. This is Presley Eubanks reporting to you live from KABC-TV News."

As Henderson switched the channel, he heard groaning coming from Skye's direction. He turned and saw that she was attempting to open her eyes. He moved in closer.

Her eyelashes fluttered. It was a great sense of relief considering how her face looked. Although her face was puffed up and bruised, her smooth, chocolate color shone through.

"Skye, can you hear me?" he whispered.

There was silence and then her mouth moved, although Henderson couldn't hear a thing. Skye's eyelashes moved, but he was yet to hear her speak.

And without warning, she opened up her eyes and stared up at the ceiling. "Henderson?" she called out, her voice a soft whisper.

"Skye, I'm right here." Henderson stood up and bent down and placed a kiss on her cheek. He brushed her braids aside and smiled.

"I feel terrible," she said.

"You're beautiful to me."

She slowly lifted her arm approximately an inch from where it rested and touched Henderson's arm with the fingers on her open hand. "Don't lie to me. My face feels like a ton of rocks are piled on top of it."

Henderson laughed. "Your face is swollen, but I'm sure it'll go down in a few days. I'm going to be by your side until you fully recover."

"Some Christmas."

Henderson forgot that Christmas was going to be in a couple of days. "You can't be worrying about Christmas. It's only another day. People are going to unwrap gifts, eat until their bellies are full, maybe go to a movie, eat some more, and the day will be over with."

"I want to see my mother."

"We have tickets to go to Kansas New Year's Eve, although you won't be able to travel."

"Henderson, I need my mother. I can't believe how selfish I've been. It's probably the reason all of these bad things are happening to me."

"Hush, Skye. Don't worry your pretty little head about Christmas and seeing your mom. Get better so you'll be able to travel in a few weeks."

Tears drizzled down both sides of Skye's face. Henderson kissed her forehead and squeezed her hand. "It's going to be all right."

The nurse came in, checked her vitals, and promised that the doctor would be in shortly. Skye's blood pressure was a little elevated, but her temperature was normal. The lab technician came in next and drew some blood, and then she was on her way. Half expecting the doctor to be the next face that waltzed through the door, Henderson was surprised when he looked up and saw Jaylin's face peep around the door.

Henderson stood, went over to where she stood inside the door, and embraced her.

"How is she doing?" Jaylin asked. Her face was sad and contemplative.

"Ask her yourself."

Jaylin walked the few feet to the bed. Skye's eyes were closed but abruptly popped open. Skye turned her head slightly and her face lit up.

"Skye," Jaylin said, bending over the bed and planting a kiss on her forehead, while caressing it with her hand. "Sis, I'm so sorry that this happened; I should've been there for you."

Skye reached for Jaylin's hand and squeezed it. "You've always been there for me. You couldn't have prevented what happened."

"Maybe not, but I should've been there for you."

"Henderson's been my rock."

Jaylin smiled. "I see; I'm glad."

For the next fifteen minutes, they were quiet and held hands. There wasn't a need for words to be spoken. They were sisters, although not biological, and they had formed a bond that no one could come between.

Jaylin stood and kissed Skye on her cheek. "Henderson, why don't you take a break? I'm going to stay with my friend. We need some girl time."

"You sure?"

Skye squeezed Jaylin's hand. "Yes, I'm plenty sure."

"Okay, this will give me an opportunity to go to the house and freshen up. I also have some things to take care of that need my immediate attention." Henderson looked at Skye and Jaylin. He smiled, leaned in, and kissed Skye on the lips. "You're in good hands. I'll be back."

Skye reached for Henderson's hand. "Thank you for being there for me."

"I'll always be here for you. Oh, I forgot to tell you that I had Jenny bring your belongings from the club. I needed your cell phone to get in touch with Jaylin, but I see that news travels fast. Your phone was locked and I couldn't get in it. And Jaylin, I need your phone number in the event of any more emergencies."

"You need to have my phone number," Jaylin said. "This will never happen again. My number is 323-242-5555. Call me so that your number will show up on my phone. Thank you, Henderson, for watching over my girl."

Henderson winked at her and exited the room.

CHAPTER 54

*H*enderson was happy that Skye and Jaylin had come together, even if it was under prevailing circumstances. It
was only a matter of time before Jaylin would come to her
senses, but regardless, Skye had the one friend she trusted…maybe
the only friend she trusted looking after her.

He jumped into his Lexus and sped away from the hospital.
Rolling the driver's side window down, Henderson leaned his arm
out of the window and smiled. He was drowning in his love for
Skye. The question Jenny asked of him, he had to ask himself.
What had Skye done to make him fall this hard?

She was real, not presumptuous. There was an innocence about
her that spoke to him. He liked the way she carried herself—a
lady with nothing to prove to no one.

Arriving home, Henderson showered and shaved. He made some
calls before finally placing a call to his favorite travel agent. That
done, he did something he hadn't done when he was married. He
went into the dresser drawer he gave Skye and picked out a few
undies to take to the hospital. She was truly his woman.

Done with what he had to do at the house, Henderson headed
for the club. He had to let Junebug know that he was taking off a
few days, maybe a week. Junebug had other friends who could
bartend in his place. The problem with Junebug was that he was
a cheap son-of-a-gun and didn't want to pay anybody.

Henderson looked at his watch. Where had the time gone? It was already one in the afternoon; it didn't seem that he was at the house that long. He called Jaylin's number to check on Skye, and all was okay. Jaylin said the doctor gave Skye a thumbs-up for a full recovery.

All was quiet when Henderson stepped into the club. There was no sign of Junebug or Jenny anywhere.

Henderson went into the bar area, set it up for the evening, and called his assistant to tell him to get to the club right away. He was anxious to get back to the hospital, and he wanted to make sure that all was in order before he left.

As he set the last glass on the counter, Henderson jumped at the sound of Junebug's voice.

"Fix me a gin and tonic."

At first, Henderson was going to tell Junebug to get it himself. He thought better of it, and got Junebug's drink.

"Where are you going all dressed up?"

"I'm on my way to the hospital to see about Skye."

"See about whom?"

"Skye, your employee who was beaten at your club last night."

"Hell no you aren't. You owe me hours from last night. I need a real bartender and not that amateur thing you got assisting you that thinks he knows how to fix a drink." Junebug took two gulps of his drink.

"Well, he's going to be it tonight and the night after that. In fact, the reason I came in was to tell you I was taking a week off."

"Now, how in the hell are you going to do that right in the middle of my busy season? I make more during the Christmas holidays than I do throughout the whole year."

"I'm sorry, Junebug. I haven't had a break in years. I'm taking one now."

"It's that girl. Women will always be the death of men. I don't understand why you want some hoe that shakes her poontang up in other men's faces."

"That girl has a name and you better watch what you say about her. It's a shame that you haven't even asked how Skye is doing."

"I'm going to call her something else if they close up my club."

"Listen to you, Junebug. They should call this place the house of ill repute, all the illegal stuff you do in this place. And while I'm at it, you need to treat Jenny with respect."

"Nigger, you need to stay out of my business, cousin or no cousin. What I do with these women ain't none of your business. If they want to show their daddy some love, I don't turn it down. I got love for all these bitches."

"I quit. I've looked the other way for far too long, and I'll not watch another minute while you disrespect Jenny, these women, and yourself."

"Get on out of here. I don't need you…you broken-down athlete. Now, fix me another gin and tonic before you go. You still owe me hours."

"Get it yourself." And Henderson walked out.

It was a good feeling to step into the sunshine and part from the place he had no desire to be. He should've left a long time ago, but he'd stayed. Junebug needed him.

As Henderson prepared to get into his car, he noticed Skye's car was still sitting where she had parked it yesterday. He'd get an old football buddy of his to ride with him to the club later in the evening to pick it up once he was able to get Skye's car keys.

"Good riddance."

CHAPTER 55

*B*enny hadn't had any luck with his contacts on finding the whereabouts of Skye Culbertson. She had to be holed up in one of the many hospitals in Los Angeles. Even his side piece, who was a nurse at one of the large hospitals in the county, couldn't get any information as to which hospital she was taken to.

He looked up as Big Sarge charged into the room. "Turn on the TV…to the ABC station. They reported on that chick Tyrone is looking for. She's at Cedars."

"No wonder I couldn't find her. I didn't expect her to be taken there," Benny said as he turned on the TV.

"There's more."

"What do you mean more? We've got what Tyrone wants."

"Listen, Benny, they put Tyrone on blast, except they called him by the name Rico Tillman."

"Well, what did they say?"

"The reporter said that Rico Tillman, aka Tyrone to us, was responsible for beating Skye and that the FBI is looking for him. Somebody dropped a dime on the L.A. location, but, of course, everything was gone by the time the police checked it out."

"Damn. We've got to tell Tyrone what's gone down and see what he wants to do with the information." Benny held out the remote and flipped through the TV stations. "They must be finished report-ing on it." Benny put down the remote.

"Getting within a few hundred feet of that girl's hospital room is a tall order. Like I said, Benny, I'm not up to killing innocent folks. It's going to be our asses in jail instead of Tyrone, and I'm not planning to wear an orange jumpsuit for nobody; I don't care who it is."

Benny looked thoughtfully at Sarge. Could it have been Sarge that rolled over on Tyrone? He doubted it. Big Sarge would be a fool to rat himself out. Truth be told, he wasn't up for killing nobody, either.

"Let's go together and give Tyrone the news," Benny finally said. "I think the nurse has been here to fix him up."

"Yeah, let's do this." They bumped fists and left the den in search of Tyrone.

Tyrone was lying in the middle of the bed in his bedroom surrounded by three beautiful women—one on either side of him and the other at the foot, dressed in midriff shirts that were cut low, tight skinny jeans, and five-inch stilettos that matched their tops. They each had a drink in their hand and were smoking off of one cigarette that they passed around.

Benny nodded at Tyrone when he and Big Sarge entered the room.

Tyrone sat up, pushing the ladies away gently with a nudge of his elbows. "My bodyguards," Tyrone shouted out. "They couldn't protect me from a pair of five-inch stilettos, but they were Johnny on the spot when they needed to be. Ladies, let's drink to Benny and Big Sarge."

The ladies lifted their glasses, clinked them together, and took a drink. Benny wasn't amused.

Benny swiped at his nose. "Yo, Tyrone, do you think we can talk a minute in private? We have some news to pass on to you."

Tyrone looked from Benny to Big Sarge, sighed, and then chuckled. "Ladies, hold it down until I get back. I've got to talk to my bodyguards a minute, but I won't be gone long. Keep my space warm."

He clutched his lower abdomen and tried to ease off the bed. "Damn, I hurt. That bitch got in a good kick, but I swear she'll never do that to another man."

With assistance from Big Sarge, Tyrone limped out of the room and followed the two men to the den.

"So, what's up?" Tyrone asked. "Were you able to get that information for me?"

"Big Sarge, tell Tyrone what you told me," Benny said with his hand cuffed under his chin.

"The girl is at Cedars-Sinai Medical Center," Big Sarge began. "They announced it on the news this morning." Sarge looked at Benny and continued on when Benny gave him the nod. "They also mentioned you by your alias, Rico Tillman."

Tyrone's face was void of expression. He sat down on the worn, brown leather couch that sat facing a large, flat-screen television. "So, what did they say?"

"They said that you were the one that beat up the girl and that you were wanted by the police and the FBI. They claimed they received a tip about the chop shop in L.A., but they didn't find anything when they went to the address they were given."

"Damn," Tyrone said, screaming to the top of his lungs. "This is all that bitch's doing."

Benny and Big Sarge traded glances but kept quiet.

"Benny, Big Sarge, I've got a mission for the two of you. Ms. Hollywood Skye has to be eliminated, and you all are going to take care of it for me." Tyrone stood up. "Make it clean as possible. Now, I've got a business to run. Pucci and ReRe hauled in a couple of top-of-the-line vehicles last night. With what we already have, we're about to get paid handsomely.

"Sarge, help me back to the room and my ladies. Call me when the deed is done."

Benny watched as Tyrone leaned on Big Sarge. Tyrone turned around and stared. Benny nodded his comprehension of what he was to do.

CHAPTER 56

Henderson high-tailed it back to the hospital, anxious to see how Skye was doing. When he entered the room, Jaylin was sitting on the bed, probably telling Skye a story. Skye's attempt to laugh was feeble, but it meant she was in good spirits.

"Hey, how's everybody doing?" Henderson asked, reaching down and placing a kiss on Skye's forehead.

Skye uttered something that was somewhat muffled. She tried again and smiled when she saw that Henderson understood.

"She's in good spirits," Jaylin said. "I've been telling her stories about the time we met in the bus station and some of the crazy antics we were involved in. It's good to hear her attempt to laugh. Her face is hurting a little more now that the anesthesia has somewhat worn off. I rang for the nurse so she could give my sister some more drugs."

Henderson chuckled. "Glad you could be here."

"I wouldn't have it any other way. By the way, my dad is going to stop in tomorrow to see Skye. I'm sure he'd love to reunion with you."

"That would be great, as long as you didn't bad-mouth me too much," Henderson said. "I haven't seen Bernard Scott in years. I'd love to see him."

"He's not aware that I've met you, and I won't tell him you'll be here. I'll call you before he comes."

"Sounds like a plan. Jaye, if you want to go home and get some rest...some food...whatever, I'm back."

"Don't try and push me out of this room, Henderson. I'm not going anywhere." Jaylin lifted Skye's hand in hers and squeezed it. "I'm not leaving my friend, even if she's a pain in the ass sometimes. I love her."

"I love her, too."

Benny and Big Sarge jumped into Benny's black 2013 Lincoln MKS and headed for Los Angeles and Cedars-Sinai Medical Center. While they didn't carry an arsenal of weapons with them, they both packed 9mm handguns with silencers.

"Do you have a plan?" Big Sarge asked. "I ain't tryna go up in there like gangbusters and get caught."

"Sarge, you need to chill out," Benny said irritably. "We have to think this thing through. She might have armed guards watching her spot."

"They didn't mention anything about guards on the newscast this morning. Don't you think they would've said something to scare any potential killers away?"

Benny laughed. "Sarge, you are funny as hell. I don't know how you got to be one of Tyrone's bodyguards, and I can't say that I feel safe with you around."

"Damn, Benny. That was a cold slam. Me and Tyrone go way back, when we were kids. I'll do my job when I hafta. But knocking off this chick is going to bring plenty heat on us. Tyrone's name is already wagging on these fools' tongues—even if it's Rico Tillman. They're going to catch his ass eventually. The PoPo is probably waiting in the cut to see if Tyrone comes around. Instead, it's going to be you and me that get caught in the dragnet...and then on to the slammer."

"Would you please shut the hell up, Sarge? You're getting on my damn nerves. Don't make me dump your ass on the street and do this job by myself. What do you think Tyrone will say when I tell him his homeboy was whining like a sissy and I had to ditch his ass so he wouldn't sabotage the mission?"

"You wouldn't do that...would you?"

"I will if you don't keep quiet. I've got to think. We'll be in L.A. in about thirty minutes. I want to get in and out. I'll have my girl go over to Cedars and do a walk-by of Skye's room. Since she's a nurse, no one will think twice about stopping her. In fact, I think it'll be smart to have her go into the room so she can report back about any visitors hanging around."

"I'm down with that."

"All right, let's do this." Benny called his nurse friend and began the first phase of their plan.

CHAPTER 57

*L*aShauna Morgan checked out of her shift at Kaiser-Permanente Los Angeles Medical Center. She had done all right for herself, especially coming from the rough side of Compton, California. With less than a fifty percent graduation rate at her high school, she had managed to go to college and get a nursing degree. For sure she would need it at some point to help her mother who was strung out on heroin. She went to UCLA, stayed on campus, and hadn't returned home since the day she'd left—at least not to sleep.

Her only vice was a boy from the hood that she hadn't been able to loose herself from completely. Benny, whose real name was Benjamin Hall, had been her boo all through high school, and every now and then, they'd still get together and kick it with each other. At twenty-seven, she'd been ready to settle down, but Benny was still stuck on the other side of the tracks. He was making good money somewhere, although when she'd ask Benny how he was able to purchase that nice ride of his, he'd only shrugged his shoulders and said that he got it working. But where he worked was always the elusive variable.

LaShauna had heard from him twice in the past two days. He wanted her to spy on some actress that was in the trauma center at Cedars-Sinai. She didn't see the harm, and since she was already dressed in her nurse's uniform, she'd blend right in.

Benny was vague as to why he wanted her to find out who was keeping the patient company and if there were any guards keeping watch. Maybe Benny had a small crush on her, but why would he go to all the trouble? Why did he want to know about the guards?

When LaShauna asked, she was told that Skye Culbertson was an up-and-coming actress and his boss might be a little sweet on her. LaShauna's job was to meander into Skye's room on the pretense of getting an autograph. Simple, however, the reason for the task nagged at her a bit. As much as she hated putting herself in the middle of Benny's business, whatever it was, and possibly jeopardizing her job, she acquiesced and granted him this one favor.

Feet tired, LaShauna dragged to her BMW SUV, a gift to herself. Being able to obtain nice things the legitimate way was so refreshing, considering how she was brought up. Her hair was laid, which was the result of being able to afford one of the best stylists in Los Angeles. She always had the latest fashions and didn't have to go to Rodeo Drive to acquire them.

She hopped in the car and readied herself for the fifteen-minute drive that would probably take thirty. She waved bye to several of the other floor nurses before taking off. It was a sunny day and she wished she was going to the beach instead.

LaShauna arrived at Cedars-Sinai Medical Center in twenty-five minutes. She'd already gotten Skye's location, although not her room number, from a fellow nursing friend of hers. Piece of cake. She'd go to the room while surveying the surroundings, ask for the autograph and leave.

Before getting into the elevator, LaShauna's cell phone vibrated. She quickly took it out of the pocket of her uniform and looked at the caller ID. It was Benny.

"Hey," LaShauna said, moving away from the elevator.

"Hey, LaShauna. You get the info yet?"

"No, Benny, I just got here. I was on my way up in the elevator when you called. Give me twenty minutes. I'll call you back then."

"Twenty minutes? Why do you need all that time?"

"I'm not sure what I'll run into. What's really going on here?" Silence. "Benny, what's up? I don't want to be part of no mess."

"Naw, you're good. Call me back in twenty…after you've left the hospital and are in your car."

"I'm not liking this one bit. I hope I'm not putting my job on the line for some crap that I'll regret."

"Naw, you're good. The patient is my boss' ex-girlfriend. I believe he wants to come and see her but without all of her family around."

"Well, why didn't you say so?" LaShauna said relieved. "You made it seem like the ordeal was shrouded in secrecy. If you were only trying to play Cupid, you should've said so."

"Something like that. Now I have to go. Call me in twenty."

"Okay."

LaShauna ended her phone call and waited for the next elevator. She'd been to Cedars on several occasions and was somewhat familiar with the lay of the land. She approached the nurses' station and put on a big smile.

The nurse at the reception counter picked up an incoming call before LaShauna was able to ask her for Skye's room number. She folded her arms and took a long look around. Everything seemed peaceful and in order. There weren't any guards of any kind that she could see.

When the nurse ended her phone call, LaShauna put back on her big smile and asked for Skye's room.

"Could you tell me where Skye Culbertson's room is?"

The nurse looked quizzically at LaShauna. "Do you work here?"

"No, I work over at Kaiser-Permanente. I stopped by to see an old friend."

"Do you know Pecolla Green? She works over at Kaiser in the surgical department."

"Yeah, I know Pecolla. We've worked together. It's truly a small world."

"I'll have to tell her I met someone she knows. What's your name?"

LaShauna hesitated, but then thought, *what the hell?* She was only scoping out the place. "I'm LaShauna Morgan. And you are?"

"Grace Evans. Tell Pecolla to call me sometimes."

"I'll make sure I tell her tomorrow."

"Oh, Skye Culbertson's room is right around the corner to your left, second door on the right."

"Thank you, Grace. I'll be sure to tell Pecolla tomorrow."

"Okay."

LaShauna rushed from the nurses' station, anxious to put some distance between her and Grace Evans. The last thing she'd anticipated was running into someone she knew or someone who knew someone she knew. No harm done, although she wasn't sure why she was fretting. She was getting information for a friend whose boss wanted to surprise his ex-girlfriend.

Coming upon the room that was marked "Culbertson," LaShauna suddenly got butterflies in her stomach. She wasn't sure why, but her confidence seemed to leave her. She looked at her watch and noted that ten minutes had already gone by. Benny would be calling in eleven minutes if she hadn't called him, and she didn't want him calling her while she was in the room.

She pushed the door open to Skye's room. A male and female were sitting next to the bed, talking about the patient when LaShauna walked in. They both turned around at the same time, although they didn't seem surprised to see her. It must have been her uniform.

The female looked up and then squinted. "LaShauna, what are you doing here? I didn't know you worked for Cedars."

"Jaye, what are you doing here?" LaShauna rushed to give Jaylin a hug.

"This is one of my best friends," Jaylin rushed to say. "She was beaten up pretty bad, but she's going to be all right. Oh, Henderson, LaShauna is one of my clients. I'm a hairstylist, as well as an actress."

Henderson got up from his seat and extended his hand to LaShauna. "It's nice to meet you."

"You, too. I'm off duty."

"So what brought you here, LaShauna?" Jaylin asked. "I had no idea you knew Skye. She's sedated right now and has been asleep for a while. Terrible headache."

"Well, I heard that a celebrity was in the house."

"There are always celebrities here. That's not news."

"True. Well, a friend of mine asked me to stop by and see if Skye was still in the hospital. His boss, Ms. Culbertson's ex-boyfriend, wants to pay her a visit."

Henderson, who'd been standing back, suddenly lurched forward. He stared at LaShauna. "Ms. Culbertson's ex-boyfriend wants to pay her a visit?"

"Well, yes, that's what I was told."

"Why didn't he come himself and what is your friend's name?"

LaShauna was suddenly tongue-tied. "Look, I don't want any trouble. I was asked to stop by and see if the patient was here. If there's something going on other than what I said, I'm in the dark."

"Listen, LaShauna, this is important," Jaylin said, getting up in her face. "My best girlfriend lying over there was beaten by her ex, who's threatened to kill her."

LaShauna's eyes rolled around in her head. "Maybe…maybe she has another ex," she rushed to say. "I'm sure the reason Benny,

I mean my friend, asked me to stop by is that I'm a nurse and could better tell how she was doing."

"Benny?" Henderson asked. "I'm going to take you at your word, LaShauna," Henderson said, enunciating every syllable. "You tell Benny that if Rico Tillman shows his ass over here, it will be hell to pay."

"Look, I'm so sorry," LaShauna said, throwing up her hands. "Whatever is going on, I have no knowledge of it. I'm a hard-working sister that wants to be left alone and enjoy life. Benny is my connection with home."

"You mean Compton?" Jaylin asked. "Is Benny your boo? If so, you're too beautiful of a person to be still attached to a hood rat."

"Benny isn't a hood rat, Jaye. Yeah, we come from the same neighborhood, but Benny always wanted the best for himself. I was lucky and got out, although my mother is still there, overtaken by drugs. There's nothing I can do for her; she doesn't want help."

LaShauna looked down as her phone began to ring. She sighed. "This is Benny. I've got to take this call."

"Why don't you take it right here?" Henderson said, watching her every move.

LaShauna said nothing but answered the call.

"Benny."

"What's taking you so long?"

"I'm still in the hospital."

"Are you still in the room?"

"Yep."

"Get out now. Call me as soon as you get to your car."

"Okay." LaShauna ended the call.

Henderson's arms were folded and he had a severe look on his face. "What did he say?"

"He told me to get out now. I swear, Mr. Henderson, if there's something going down, I'm not aware of it."

There wasn't a smile on his face. "Okay, I'll make a mental note of it. Now, you better go before this Benny does something crazy to you. I suggest that you don't tell him what you told us."

"I won't." And LaShauna was gone.

CHAPTER 58

Another few feet and LaShauna would be at her car. She almost raced to it, in a hurry to get far away from Cedars-Sinai.

Releasing the alarm, she opened the door to the driver's side, but was unable to move. She swung her head to the right and looked into Benny's face. LaShauna tried to jerk her arm away from Benny, but he had such a tight grip on it, that purple bruises were beginning to show on her caramel-colored skin.

"Take your hands off of me, Benny. What's wrong with you?"

"Why did it take you so long to go in and come out?"

"First of all, Benny, I had to find out where Ms. Skye's hospital room was, and when I finally got to the floor, I had to wait on the nurse who was on a five-minute phone call to get off the phone. I was trying to act normal and not cause attention. What else did you want me to do?"

Benny eased his grip but didn't completely release LaShauna's arm. "Was the girl in the room?"

"You mean Skye, the actress?"

"Don't get smart with me. We've been buds since we were in diapers. Don't let me have to go off on you. And I will."

LaShauna couldn't believe her ears. Was this the Benny she'd been holding out for something good to happen to? His time was up. The bell had rung: it was a TKO. If the Lord blessed her to get out of this mess, Benny was history.

"Yes, she was in there."

"What did she say?"

"She was sleeping. She wasn't even aware that I was there."

"Who else was in the room?"

"Nobody," LaShauna said with a straight face. "She was in there all by herself."

"You didn't say if there were any guards hanging around."

"You didn't ask, but I wouldn't have forgotten that minor detail."

"Whatever you've got stuck up your butt, you need to let it go."

"I did you a favor, but I'm the one whose arm is in a vise. Maybe you've forgotten that I don't take too kindly to being roughed up by assholes who abuse children, mothers, and those who can't defend themselves. Did you forget that, Benny? Huh?"

"Sorry, LaShauna. It shouldn't have taken you damn near thirty minutes to go in and out of the hospital," Benny muttered. He released LaShauna's arm. "All right, go on and get out of here. I'll call you tonight."

LaShauna got in her car without saying a word. For the first time since Benny had contacted her, she was suddenly afraid. Had Benny been a party to what had happened to Skye?

She drove from the parking lot as fast as she could, burning rubber all the way. Tears streamed down her face. "I hate you, Benny. You and no one else will ever hurt me again."

CHAPTER 59

"You stay here with Skye. I'm going to contact the police and alert the nurses at the station. No one else will be allowed in the room without our knowledge."

"Okay, Henderson. Who would've thought that Rico would try some foolishness like this?"

"It amazes me that he'd be fool enough to show up when he knows the police are after him."

"Maybe he's not going to show up. It's Benny. He's sending this Benny guy that LaShauna was talking about to do his dirty work."

"You're probably right, Jaye. I've got to move. We may not have much time to get something in place."

"Okay, I'll be here."

Henderson left the room and dialed nine-one-one. He explained to the operator what had transpired and that he was in fear of Skye's life. They said they were on it.

Next, Henderson rushed to the nurses' station. He quickly told Grace Evans what had gone down.

"I should've known there was something suspicious about that woman. She acted so natural—cool as a cucumber. I remember her hesitating when I asked her name."

"What did she say her name was?"

"LaShauna Morgan. The reason I remember is that she knows a friend of mine, Pecolla Green, who works at Kaiser."

"I believe LaShauna doesn't have any idea as to what's going on. She was a pawn in a larger scheme."

"Oh, that's too bad," Grace said.

"Thanks, I'm going back to Skye's room. Please let me know when the guards show up."

"Will do."

Several minutes passed. Grace looked up as two gentlemen dressed in black approached the desk. The specimens standing in front of her were delicious. The burley one of the two with his rich, black complexion excited her. Grace loved them dark and chocolate. He could've easily been on the WWE circuit. The shorter one was a looker too, but he was too thin for her taste.

Grace batted her eyes and licked her lips. "Are you the guys sent to guard…?" Grace hesitated and took a better look at the two. They were dressed in black, but they didn't have on police uniforms. She needed to get her head out of the clouds. The shorter one of the two opened his mouth to speak.

"What was that you were saying?" Benny asked, presenting himself as spokesman for the duo.

"Ah, are you here to see someone?"

Benny looked at Big Sarge and rolled his eyes. He leaned in close so that only Grace could hear him speak. "Yes," Benny hissed, "although that wasn't what you said."

Grace began to shake. The other two nurses on her shift were making rounds and she was by herself. "Who are you here to see?"

"Skye Culbertson."

"She is not allowed to have visitors," Grace said nervously. "Strict orders."

"You're making that up," Benny pushed.

Suddenly, for a smidgen of a second, Grace got her nerve back and looked dead at Benny. "Buster, I take my job seriously. When I said that Ms. Culbertson can't have visitors, that's what I meant."

Benny moved closer and got up in Grace's face. "I have a friend who was in Ms. Culbertson's room a few minutes ago. Are you calling her a liar?"

"And who are you? Why do you want to see Ms. Culbertson?" Grace's nerves were now getting the best of her. Where were the guards who were supposed to protect the patient? Damn, why on her watch?

"I'm a friend of Skye's and you're going to give me her room number, now."

Grace looked from the buffoon who was standing in her space to her delicious WWE wannabe, except the two no longer appealed to her. "I'm not giving it to you."

"I guess I'll have to use reinforcement." Benny looked at Big Sarge who only sighed. From out of nowhere, Benny produced the 9mm gun he had hidden in the waistband of his pants and pointed it at Grace.

"Jesus," she said. Sweat began to pour from Grace's face.

"Not so brave now, are you? My, my, my, where is Jesus when you need him? Now give me the damn room number. I won't hesitate to blow your brains out."

"Come on, Benny," Big Sarge said.

Benny rolled his head in Big Sarge's direction. "Did you call out my name, fool?"

"Get the number, but don't hurt the woman. Let's do what we came to do and get out of here."

"I don't need you. You can go on back to the car. I'll handle this by myself." Benny turned back to Grace with the gun still pointing at her temple. "Give me the damn room number."

Grace rambled off the number, tears streaming down her face. Before she knew what was happening, Benny had jumped on the desk and into her area, grabbed her by the neck, and dragged her out of the cubicle. "If the number isn't right, your lights are out."

Benny dragged Grace in the direction she indicated with Big Sarge right behind them. As they turned the corner, a nurse walked down the hall in their direction, seeing the commotion. The nurse shouted. Benny turned the gun on her and pulled the trigger. She dropped to the floor.

"Oh my God," Grace screamed. "Oh my God."

"Shut the hell up," Benny said, "before I turn the gun on you."

Grace looked at her fallen comrade. Blood began to saturate the floor where the nurse fell, the blood so red that Grace couldn't stomach it.

Finally, they stood before the room with Skye's name on it. But before Benny was able to open the door, others who had heard shots descended into the hallway. All hell broke loose as screams began to permeate the corridor.

Benny fired off a few shots and pushed Grace away. She fell to the floor right next to her fallen comrade. Unmoved by it all, Benny pushed his way into Skye's room.

She was sitting upright in the bed, her face a swollen mess with the top half of her body bandaged up. Benny moved toward the bed, holding the gun straight at Skye, his finger on the trigger. Big Sarge entered the room when all of a sudden, the gun went off.

Benny dropped the gun and fell to the floor. Jaylin hit him once again in the head while Henderson retrieved the gun. Big Sarge pulled his pistol out of his pants, but Henderson was already pointing Benny's gun at him. Skye looked on in disbelief.

"Put the gun down," Henderson said, unwavering from his position. "You must not have gotten my message."

Big Sarge looked at Henderson not understanding what he was talking about.

"I told your carrier pigeon that there was going to be hell to pay if anyone tried to hurt Skye."

Suddenly, Jaylin began to thrash her arms, trying to unleash her leg from Benny's grasp. Having quickly recovered from the blow to the head, he pulled himself up and grabbed Jaylin by the neck. "Blow her ass away," Benny said to Big Sarge.

Henderson still had Benny's gun aimed at Big Sarge. "Touch one hair on Skye's head and you're a dead man."

"And I'll snap this one's neck," Benny said with a scowl on his face. "I promise you."

In the midst of the standoff, Skye pulled the IV out of her arm and got up out of bed.

"No, Skye," Jaylin said, screaming. "No."

Through all of the swollenness, Skye went to Big Sarge. "Kill me, coward," she muttered. "Kill me, you sorry son-of-a-bitch. What is Rico going to give you? A pat on the back?"

"Back up," Big Sarge said, his gun pointed toward Skye's heart, while Henderson had the other gun still aimed at Big Sarge's head.

"Kill her," Benny shouted. He squeezed Jaylin's neck.

"Oh God," Jaylin whispered.

In the next instant, Benny was lying on the floor. Skye had snatched the gun out of Big Sarge's hand, aimed it at Benny, and pulled the trigger.

Henderson pushed Big Sarge against the wall. "Don't move. Where in the hell are those cops?"

The door to Skye's hospital room flew open. Six uniformed officers rushed in. Big Sarge was immediately handcuffed and a doctor was called in to check Benny's vitals and issue, in this case, a time of death.

In the door was Grace. "Is everyone all right?" She huffed, as she clutched her chest, with a weary look on her face. "Those bastards pulled a gun on me and killed one of my dear friends. I'm so sorry about this, Mr. Henderson."

"It's all right, Grace. We should've had an armed guard in the first place. Will you help me get Skye back into bed?"

"Ms. Skye, why are you out of bed? You have cracked ribs and shouldn't be moving around."

"Nurse Grace," Jaylin began, "she was trying to fight the bad guys too."

"Lord, have mercy. When I first saw those two guys come onto the floor, I thought they were some real handsome brothers. The things that make you shake your head."

"You're right, Grace," Henderson said. "Unfortunately, the mastermind behind all of this is still at large. Skye won't be able to rest until they find this Rico Tillman or whatever his name is. We're going to have to move her to a more secure room." Henderson went on to explain the events that brought Skye to the hospital.

"Strange thing," Grace began, "one of my coworkers had to make a house call earlier today. I believe she said in Riverside. Someone she knows had a close call with a killer shoe. Do you think that could be the person?"

"I need you to tell all of what you told me to the police. I don't know, Grace, but it certainly could be the person in question. A tip is a tip. If we don't act on it, and Rico Tillman is the man in Riverside, he'll get away again. If it's not him, at least we tried." Henderson kissed Grace on the cheek. "Thanks for having my girl's back."

"We're going to take good care of Ms. Skye."

CHAPTER 60

*C*haos was rampant throughout the hospital. Doctors and nurses scurried here and there, moving out of the way of the police who'd been summoned by a frantic caller about two men who were possibly targeting a patient.

Henderson heaved a sigh of relief as several orderlies removed Benny's body from Skye's hospital room. Big Sarge, Benny's accomplice, had been placed in handcuffs and taken away by the police. He looked at Skye who seemed to be in a daze—in a frozen state— her eyes fixed on nothing in particular.

The room now quiet, Henderson went to Skye and put his arm around her shoulders. She began to shake and then cry, traumatized, no doubt, by the events that had unfolded in the room. Jaylin had gone to the ladies' room to freshen up, probably to get her nerves straight. Henderson had seen the fear in her eyes as Benny's fingers grasped her throat, threatening to snap her neck.

"I'm here for you, Skye. I'm not going to leave you."

Skye momentarily closed her eyes and the tears ran down. She seemed so helpless and vulnerable. Henderson wasn't sure what to do. Skye refused to speak, and the only thing he could do was watch over her to make sure she was safe from harm.

Grace, along with another nurse, came into Skye's room. "We're going to give Ms. Skye a sedative and move her to a private room."

Thanks, Grace. It's in her best interest."

News of the shootout at Cedars-Sinai flashed across the television screen. Rico/Tyrone sat up in his bed, motioning with his hands for the ladies to get up and leave. Tyrone sat transfixed as the newscaster began to broadcast what had transpired.

"Today, only moments ago, Cedars-Sinai Medical Center was the scene of a horrific shooting in which a nurse was shot and killed, gangland style, in the Trauma Unit of the hospital. The shooting took place in the hallway outside of several patients' rooms. We understand the nurse was not, I repeat, not the intended target.

"However, we've learned that patient Skye Culbertson, an up-and-coming actress in Hollywood, was brought into the hospital on last evening after she was beaten by what a witness said was an ex-boyfriend. It has been confirmed that she was the target. The ex-boyfriend, a Mr. Rico Tillman, which is said to be an alias, is wanted by the police and the FBI for running a chop shop in the city, stealing and selling refurbished high-end cars and parts across the U.S. and abroad. At this time, the LAPD isn't sure if what took place here is related to what happened to Ms. Culbertson last night.

"Two would-be assassins entered Ms. Culbertson's room with the intention of killing her. It is apparent that the pair was unaware that ex-football pro, Corlis Henderson of the former L.A. Raiders and friend of Ms. Culbertson, was in the room. While we don't have the full account of today's events, one of the gunmen, whose name is being withheld for verification, was shot and killed by the other gunman's weapon. The other gunman, a Maurice Whitaker who goes by the name Big Sarge, was taken into custody and will be charged with attempted murder."

Tyrone picked up the remote and turned the television off without listening to the rest of the broadcast. His nostrils flared and he beat the bed with both fists.

"I should've done the job myself. I can't believe I sent a bunch of weasels to do a simple job."

Tyrone tried to rise from the bed. He grabbed his groin, the pain still intense. He limped over to the dresser and pulled out fresh underclothes and limped into the bathroom. It took him longer than usual, but he managed to shower and dress himself. He couldn't get the telecast off of his mind. He had to take matters into his own hands and take care of Skye Culbertson himself.

Without a single, available bodyguard, he took a set of keys off the key rack in the kitchen and jumped into his cousin's late-model Ford truck. It was probably suicide, but Skye had to be silenced. Her existence seemed to always lead back to him, and staying under the radar while he continued his lucrative business was in jeopardy.

Tyrone hated that he had to drive from Riverside to L.A. If he was lucky, he could do it in an hour, but with traffic at a premium, it was highly unlikely. His blood pressure was up and he could feel the tension that fueled his anger. "Damn," he said, pounding the steering wheel. "I've got to get rid of the bitch."

As if he had a sudden memory jolt, Tyrone remembered that Big Sarge was now locked up in the city jail. What if he told the police about their operations and where he could be found? Information like that would be more incriminating than anything Skye Culbertson could produce. She didn't know a damn thing. But no, Big Sarge wouldn't do that. He was on the payroll and they were brothers. There was a code. Blood is blood even if they weren't biologically from the same womb.

CHAPTER 61

*H*ospital personnel swiftly moved Skye out of her present room to one that was more secluded. Two armed guards were to be stationed around the clock. With the information the police now possessed, there was the likelihood that Rico/Tyrone might show up in person. No one could be certain, but his failed attempts to eliminate Skye may have aroused him to action.

While the nurses worked to get Skye settled into her new room, Henderson went out into the hallway to answer his cell phone. Even Junebug was concerned about Skye's safety after hearing about all the commotion that had occurred at the hospital.

His eyes gleamed when he saw the number pop into his caller ID. "Hello, Mrs. Taylor."

"Is this Mr. Henderson?" Nona Taylor asked meekly.

"Yes, yes, it is. I was going to call you later to give you the status of Skye's condition. I was hoping you'd call me before now."

Ignoring Henderson's comment, Nona continued. "Is it true? It's all over the news about the shootout at the hospital. When I heard Skye's name, I knew it had to be my daughter."

"Yes, it's true. She's been through quite an ordeal. She's been given a sedative and is resting."

"Oh my God. My poor baby has been through so much."

"Her prognosis is good."

There was a sigh of relief at the other end followed by a slight pause. "She probably brought a lot of this on herself; she's so stubborn."

"Well, she didn't ask for this, Mrs. Taylor. I'm going to make sure nothing else happens to her."

"I want to thank you for the offer of the tickets. I'm sorry that I'm just now calling. I do want to come. Skye's sister and her husband will join me."

"How soon are you available?"

"Whenever you can arrange it. Oh, and if you can tell me what hotel is close to the hospital, something cheap, I'd appreciate it."

"I have plenty of room at my house. There's no need to get a hotel."

"No, I don't want to inconvenience you, no more than I already am. I'll appreciate you getting the ticket for me, though."

"It's not an inconvenience at all. Tomorrow is Christmas and there may be some available seats at a lower price. I'll get all three tickets. Your daughter and her husband can reimburse me later."

"Thank you. You are so kind."

"I don't mind doing it."

"My baby needs me." There was another moment of silence. "Uhh, Mr. Henderson, I want this to be a surprise. Please don't tell Skye we're coming."

"It will be our secret. Before you go, I'll need everyone's name so I can contact my travel agent and book the tickets. I'll call you back with the information as soon as everything is confirmed."

"Sure, that will be fine." Nona gave Henderson the information which he wrote down on a business card he had in his pocket. "I'll be waiting to hear from you."

"All right." Henderson hung up and called his personal travel agent and ordered the tickets. Then he called Nona Taylor. They'd be arriving from Kansas City tomorrow afternoon.

Henderson breathed a sigh of relief. It felt good to be needed. He hadn't given anyone his all in a long time. He truly was in love with Skye and he wanted to do everything within his power to make things right for her.

He looked up when he saw Jaylin round the bend. "You need a break. I've got this if you need to run home and freshen up."

"First of all, I'm not going anywhere, Mr. Henderson. I've already told you this, so don't try to keep Skye all to yourself. And I did freshen up." Jaylin smiled for the first time today.

"Okay, okay. I got it."

Henderson hugged her. "I'm glad you're here."

"I still don't understand it, but God put her in my path for a reason. Our friendship was meant to be. I love that girl."

"I've got some good news."

"What is it? I need to hear some good news about now."

"Skye's mother, sister, and brother-in-law are flying in tomorrow." Jaylin covered her mouth with her hand. "For real, Henderson? You're not fooling, are you?"

"No. I just got off the phone with Mrs. Taylor and my travel agent; everything has been arranged. I called her early this morning and made the offer. Her mother wants it to be a surprise."

"That's wonderful news. Skye is going to be so happy. She really misses her family, although she doesn't say it out loud. Henderson, you're the man."

"Who's the man?"

Both Jaylin and Henderson jumped and turned around.

"Hey, Daddy," Jaylin said, going to her dad and putting her arms around him. She gave him a big kiss on the cheek, and he on hers. "Daddy, I want you to meet…"

"Corlis Henderson, I'll be damned."

"Bernard Scott. Man, where have you been?"

The two men gave each other a brotherly hug and pushed back. "When Jaylin said there was someone she wanted me to meet, the last person I expected to see was an old college friend."

Henderson was puzzled. The last thing Jaylin said was that she wasn't going to tell her father that she knew him. "You're a sight for sore eyes. It's been a long time. "

"Yes it has. And how is it that you happen to be at the hospital? Don't tell me you're related to Skye."

"No, Skye and I are friends."

"As in...you and Skye are an item?" Bernard Scott smiled. "It doesn't take me long to put two and two together."

A sly smile crossed Henderson's face. "Bernard, it was supposed to happen. Life happens and here I am."

"I guess you don't want to talk about it in front of my daughter." Bernard slapped Henderson on the shoulder. Jaylin sneered at him.

"It's not that. In fact, Jaye knows our story. Right now, my concern is for Skye in there." Henderson pointed toward the door.

"How is she?" Bernard asked. "She and my little girl have forged quite a friendship."

Jaylin shook her head. "That's my girl in there. She's a fighter and she's going to be all right."

Henderson clasped his hands together. "As soon as they catch this crazy person who's been after her, she may be able to catch a break."

"Yeah, I noticed the guards," Bernard added.

"Speaking of guards, how did you get through the dragnet?" Henderson asked.

Jaylin spoke up. "Daddy called to say he was on his way to the hospital. I went to the nurses' station and told them to allow Daddy to come through. That's where I was coming from."

"Oh, I was wondering if we had a breach already."

"I heard the news account of the shooting on TV," Bernard said. "When Jaylin told me she was going to the hospital to be with Skye, her mother and I were shaken up. We didn't relax until after Jaye called to say that she was all right and what happened. I had planned on coming anyway."

Henderson glanced over at Jaylin. It was apparent that she hadn't told her father everything that had gone down in the room. And he wasn't about to expose her.

CHAPTER 62

*F*rustrated, Tyrone blew his horn at a driver who tried to pull in front of him. He couldn't believe that he was still sitting in the parking garage, aka the interstate. An hour had passed and he still hadn't made it into the city.

It was Christmas Eve, and it seemed that every Tom, Dick, and Jane were on the road going somewhere. He was anxious to get the deed done that he'd sent his bodyguards to do. The more he thought about the botched job that Benny and Big Sarge did at the hospital, the madder he got. And then he remembered that Benny, his best friend, was dead.

Unable to move ahead, Tyrone turned on the radio. He wasn't in the mood for easy listening music or some rapper that he couldn't understand rap about getting down with his woman. Nothing seemed to satisfy him until at the top of the hour, the local news came on.

At first, Tyrone halfway listened to the news commentator. The longer he sat on the freeway, the angrier he got. And then he sat up straight, drawing his face closer to the speaker, as if he were hard of hearing.

The LAPD has learned that Rico Tillman, whose real name is Tyrone Rogers, masterminded the attempted hit on Skye Culbertson's life. Ms. Culbertson was an up-and-coming actress in Hollywood. Maurice Whitaker, an associate of Rogers and better known as Big Sarge,

*arrested at Cedars-Sinai Medical Center earlier today when his attempt
to kill Ms. Culbertson went array, told police that Rogers ordered the
hit. Whitaker's accomplice, a Mr. Benjamin Hall, was shot and killed.*

*From eyewitness accounts, Tyrone Rogers beat Ms. Culbertson up at
a strip club two nights ago and she was brought to Cedars-Sinai shortly
thereafter. While we don't have all of the details, Rogers wanted Ms.
Culbertson dead so that she wouldn't turn the police onto him. This is
according to Maurice Whitaker. Mr. Whitaker also told police that Tyrone
Rogers was operating a car theft ring in Los Angeles last year when Ms.
Culbertson, who was his girlfriend at the time, was arrested for driving
one of Rogers' stolen vehicles. Ms. Culbertson was later exonerated as
police learned that she had no knowledge that the car she was driving
was stolen nor had any prior knowledge that the man she knew as Rico
Tillman was involved in any illegal dealings. Tyrone Rogers moved his
operation to Riverside, California.*

Tyrone turned off the radio and stared straight ahead. His teeth
gritted as he recounted the news story in his head. He couldn't
believe his ears. He and Big Sarge went way back—they were true
boys from the hood...the same hood. How in God's name could
he drop a dime on him like that?

As the traffic inched forward, Tyrone positioned himself to get
off the freeway. To take care of the dirty deed at this time would
be definite suicide. The person he'd really like to put out of their
misery was Big Sarge.

CHAPTER 63

hristmas finally arrived in the City of Angels. All was quiet except for the few people who ventured outside to visit relatives and friends for Christmas dinner. It was a moderately warm day, nothing like the true winter the East Coast was experiencing.

Today was the day that Skye's family would be flying into town. Skye had begged to go home, except that the doctors wanted to keep her a few more days, especially since the previous day had been so traumatic. Henderson was excited to meet Skye's family and was satisfied that Yee Ling, his housekeeper, had the house in tip-top shape. He wanted to go to the hospital and see Skye, but he was afraid that if he went, he wouldn't be able to get away. Her family's arrival would be her Christmas gift.

Henderson looked at his watch. It was about time to go to the airport and pick up his visitors. He grabbed his keys from the coffee table where he'd laid them when he got in last evening. He stopped short when he heard the doorbell ring.

Hurriedly, Henderson flew to the door, hoping that his unexpected guest would leave right away. When he looked through the peephole, he froze and took a long, deep breath. He couldn't believe his eyes. Without wasting another minute, Henderson reluctantly opened the door and faced his ex-wife, Stacy, with his sons, Torian and Corlis Jr., who stood behind her.

She looked like a black Barbie doll that had recently come from the factory. Her toned features made her look younger than her true age. Her hair was cut close to the scalp on one side, while the length of her hair on the other side of her head dropped just below her chin. She wore a navy-blue-and-white shift dress and a navy, bolero jacket. Henderson refrained from looking at her legs—the legs that got him into trouble in the first place.

Henderson was happy to see his boys. He couldn't remember how many times he'd begged his ex-wife to let the boys come and stay with him. When she felt like it, she'd let them stay a minute, regardless of what the court order said. His sons were a sight for sore eyes.

The amount of alimony and child support Henderson paid for his freedom was staggering; however, he was always going to take care of his boys. Stacy, on the other hand, didn't deserve the alimony check she got. While she was well taken care of as a wife, she hadn't been the least bit faithful. Henderson had nothing but disdain for her, as she controlled when he could see his sons.

Stacy looked at him with admiring eyes. "Merry Christmas. Well, aren't you going to invite us in?"

"Hello, Corlis and Torian. This is quite a surprise."

"Hi, Dad," the young men said in unison.

"Look, I'm actually on my way out. You all can come in for a minute."

The crew of three walked past him into the foyer. Stacy rolled her eyes at Henderson but moved further into the house, rotating her head back and forth while examining the contents, as if she half expected to see someone. Henderson smiled at his boys; they looked like grown men, handsome men, and gave them each a pat on the back. They were almost like strangers to him, although they communicated with him through FaceTime ever so often.

It was the reason he had sent both boys iPhones in the first place.

Stacy continued to look at Henderson with seductive eyes. She ran her finger down the side of one arm. "You look nice. Smell good too. You must have a hot date."

Henderson moved away from Stacy. "I'm on my way to the airport. I have visitors coming in and I don't want to be late."

"I brought your boys so they could spend some time with you. After all, it's Christmas. You've been so disappointed in the past."

"Don't you think it would've been courteous of you to let me know in advance that you…they were coming?"

For the first time, one of the boys spoke up. "Dad, it's okay. I told Mom that this was a bad idea."

"Corlis, it isn't that I don't want to spend time with you. Lord knows, I do. I can't remember the number of times I've asked—no, begged—your mother to let you all come and spend Christmas and the summer with me. I love you guys with all my heart."

"But now is not the appropriate time for you to see them," Stacy chimed in.

"I didn't say that, Stacy. Please don't put words in my mouth."

"You're still a spineless fool."

"Mom, why do you have to be mean to Dad?" Torian asked. "Can't you see that he already has plans? You've succeeded in spoiling our Christmas." Torian turned around and walked out of the house.

Henderson followed behind him. "Torian, please don't be angry."

"I'm not angry at you, Dad. Mom keeps trying to manipulate our lives."

"Whoa, those are strong words, Torian. Regardless of the relationship between your mother and me, she's been the one who's taken care of you."

"Dad, we begged to come and live with you, and that's why she won't let us come and visit."

Corlis Jr. walked up behind Henderson, leaving his mother stand-ing on the front porch. "I heard what Torian said, and it's true. Mom hates your guts, but we never saw you treat her any kind of way."

Henderson grabbed his boys and hugged them to his chest. "How long are you going to be in Los Angeles and where are you staying?"

"We're staying with one of Mom's friends. I'm sure she was only trying to get rid of us today so she can do whatever it is she does when she stays out all night...sometimes for two and three days."

Henderson looked back at Stacy who was still on the porch talk-ing on her cell phone. "If you guys want to come and live with me, you're welcome to do so. I'm going to let you in on something. I do have someone special in my life and I'm going to ask her to marry me. The only thing I ask is that you not tell your mother about me getting married. I haven't even asked my intended. How-ever, you are my young men, and it's high time I get to spend time with you."

"Are you for real, Dad?" Corlis Jr. asked. "My bags are packed now. Only thing, I'll be going off to college in the fall."

"So that means we've got six months. And where are you going?"

"Stanford. I'm going to Stanford."

Henderson looked at his son in amazement. "My boy is going to Stanford. Yes!" Henderson kicked his heels and drew his arm back and punched the air. "Stanford! Going to Stanford costs a pretty penny."

"I've got scholarships, but, of course, I'll need a little more money."

"Son, you have my full support." The boys and their father bumped fists. They looked up when they noticed Stacy had ended her phone call and was walking their way.

Stacy smirked when she stood in front of the trio. "What's all this male bonding about? Did your father decide to let you stay?"

"Stacy, I have prior plans today, and I have to get going. Corlis and Torian, how about we have a father/son day before you leave. We can spend the whole day and do whatever you want."

"That's cool, Dad," Corlis Jr. said.

"Yeah, I'd like that," Torian uttered.

"But they can't stay today," Stacy said, her nostrils flaring.

"As I said, Stacy, I have guests coming in and I'm already late picking them up from the airport."

"Who is it?"

"It's none of your business."

"It's my business if you plan on seeing your sons."

"Mom, please," Corlis Jr. said, as he let out a large sigh. "Dad, we're cool. Let us know when you want to get together." The boys walked toward their mother's rental car.

"So, you've succeeded in disappointing your sons on Christmas Day."

"No, you did that all by yourself. You show up on my doorstep unannounced and think that I'm going to succumb to your demand."

"It's the girl, isn't it?"

"What are you talking about? What girl?"

"I talked to Junebug. He told me you've been pining over some stripper that almost got herself killed. Is that the best you could do? I know you had the best, but please, you didn't have to fall in the gutter."

A mean glare crossed Henderson's face. "Listen to me, and listen well. You and I were done years ago. What I do with my time and who I see is my business. I will pick up Corlis Jr. and Torian the day after tomorrow."

"And if I don't let them come?"

"I will take your sorry ass to court. And I mean that."

"You wouldn't. You don't have the guts to take my sons away from me."

"After I tell the judge that you haven't adhered to the custody court orders the past ten years, they might have another way of thinking. And you can never say that I've not been a responsible parent. So think on it."

With remote in hand, Henderson opened the garage, got in his car, and set the alarm.

"I will be back," Stacy said as she walked away. "I'll be back."

"You can come as long as you're delivering my sons to me. Now, I have to go."

Henderson watched as Stacy sashayed to the car. She gave him a hard stare before she got in and drove off. Was it fate that his once uncomplicated life was suddenly getting even more complicated?'

CHAPTER 64

*H*enderson drove like a bat out of hell. Navigating through L.A. traffic at this time of day was brutal. If he had left home an hour earlier, he would've missed Stacy and wouldn't have to rush. He exhaled, still recovering from seeing his sons and ex-wife on his doorstep.

Trying to regain that wonderful feeling he had when he woke up seemed futile. Every time he thought about his surprise for Skye, he kept thinking about his sons and how he'd dismissed them. He truly hoped they understood why he couldn't entertain them today, but he'd make it up to them.

Finally, he arrived at the airport. Henderson hated to park, but there was no way he could drive curbside and leave his car to retrieve Skye's family from baggage claim. Shucks, he didn't even know what they looked like.

Right on cue, his Bluetooth buzzed in. He looked at his cell and it was Skye's mother.

"Hello," Henderson said after activating the Bluetooth.

"Mr. Henderson, this is Skye's mother. We're at the airport and have our luggage."

"That's great, Mrs. Taylor. I'm at the airport now and will drive around and pick you up. What are you wearing so I can identify you?"

"I have on a red pantsuit and my daughter has on a white pantsuit. Her husband and baby are with us."

"I'm sure I'll be able to find you. I'll be there in a jiffy." He hung up.

Baby? No one had mentioned a baby when Henderson spoke with Skye's mother on the phone. Oh, well. This was going to be interesting.

Henderson looked at his watch. It was one forty-five. The flight was supposed to arrive at one twenty. He pulled into the ARRIVAL section of the American Airlines terminal and immediately saw Skye's family, fitting the description that Mrs. Taylor had given him.

He eased his car curbside and stopped in front of them. He swallowed hard when he saw the amount of luggage they had with them. He wasn't sure that he was going to be able to fit all of it in his Lexus. If he'd been thinking, he would've driven his Lincoln Navigator.

Henderson jumped out of the car and rushed to greet Mrs. Taylor and her family. Skye's mother seemed frail. They seemed to be a happy group, though. He couldn't get over how Skye's sister, Whitney, looked so much like her. Her husband, Jeffrey, was tall and slender and shook his hand with a firm grip. They held the baby, a little girl, in a car seat, another obstacle for Henderson. He managed to get luggage and family into the car. He would struggle getting his car up and through Baldwin Hills later.

"Would you all like to go to the house and freshen up first?" Henderson asked.

"I would like to go straight to the hospital to see my daughter," Nona Taylor said matter-of-factly. "It's been a long time; she needs her mother's love."

Henderson smiled to himself as he ingested Nona's words. It

was comforting to know that there were mothers who loved their children and truly cared about their well-being.

"I haven't seen my sister in almost three years," Whitney said. "Skye was going through some abandonment issues after our father was killed in the war. I got married and left home; too many memories. I guess in a way, I was escaping my dad's memory...in that house...in that military town.

"Mother told me what she was going through with Skye, but I didn't want the responsibility of worrying about my sister; and I never tried to contact her. We were both suffering."

This was heavier than Henderson had thought. "Although Skye is in the hospital, I hope this will be the time that you all can bond...find your way back to each other. She misses you all."

Nona fetched a tissue out of her purse and dabbed her face. It was apparent that what Whitney had said about everyone running away had gotten to her.

"And Mother," Whitney interjected, "please forgive me. I'm not sure why I chose this time to say this, but I need to say it. I ran like a banshee. I practically did the same thing that Skye did, except that I handled it much better. You needed someone, too, after Dad died. I'm sorry for not being there."

Nona wiped her face some more. She patted Whitney's hand that was laying on her shoulder. "It's all right, baby. Your heart was hurting too, and you handled it the best way you could. Your mother will never hold a grudge against her children. Now, let's not bore Mr. Henderson with our family issues. We don't want him to think that we're as dysfunctional as we sound."

No one said a word right away. Then Whitney reached up from behind and gave her mother a kiss on the cheek. Her husband, Jeff, was quiet, listening to mother and daughter find peace. And then there was quiet for the next thirty minutes or more.

"Well, we've finally arrived at Cedars-Sinai Medical Center. Skye is getting the best care possible."

"Thank you, Mr. Henderson, for taking care of my baby."

"You're welcome. I wouldn't have had it any other way, Mrs. Taylor."

"Call me Nona."

"Okay, Nona."

CHAPTER 65

hey looked like the shepherds searching for the baby Jesus. Nona, Whitney and baby, and Jeffrey followed behind Henderson as they walked through the corridors of Cedars-Sinai Medical Center. For Christmas Day, it was eerily quiet.

As they approached Skye's room, Henderson heard laughter coming from inside. He knew at once that Jaylin was there. Henderson turned around and looked at his band of followers, Skye's family, as they braced themselves to see their long-lost loved one.

"Wait outside," Henderson said, holding up his hand. "I'm going in to prepare Skye...tell her that I have a special Christmas present."

"Okay," Nona whispered. Her nervousness was evident in her voice. Whitney and Jeffrey shook their heads.

Before they could say another word, Henderson disappeared through the door. Two minutes went by and then another before Henderson stepped into the corridor. "Okay, it's time."

The group followed Henderson into the room. Skye was sitting up in bed, waiting for her surprise. She was still bandaged up although most of the swelling had gone down on her face; however, the purple bruise marks were still visible. Her eyes bulged, and she brought both hands to the sides of her head like crashing cymbals when she saw her mother, sister, a man she'd met briefly, and a baby walk into the room.

"Mother! Oh my God, Mother," Skye cried, reaching out her arms.

Nona Taylor ran to Skye. "Skye, oh my baby, Skye, Mother is here now." Nona held Skye for a moment, pulled back and looked at her bruised face, and then kissed her on the cheek. "Baby, I've missed you so much."

"I've missed you, too. Every time I tried to call you, I felt so guilty. I'm so sorry."

"Mother is here now and I'm going to take care of you."

Whitney pushed her way to her mother's side. Nona moved back so Whitney could embrace her sister.

"Whitney, I missed you too. We were so close once. You left me…"

"Shhhhh. Skye, that was in the past. We're here now. I love you, little sis. Love you with all my heart. I have someone here I want you to meet." She motioned for Jeffrey to come forward. "You remember my husband, Jeffrey, and this is our baby girl, Salina."

"Hi," Jeffrey said. "It's been a long time. The family resemblance can't be denied. You look a lot like Whitney."

"It's good to see you, too, Jeffrey. May I see my niece?"

Whitney picked the baby out of her carrier and held her for Skye.

"She's so beautiful. I'm guessing she looks like the both of you."

"More like her daddy," Whitney said.

Skye looked past her mother and sister. "Where is Jermaine?"

"Your brother met some girl that he's head over hills in love with. He's spending Christmas with her," Nona said, taking ahold of Skye's hand. "But he asked me to give you his love."

Skye squeezed Nona's hand. "I don't blame him. And he's going to be a college grad soon."

"Yes," Nona said with a smile.

"Oh, let me introduce you to my best friend." Everyone turned around and stared at the young woman, who looked to be about Skye's age, standing at the back of the room. "This is Jaylin, but she goes by Jaye. She rescued me the night I rode into Los Angeles as a lost soul. I owe her everything."

"She doesn't owe me a thing," Jaye said, trying to act shy. "The Lord appointed me as her guardian while she's out west; that's all. It's nice to meet you all."

"It's nice to meet you, too," Nona said. "And thank you for being a friend to my child. She desperately needed a good friend."

"So how did you all get to Los Angeles?" Skye asked, her inquiring eyes roving around until they landed on Henderson. "This is a total surprise."

"Henderson took good care of us," Nona said.

"But you don't know Henderson."

"I do now, and, Skye, he's a keeper, if you know what I mean." Nona smiled.

"What do you mean, Mother?"

"That Bryan boy wasn't husband material. I couldn't get you to see it, but it doesn't matter now."

Skye smiled. "I've grown up a lot. Your baby has learned a lot about life in the few years I've been gone from Junction City. And I'm still learning."

"That she is," Jaylin chimed in. "Look, I'm going to go and spend some time with my parents and get a Christmas meal. It'll give you all a chance to catch up in private. What are you going to do about feeding them, Henderson?"

"I'm going to take them out to a nice dinner before we go to the house. Thanks, Jaye, for staying with Skye."

"Love that girl. I was glad to be here. It was nice meeting you all." Jaylin waved at them.

"You too," the trio said in unison.

Jaylin walked out and now it was only the family.

The family talked on and on while Henderson looked on. He was happy that Skye was happy; their healing had begun.

An hour passed before Henderson decided to interrupt. "Excuse me, folks. I hate to interrupt your reunion. However, as today is

Christmas, I have another gift for Skye. You all coming was her special gift, but I have another important one." Nona gave Skye the eye.

Henderson took Skye's hand. "Skye and I have known each other for a short time, but in that time, I've grown to love her. All I want to do is love, protect, and treat her like the woman she is." Skye looked on with water in her eyes.

"Amen," Whitney said. "I like him, Skye."

"Well." Henderson stopped and put his hand in his pants pocket. He drew out a black velvet box. He opened it up and pulled out a beautiful custom-made ring with three one-carat diamonds placed side by side, with smaller diamonds that weighed in at two carats that encircled the larger ones.

Everyone gasped, including Skye.

"Skye Culbertson, I love you," Henderson continued. "Before these witnesses…your family, will you be my wife?"

Tears of joy ran down Skye's face. Everyone else hung on to hear her reply. She cried and cried and then the words slipped out.

"Yes!"

CHAPTER 66

*T*yrone and his cousin, Linda, sat in front of the small Christmas tree that sat in one corner of the living room near the fake fireplace that was complete with a fireplace tool set that consisted of a small broom, shovel, and poker. It was a functional tree, pre-lighted, that Linda had purchased the previous year from Walmart. It served the purpose. The holidays weren't big events like in other households—families gathered together with the big Christmas spread that consisted of either turkey, ham, or a rack of lamb accompanied by all of the trimmings.

Linda was an older, second cousin on Tyrone's mother's side of the family. She had half raised him growing up as a young boy in Compton, bouncing between Linda and his grandmother. Memories of Tyrone's mother never stayed with him for long, especially since the only vision of her was as a strung-out drug addict that had to have her crack.

"I got you something for Christmas, Ty," Linda said, going over to the tree and lifting a small package from underneath that was wrapped in pretty foil Christmas paper. "I hope you like it; it isn't much."

Tyrone wasn't in the Christmas spirit. He kept thinking about the news report he'd heard yesterday, the part about Big Sarge fingering him and his operation. It was bad enough that Big Sarge and Benny had not carried out his request to kill Skye, but now he was a sitting duck and had to dismantle his operations once again.

"Thanks, Linda. You shouldn't have. I've been so preoccupied with other things lately that I'd forgotten all about Christmas. But I'm going to get you something nice."

"No need. I'm blessed to be alive. Do you want some coffee or something?"

"Naw. I'm going out in a few. Gotta check on a couple of things."

"Oh, okay. Thought maybe we could hang out and enjoy the day together."

"I'd love to, cuz, but I need to take care of a few things. Maybe when I get back we can go out to dinner. How's that sound?"

Linda smiled. "I'd like that."

All of a sudden the doorbell rang and then banging on the door. Tyrone flinched. Without thinking twice, he jumped up from the seat he was sitting in.

"Police. Open up," the voice shouted from the other side of the door.

Tyrone went into the kitchen, opened a drawer, and pulled out the 9 mm pistol he'd hidden inside.

"What's going on, Ty?" Linda asked, her body shaking.

The banging seemed louder than before. "Open up or we're coming in."

Tyrone motioned for Linda to remain quiet, as he aimed the pistol at the door, all the while inching his way back toward the kitchen.

A few seconds went by and then a loud crash. A long cylindrical object crushed in the door.

Linda screamed and ran into a back bedroom as the Riverside Police Department rushed in. Tyrone fired a volley of shots, hitting one of the officers, while blasts from several other officers' guns riddled the living room wall. He ran through the kitchen and disappeared through a side door that led into the garage and cracked open a door that led outside. With keys in his pocket, he quickly opened the trunk and got in, pulling it shut. In a matter of seconds, he heard footsteps enter the garage and retreat out of the side door.

He was sweating profusely, but with gun in hand, he remained in the belly of the trunk for more hours than he had anticipated.

Inside the house, the others searched through every nook and cranny, guns drawn in SWAT style.

"Call an ambulance," the officer who seemed to be in charge said, forging ahead. "It looks like the bullet exited Nelson's arm. He'll be all right. Find anything? "

"Enough to bring an indictment against him," an officer replied. "All kinds of papers were laying on a dresser detailing car transactions. Also, there's a woman kneeling behind a chair in a back bedroom." The officer pulled on Linda's arm, dragging her through the hallway.

"What is this all about?" Linda inquired, trying to pull away. She shook like a leaf on a tree that was bracing the elements and the terrified look on her face said even more. "Where is Tyrone?"

"Ma'am, calm down. Please calm down," the officer who found her said, still holding onto her arm with one hand, while holding the confiscated papers in another.

Linda tried to struggle free as several officers cuffed her hands. "I have done nothing wrong."

"Tell us where Tyrone is," the officer in charge said, peering into Linda's eyes.

"I...I...I don't know. He was here a minute ago."

"What is your name?"

"Linda…Linda Neal. I'm Tyrone's cousin. Can you tell me what this is all about?"

"I was hoping you would be able to. I'm Sergeant Crunk with the Riverside Police Department. We were informed by the Los Angeles County Federal Bureau of Investigation that one, Tyrone Rogers, was hiding out here."

"Hiding out? He's my nephew and lives here."

"How long has he been here, Linda—a week, month, possibly a year?"

"May I sit down?" Linda asked. "Honestly, sir, whatever it is you think is going on at my residence, I'm none the wiser."

"Anything suspicious that may have caused you to wonder?"

"No, no more than a lot of Tyrone's friends came around. But that was always his nature—he had to have a lot of people around him."

"Why was he living with you?"

"He asked, and I said he could." Arms cuffed behind her, Linda sank back into her seat.

Sergeant Crunk looked at one of the other officers and nodded his head. The officer, whose face was less than friendly, reluctantly took a key from his pocket and released the handcuffs from around Linda's wrists. She rubbed them, sat back, dropped her head and sighed.

"Ms. Neal, what can you tell me about Tyrone's businesses, who he hangs out with, and whatever else you can think of that might be of interest to the Riverside Police Department?"

"If Tyrone is involved in anything, I'm totally unaware as I've already said. He comes and goes as he pleases. He has female company from time to time, like any man his age. I mind my business; he minds his. Tyrone is not the sharing type."

"Is there anyone in the neighborhood he converses with?"

"Sergeant Crunk, I've been honest in my answers to you. Tyrone is from Compton. He lived with me as a little boy growing up, but that was years ago. I don't even know the names of the women he brings to the house. The only persons I remotely knew, and that was only through association, were Big Sarge and Benny. They lived in the same neighborhood as kids."

"If Tyrone lived with you, does that mean Big Sarge and Benny are from Riverside?"

"No, Sergeant. It doesn't mean that at all." Linda hung her head. She sighed and looked into the faces of the cops that still lingered. "Tyrone's mother is my first cousin. We were close as children. After high school, she went her way and I went mine. She hung around a lot of…of not-so-good people. She got hooked on drugs and has never recovered…well, I mean, she's still hooked and will probably die in the streets.

"When she birthed Tyrone, she was only doing little drugs at the time. But after Tyrone reached four and five, she was a straight-up addict. My aunt, Tyrone's grandmother, lived with them, and sometimes she felt for the boy and would send him to stay with me. Mind you, I had barely graduated from a junior college and was doing secretarial work, and now I had the responsibility of helping to raise this kid. Tyrone was back and forth from Compton to Riverside. But I don't understand what that has to do with whatever's going on with him now. Why are you looking for him?"

"Ms. Neal, he's been running an auto theft ring right under your nose. He moved his operation from Los Angeles a little over a year ago after an ex-girlfriend was arrested driving a stolen vehicle that belonged to Tyrone, although she only knew him as Rico Tillman."

"Rico Tillman?"

"Yes. Does the name mean something to you?"

Linda sat back and pondered the question. "Rico Tillman is the name of a dead uncle. I haven't heard his name in years. In fact, he and Tyrone had gotten into a big fight before Uncle T, as we called him, suddenly disappeared. And then, if I recall correctly, about a year later, someone found a dead body in a freezer inside a warehouse in L.A. And after matching dental records, the human remains belonged to my Uncle T. It's crazy that Tyrone would use that name as an alias, if that's the case. He hated Uncle T."

Sergeant Crunk looked thoughtfully at Linda. "You've been helpful, Ms. Neal. We have several officers out scouring the neighborhood looking for Tyrone, but they have yet to locate him. If he should show up, although we will have your house on twenty-four-hour surveillance, please let us know. I may be back with some follow-up questions." Sergeant Crunk handed Linda his card.

Linda took the card and brought her hands to her chest. "I don't believe this...and on Christmas Day."

Sergeant Crunk looked at Linda and turned away.

"The ambulance is here to pick up Nelson," one of the officers said.

"Let them in."

The EMS team quickly wrapped the downed officer's arm to stop the blood flow. They took his vitals, put him on a gurney, and whisked him away to the ambulance. And then they were gone.

Sergeant Crunk gave the other officers the nod and they retreated the way they had come. "Oh, call the City to see about getting your door fixed," he said to Linda. Then Sergeant Crunk went to the door and closed what was left of it behind him. And the room was suddenly quiet.

Linda watched with a stoic face as the officers retreated. She fumbled with the card in her hand. She looked at it for a few moments and then threw it down on the living room floor. Mad as hell, Linda rubbed her wrists and then got up from her seat and began to walk around the house, looking behind doors and under beds. Puzzled, she walked back into the living room with her arms crossed over her stomach. She looked at the Christmas tree that had fallen to the floor in the brief melee and huffed.

"I have no idea where you are, but it's time for you to go, Tyrone. You have overstayed your welcome."

CHAPTER 67

For the next thirty minutes, Linda sat on the couch sulking. She sulked not only because the cops had come up into her house like gangbusters and wreaked havoc, knocking things over and plastering her walls with bullet holes, but Tyrone had disrespected her with some nonsense she wasn't privy to, disturbing the peace in her otherwise happy home. She'd been a loving cousin who'd allowed a member of her family to rest his head at her place for a while, although a year had passed, only to find out that he had used her all along for some dirty business that had the cops knocking down her door. Where in the world had he disappeared to?

She jumped when she heard the squeaking sound of a door. On instinct, Linda looked around the living room and spotted the poker sitting by the fireplace. It was small, but it would do. She picked it up and headed toward the sound.

Ears on alert, Linda walked stealthily toward the kitchen, her feet moving only a half inch at a time. She stopped short when she heard the noise again. This time fear took over and prevented her from moving.

Linda stood still with her arms up in the air, poised to strike whatever...whoever was around the corner. "Tyrone, is that you?" Not hearing a response, Linda inched forward. And then the intruder came around the corner into view, and Linda lunged forward bringing the poker down with all of her might, missing the target completely.

"Damn, Linda, were you trying to kill me?"

Linda looked at Tyrone with hatred in her eyes. She pulled her arms back with the poker still in her hands and tried to hit at him again. She missed. Tyrone tackled Linda to the ground and jerked the poker out of her hands and threw it on the floor.

"You damn bitch. You could've killed me."

"Get your sorry ass out of here right now, Tyrone. They told me what you've been up to. The cops nearly destroyed my place, upset my Christmas, and sent my blood pressure sky high."

"Calm down, cousin."

"Don't tell me to calm down, Tyrone. Where in the hell have you been? How did you elude the police? They covered this place with a fine-tooth comb, and here you are without a scratch on your face, looking as if you don't have any idea about what happened."

A slow grin began to cross Tyrone's face. He tried to keep from laughing, but it escaped anyway. He threw his hands up when he saw Linda about to retaliate. "I'm in some deep sh…"

"Get out now, Tyrone. Get out. Your lease is up, although you didn't pay a single dime to help me out around here."

Tyrone reached in his pocket and pulled out a wad of dough and threw several hundred-dollar bills on the coffee table. Linda's eyes lit up brighter than the lights on her Christmas tree.

"Where did you get that from, Tyrone? I thought you were bankrupt."

"No more questions. You've got to help me get out of here."

"And how do you propose I do that? And don't try to avoid my question."

"I have a plan, but we'll have to wait awhile to execute it. I'm sure the cops are watching your house."

"No thanks to you."

"Come on, Linda. I didn't mean to get you involved in my troubles."

"I thought you were going to make something of yourself, Tyrone. Yes, you've invested in real estate and had other ventures, but were they legitimate at all? A legitimate businessman keeps his roll of dough in the banks downtown—not in wads stuffed in his pocket."

"I'm a different kind of businessman. I roll both ways."

Linda huffed and puffed. "I don't know what you're going to do, but you've got to get up out of my house today. The end."

Tyrone watched Linda until he felt his cell phone vibrate in his pocket. He withdrew it and looked at the caller ID.

"What's up, Pucci?"

"The cops raided the chop shop. They arrested ReRe and the others. I slipped out the side door before they could capture me. The whole place is on lockdown."

"Damn, damn." Tyrone clicked off the phone and threw it at the fake fireplace.

Linda refrained from asking about the bad news. She turned her back and went into the kitchen and poured herself a cup of coffee. For more years that she could count, she had nurtured and been a mother to her addict cousin's son. Now, he was a grown-ass man, and he would have to work out his own problems. They were no longer hers. Tyrone was no longer her responsibility. Whatever it took to get him out of her house, she would do it.

CHAPTER 68

*S*kye was enjoying her family. They had no idea how happy their presence made her. Could good luck finally be hers? Had God forgiven her for all of the bad things she'd done so that she could now reap the joy that had found its way into her life?

It was amazing how gentle and caring Henderson was with her family. Even her mother seemed to be a new person. There was a sparkle in her eyes that she hadn't seen since her daddy had died. Whitney and her husband seemed to take to Henderson as if they'd known him all of their lives.

Skye looked at her engagement ring and smiled. It was beautiful. She couldn't believe she'd met the man of her dreams on a humbug. Who knew that her knight in shining armor would be posing as a bartender in a strip joint, only to find out that he was a Pro Football Hall of Famer?

"What are you thinking about?" Henderson asked, catching Skye off guard.

"I was thinking about how good God has been to me."

Nona Taylor reached over and brushed her daughter's face with her hands. "He sure has, baby girl. He's been good to all of us. I prayed and prayed for a day like this to come. And along with his gift of the Christ child, He gave us peace and harmony within our family." Nona kissed Skye and she held on to her mother's neck for dear life.

"I love you, Mother, and I don't ever want us to be apart. Maybe you can come to L.A. and live with us."

Nona raised her head and patted Skye's hand. "I don't know about that, baby. I have my job…"

"At the Walmart, Mother?"

Nona eyed Skye with a different set of eyes. Berating her about where she worked was a bone of contention between them.

"Mother, I wasn't trying to minimize what you do. I apologize if it sounded that way. You've always worked hard for us kids. Now it's time for you to chill out and have some fun. You never traveled when Daddy was in the service. In fact, this is probably the first time that you've left Junction City."

"Skye," Whitney said, challenging Skye with her voice.

"It's okay, Whitney. Maybe Skye is right. Maybe it's time for me to do something else. I can always take an early retirement."

"But, Mother, you love what you do at Walmart. What are you going to do out here in big, ole Los Angeles?"

"Whitney, are you jealous?"

"Mother, I don't believe you said that. No, I'm not jealous. You've always said that your identity was your own and that you'd never let anyone take it away from you."

"I still feel that way, but what Skye said has got me to thinking. You and Jeffrey will be going to a new duty station in the next eighteen months. Jermaine is his own person, and no telling where he'll end up, especially since he's about to graduate from college. It'll be nice to be around at least one of my children. And you can always bring my grandbaby to see me."

Whitney exhaled. "Have it your way. Skye has always been your baby anyway."

Skye looked at Whitney. "That's not true, Whit. Mother loves all of us the same. When you and Jeffrey got married, that's all I heard about. Whitney is going to see the world. Whitney is going to do this and that." Skye stopped when her sister began to laugh.

Whitney couldn't stop laughing. And then she pointed her finger at Skye. "You must be feeling much better. You should've seen how animated you were."

The men, who had remained quiet, joined in the laughter. They were so loud that a nurse passing by the room poked her head inside. She smiled and left.

"Mother, if you want to come to L.A. and stay with us, it's entirely up to you. I'm not going to force the issue, but I'd love for you to come." Skye turned her head and looked toward Henderson. "Right, Henderson?"

"Of course, we'd love to have you in L.A. We may need a nanny for our baby."

"What baby?" Whitney said, shrieking with excitement.

"There's no baby, you crazy girl," Skye said. "In the future, I'd love to have a child."

"Oh, okay. Too much excitement for one day."

"Skye, I'm going to take your family home, get them situated, and take them out to eat. I'll be back later."

"Okay. I have a Christmas present for you, Corlis. I left it in the glove compartment of my car. I bought it the day of the incident. By the way, is my car still at work?"

"I picked up your car; it's at the house. And don't worry about my gift. In fact, seeing you with a smile on your face with family all around is my gift. I do have a question."

"What is it?"

"Do you realize you called me Corlis?"

"I did. It is your name, isn't it? Now take care of my family and don't worry about me."

"I will, but I'm going to call Jaylin to see if she can come back and sit with you. I really don't want you to be by yourself. I'll be back later." He leaned over and kissed her lips. "You need some lip balm."

Everyone laughed.

"We'll see you later, baby," Nona said. "I love you." Nona gave Skye a kiss on the cheek.

"I love you too, Mother."

Whitney and Jeffrey kissed Skye too, and then they were gone.

Skye looked up at the ceiling and the tears rolled down her face. "Thank you God for blessing me this day."

CHAPTER 69

Skye's family enjoyed the view as Henderson drove up the incline en route to his Baldwin Hills estate. They ooh'd and ahh'd as the view of the city opened itself up to them. Before he forgot, he called Jaylin, who agreed to go back to the hospital to sit with Skye.

"My, my, my," Nona Taylor said. "I'm so used to looking at the flint hills of Junction City, Kansas, that I hadn't imagined that I would see anything as breathtaking as this."

"I see why Skye hasn't made any attempts to come home," Whitney added. "The city seems to grab you into its arms." She looked at Jeffrey. "I could live here."

"L.A. is a different animal from where you come from, baby," Jeffrey offered. "You'd get swallowed up easily. The life here is so face-paced, almost as if you're in another world. The people are so into themselves, what they're wearing and who they should impress today. Everybody wants to be a mover or shaker—Hollywood style."

Whitley looked at Jeffrey in disgust. "And what in the world could you possibly know about living in Los Angeles?"

"Out here you say L.A. If you're going to blend in with the natives or those who've made this their home, you have to act like you know."

"Please, Jeffrey. You're two steps from the country road yourself. You don't know a blank thing about big city living."

"Ouch, that hurt. However, for your edification, I may have lived in the clay hills of Georgia, but I was only thirty minutes from the big city called Atlanta." Jeffrey laughed at his own attempt to be funny. "I've smelled and lived big city life. I went to Morehouse College before I was commissioned as an officer in the United States Army, and ..."

"We get it."

"A Morehouse man," Henderson said matter-of-factly. "Can't mess with a Morehouse man, Ms. Whitney."

Nona began to laugh.

"Why are you laughing, Mother? Your son-in-law doesn't have any idea what I can tolerate and how I would fare in a big city like...like L.A."

Now everyone was laughing except for Whitney. And then baby Salina began to cry. "See what you all have done? Salina's going to be up all night."

"I'm going to let you in on a secret. Baldwin Hills is one of the oldest and largest middle and upper middle-class African-American communities in Los Angeles. It was dubbed 'the Black Beverly Hills' back in the day as many of the black celebrities/entertainers like Ray Charles, Ike and Tina Turner, Loretta Devine, and Nancy Wilson, who weren't allowed to move into the other affluent Los Angeles neighborhoods, moved here. Baldwin Hills is still considered an affluent African-American area although it borders Crenshaw...South Central Los Angeles, and Leimert Park, but it also is connected to Hollywood. The price was right when I bought, and I'm not paying half of what those other folks are paying to live in Beverly and the Hollywood Hills, although my place is considered to be a nice piece of real estate."

"I'm impressed," Jeffrey said, his nose pressed to the car window.

The group continued to laugh and then eased into a peaceful quiet. At last, they finally reached Henderson's house. He let up one of the garage doors, and all you could hear was Jeffrey's loud *ahh*—a big garage with a couple of luxury vehicles parked inside.

The tired and weary travelers were excited about their accommodations.

"I'm loving it already and we have yet to go inside," Whitney said, looking all around the garage as Henderson and Jeffrey pulled luggage from the trunk and assisted Nona out of the car.

"Yeah, I could get used to this," Jeffrey lamented. "I'm going to have to agree with you on that, baby."

Whitney smiled. "I see you had a quick change of heart." Turning to Nona, Whitney patted her back. "Are you all right, Mother?"

"Yes, I was thinking about your daddy. I miss him so much. I felt his spirit come over me. It was a weird feeling that I can't explain."

Whitney hugged Nona. "I miss Daddy too. I believe Skye has missed him more than the rest of us."

Nona sighed and followed Henderson and the rest of her family inside. She smiled at Salina and rubbed her chin. "I wish your grandpa could have seen you," she whispered.

"Oh, my goodness," Jeffrey shouted. "Look at this place."

"Well, let me get you all settled into your rooms and then I'll take you on a tour," Henderson said, smiling. "You'll love my NFL room, Jeffrey."

"NFL room? Football is my favorite sport. I can't wait!"

"Nona, I'll take your bags to your room. And when you've freshened up, I'll take you all out to dinner."

"Thanks, Henderson. I appreciate…*we* appreciate everything."

Henderson showed everyone to their rooms and pointed out all the accommodations—bathrooms, linen closets, and all that they would need to make their stay comfortable. While the group freshened up, he called the hospital to see if Jaylin had returned to sit with Skye. Satisfied that Jaylin was there, he hung out in the kitchen and waited for the refreshed crew to appear.

"I have to take back everything I said to Whitney," Jeffrey said to Henderson, as he walked into the kitchen. "I definitely could get used to this place. You may have to push us out of the house when it's time for us to leave. The view from our room is awesome."

"I'm glad you like, my brother. I want your stay here to be as comfortable as possible."

"It is," Whitney remarked.

Henderson took them on the tour of the house. Nona, Whitney, and Jeffrey touched and felt everything in sight. They couldn't keep their bottom lips from off the floor. They ooh'd and ahh'd during the duration of the tour, and when they got to Henderson's NFL room, there was no breaking Jeffrey away. Even the ladies were excited by what they saw—the awards and trophies that either lined a wall or sat in a glass case.

Henderson looked down at his watch. "It's late. We better go before all the restaurants close up. After all, this is Christmas Day."

"I'm ready," Nona was first to say.

All refreshed and dressed in clean clothes, the group gathered at the door and prepared to leave through the garage. As Henderson began to set the alarm, the doorbell rang. Henderson frowned and exhaled, recalling the last time, which was only that afternoon, when his doorbell rang.

He started not to answer it; however, heads were turned in his direction, waiting to see if he was going to get the door.

With keys in hand, Henderson moved through the kitchen into the butler's pantry and into the adjoining dining room. The doorbell rang again as soon as he set foot in the foyer. He had a sneaking suspicion as to who the caller might be at the door, however, he'd never know unless he answered it.

Slowly, he opened the door. As he thought, there stood his sons and ex-wife, Stacy. She had a scowl on her face. She pushed the boys forward into the house and followed.

"What are you doing here, Stacy?"

Stacy followed Henderson's gaze as he glanced to his right. Seeing no one, she went into her reason for coming.

"I have plans this evening and the boys will have to stay with you tonight. They have clothes for their overnight stay in their backpacks."

Henderson looked at Stacy but didn't respond. He put his hands on each of his sons' shoulders. "Mighty presumptuous of you to come without calling first. Come in, Torian and C. J." The boys walked further into the house.

Stacy bucked her eyes and put her hands on her hips. "No lip, no back talk, no 'why did you come here unannounced, Stacy?'"

"They're my sons and are welcome to stay," Henderson said, looking straight through her.

"Umph, if I knew it was going to be this easy, I would've dropped them off earlier. I'll pick them up first thing in the morning." She stood still and stared at Henderson, probably not able to understand why he was being so agreeable.

"Don't bother. They'll be fine with me. Have fun with your friends or whatever it was you came to L.A. to do."

"I don't get you. Why the sudden change in attitude?"

There were no words Henderson needed to express. He waited for Stacy to leave.

"Well," Stacy said, realizing Henderson had won this round, "I guess I'll be on my way."

"I'll take care of my sons."

"I wouldn't have it any other way. Bye, Torian and C. J."

"Bye, Mom," the boys said simultaneously.

Henderson watched as Stacy strutted to her car, got in, and drove away.

CHAPTER 70

*T*orian and C. J. followed Henderson, their backpacks still strapped to their backs. When they reached the kitchen, Henderson stopped.

"Lay your backpacks over to the side. We're going out to eat."

"I'm not hungry," C. J. said.

"Well, I have guests who are hungry and are waiting for me to take them to get something to eat. That means you'll have to go with us."

C. J. and Torian did as Henderson instructed and followed him to where the others were waiting in the pool room.

There were surprised looks on the faces of Nona, Whitney, and Jeffrey when Henderson entered the room. "These are my sons, everyone—C. J. and Torian. My ex-wife dropped them off a moment a go. They're in California for the Christmas holiday. They'll be joining us for dinner."

"The more the merrier," Nona said with a smile.

Everyone hopped into Henderson's Lincoln Navigator. The ride to the restaurant was met with silence. Shallow breathing was all that could be heard. It was an awkward silence until Henderson finally spoke up.

"I hope you all are comfortable," Henderson began. "I haven't seen my sons in a good while. It was a surprise when they showed up on my doorstep this afternoon; I had no idea they were even in L.A. They've grown so much since the last time I saw them."

"How old are you?" Nona asked, as she looked behind her.

The boys passed looks between them, and Corlis Jr. became the spokesperson. "I'm seventeen; I'll be eighteen in February. Torian is sixteen."

"Wow, my daughter isn't much older than you boys."

"Who's your daughter?" C. J. asked.

"She's a friend of your father."

Silence ensued. It almost felt as if the air had been sucked out of the car. Henderson wasn't sure of the vibes he was receiving. Nona was looking straight ahead, and there was no sound from Whitney or Jeffrey.

They reached the restaurant and the group slipped quietly from the SUV and went inside.

Nona watched Henderson. He was gentle, handsome, built like an athlete, and had the nicest smile. She wasn't sure of his age, but from what she was able to deduce, he couldn't be much younger than she or about the same age. Nona wasn't sure why she hadn't given his age a thought when she first viewed him at the airport. His generosity had undoubtedly overshadowed any negative thoughts and/or reservations she may have had about him, but in all honesty, she had none—at least not until his sons had shown up at the house.

Tension mounted in the room—Whitney and Jeffrey no doubt feeding off of the strange vibe Nona was distributing. Everyone was extremely quiet, the laughter long gone from the group. Nona kept looking from Henderson to his boys, trying to make sense of it all. Curiosity getting the best of her, Nona let her thoughts roll onto her tongue and out of her mouth for the whole world to hear. There was no biting her tongue.

"Henderson, your boys are handsome. You must've been a baby when you had them. You can't be a day over thirty."

Henderson hadn't anticipated this. After all, he'd made her trip possible…possible so she could be with her daughter who'd been severely beaten up.

He smiled. "I'm thirty-seven. I've been out of the NFL for some time. Is there something wrong?"

"No," Nona said with some hesitation. "Well…" Nona wasn't sure how to say what she wanted to say. And then she looked up and Whitney and Jeffrey were staring at her. "Skye is so young and naïve. She hasn't had a real chance to experience life."

"No disrespect, Mrs. Taylor, although I hear what you're saying and may understand where you're coming from, but Skye has experienced a lot more of life than you can possibly imagine."

"What do you mean by that, Henderson? Are you insinuating something about my daughter that I'm not aware of?"

"I wasn't trying to insinuate…"

Whitney quickly jumped in to save the day. "Mother, this is Christmas and Mr. Henderson's sons are with us. He's only saying that Skye isn't the girl you remember from Junction City. Being in L.A. has probably made her grow up a lot. Am I right, Henderson?"

"You're right, Whitney. In fact, prior to my meeting her, she was a working actress and starred in a couple of movies. In fact, she was on a sitcom when she ran into a bad streak of luck that has haunted her ever since. She's gone through a lot, Mrs. Taylor."

"Call me Nona. I'm sorry, Henderson. I still haven't quite gotten over Skye leaving home. She married some guy who didn't want to marry her to spite me and…"

"Mother, please."

"Okay. I'm sorry," Nona said. Then she put on a smile. "Merry Christmas, everyone."

"Who's Skye?" Torian asked, now even more confused.

"Remember this afternoon when I told you and C. J. that I was getting married again?"

C. J. tapped Torian lightly upside the head. "Yeah, Dad, we remember."

"I'm going to marry Skye, and Mrs. Taylor is Skye's mother. Whitney and Jeffrey are her sister and brother-in-law, and baby Salina is her niece."

"Ohhhhh, I get it now," Torian said. C. J. tapped him on his head again.

"So, when are we going to meet Skye?" C. J. asked. "Will she be our stepmother?"

"Lord, Lord," Nona said, fanning herself with a napkin.

"Skye will love both of you. We're going to the hospital to see her when we've finished eating."

"Why is she in the hospital?" Torian wanted to know.

"She had some pains that the doctor had to see about. Now eat your food."

Nona looked at Henderson and patted his hand. "Sorry about that. I'm a mother acting out. I want the best for my baby, but it seems she already knows what she wants. I wish you both all the best. And I mean that."

"Thanks, Nona. I needed to hear that from you."

CHAPTER 71

*N*ervous energy kept Linda jumping up and going to the window to peek outside. The neighborhood was still, almost too quiet for her liking. Tyrone remained in a back bedroom, trying to formulate some kind of plan to escape the prison he now found himself in. He had no place to go, but it was imperative that he make a move tonight to get out of Riverside.

Pucci was holed up in one of his baby mama's apartments, knowing that a dragnet was out there to capture him. His last call to Tyrone was two hours ago; he was scared as hell and on pins and needles.

"Tyrone," Linda said, as she walked toward the back bedroom. "What are you going to do?"

"I've got to get out of here, Linda, but I'm not feeling it at the moment. Even though they aren't visible, the cops are out there waiting for me to slip."

"Why don't I turn on the TV? At least we'll know what they're up to."

Tyrone reached for the remote on the nightstand and flicked the television on. Linda sat on the edge of the bed with her arms wrapped around her waist. Tyrone flipped through the channels until he found a local twenty-four-hour news station and waited to hear if there was any word about the raid on the house earlier today.

There was nothing and they relaxed. The news began again.

"Our top story this evening comes from Riverside." Linda and Tyrone sat up straight and looked dead at the TV without blinking an eye. "A raid was conducted at a home in Riverside, California, that was believed to be the temporary residence of Tyrone Rogers, also known as Rico Tillman, who conducted a chop shop in Los Angeles and as recently in Riverside. The chop shop, which housed several stolen luxury cars, was also seized. Several employees at the chop shop, owned by Tyrone Rogers, were apprehended. We have learned that one of Rogers' lead men at the chop shop escaped."

Both Tyrone and Linda gasped as Tyrone's and Pucci's pictures were splashed on the screen. "If you know the whereabouts or have seen these two men, call either the LAPD or the RPD at once. Tyrone Rogers is armed and dangerous. He shot a police officer earlier in the day before he magically disappeared from the scene. Police are still reeling as to how he was able to elude them..."

"Where did they get those pictures from? Damn, they could've gotten a better picture that was representative of the way I really look."

"Shut the hell up, Tyrone. Why don't you be a man and turn yourself in? It appears that you are involved in all of this mess. Face the piper."

Tyrone jumped up from where he was sitting and lunged at Linda, catching her around the throat. "What you should be thinking is how you're going to get me out of this, bitch. And if you double-cross me, you'll have hell to pay, cousin or no cousin. I'm not turning myself in. They'll have to kill me first, do you understand?" And then he released Linda's neck, and she fell backward onto the bed.

Her breathing was labored as she grabbed her neck, feeling it to make sure it was still intact. Tears sprang to her eyes as she stared at the man she loved and took care of for most of his life. Linda sat up, slid off the bed, and walked out of the room.

"They've got to come and get me, if they want me," Tyrone yelled. "Those bastards always mess with a brother's dream. Well, before they take all of mine, they'll have to shoot me first, but you best believe I'm going to be shooting, too."

And then all was quiet.

CHAPTER 72

*F*inished with their meal, Henderson loaded up the crew in the SUV and proceeded to the hospital. He'd have to hurry if they intended to arrive before visiting hours were over. Henderson drove the back streets, and in a little under thirty minutes, they arrived at Cedars-Sinai.

Anxious to see Skye before the night was over, Nona moved ahead of the crowd. The others moved right along with her. Approaching the door, Nona knocked on it, and after hearing a faint "come in," they all rushed inside the room.

Jaylin stood to one side as Nona rushed to Skye's side. She placed kisses all over Skye's face and gave her a hug. The others followed, while Henderson stood back until Whitney and Jeffrey were done.

"And who are these good-looking young men?" Skye asked in a soft voice.

Jaylin watched Henderson and the two young men thoughtfully.

"Skye, these are my sons, Corlis Jr. and Torian."

Skye smiled. "Hi. Your dad has told me all about you."

Jaylin twisted her lips and made faces, as if she were searching her memory bank.

C. J. spoke up. "My dad says he's going to marry you. Does that mean you're going to be our stepmother?"

Skye smiled and then looked approvingly at Henderson. "So your dad has already told you about me?"

"Yes, and he said he loves you."

"I love him, too. I hope to get to know you both much better."

"So does that mean you're going to be telling us what to do?" Torian asked concerned.

"No, not at all. I understand C. J. is going off to college soon, which means he'll probably be living in a dorm on campus. And for you, Torian, whenever you come out to visit, we'll be friends and do some fun things. Is that all right?"

"Yeah…I guess."

C. J. spoke up. "We want to come and live with you and Dad, now."

Surprise registered on Skye's face. She looked over at Henderson who only raised his eyebrows and hunched his shoulders. "That will have to be something that is worked out between your mother and father. But sure, we'd love to have you if everything works out."

"Yes!" C. J. said, clenching his fist, raising it in the air, and bringing it down in an ultimate triumph.

"That's if our mother will let us come," Torian said a little bewildered.

"Okay, enough of this talk," Henderson said, cutting in. "I wanted you to meet Skye before your mother picks you up in the morning. She might not let you come over again."

"We don't want to go back with her." Torian looked at Henderson, pleading with his eyes.

"I can't promise anything, guys, but I'll do what I can."

"Oh, I almost forgot," Skye said, cutting in. "The doctor said that if I promise to be careful, I could go home tomorrow. Didn't he say it, Jaye?"

"He sure did."

The room erupted. There were happy hearts and faces.

"I can't wait to get out of here."

"We can't wait for you to come home," Henderson said. "Thanks, Jaye, for looking out."

"No problem. In fact, I'm going to stay the night." Jaylin gave Henderson the eye.

"Okay, everyone, get your last kisses in. Visiting hours are over, and I'm sure the staff will be herding us out in a few. I'm going to step outside with Jaylin for a few minutes." And he and Jaylin left the room.

"What's up, Jaye?"

"Skye is putting on a brave face. We were watching the news and they reported that Rico got away when they tried to arrest him earlier today. The reporter said he was armed and dangerous, and after what happened the other day, she is scared out of her mind."

"Jesus. I should be here instead of you."

"Don't worry. I informed the doctor and police protection is still intact. They don't want another incident. But Skye is still scared. Those fools got in the room before, and if Rico is intent on trying to kill her, he may try again."

"Jaye, we're going to have to bank on the fact that this Rico character doesn't want to get caught. If he comes to the hospital, he will be a sitting duck. I'll talk with security before I leave. Let me take everyone home. I'll have my cell phone next to me. Call me if you need me."

"Okay, don't worry. I pray that we'll be all right."

Henderson gave Jaylin a hug. "Thank you, thank up, thank you."

CHAPTER 73

"Linda, you're going to drive me out of here tonight."

"What are you talking about, Tyrone? The police are looking for your ass, and you want me to risk my life after you had the nerve to put your hands around my throat?"

"You want me out of here, don't you?"

"The sooner the better."

"You don't have to be sarcastic, Linda. I know I've overextended my welcome and now I'm ready to do something about it."

Linda rolled her eyes and threw down the magazine she was reading. She gazed over at the Christmas tree, whose lights were now dim. She looked around the living room and reflected on how the bullet holes that graced her walls had come to be. The longer she sat, the madder she got.

"What do you want me to do?"

"I want you to drive the car into L.A. while I ride in the trunk."

"Where in L.A. will I be driving you?"

"I haven't figured that out yet."

"This doesn't feel good, Tyrone. The police will be crawling all over my ass and it doesn't sit well with me that they're going to have firearms while I'll have nothing."

"Keep your cool, cuz. I've got to think about this a little more. I'll have it worked out in a minute."

Linda sighed. Tyrone had worked her last nerve. If she weren't afraid he'd retaliate, she'd turn him in herself. She'd wasted enough time on Tyrone and his sorry-ass momma. Linda was all about family, but there came a time when you had to cut the umbilical cord, she thought.

"Let me know when you've made a decision."

As Tyrone was about to turn around and head back to his bedroom, his cell phone vibrated. He lifted the phone from out of his pocket and read the caller ID. He moved with lightning speed to the bedroom before he answered.

"Pucci, what's up?"

"Man, Five-O is lined up around the block. Somebody dropped a dime on me...probably Desmond and them...trying to save their asses now that they're locked up."

"Don't sweat it, man. We'll get out of this and go somewhere no one knows us. I'm trying to come up with a plan now to get up from Linda's crib."

"Be careful. These fools are ready to mop us up with a biscuit. They want blood, our blood, and they don't give a damn that it's Christmas Day."

"Yeah, Pucci, our mugs were plastered on the TV screen earlier. Now, Linda is in a tizzy and wants my ass out of her house. Can't blame her, though. Five-O riddled her crib with bullets and knocked stuff over like they were in a Vietnam jungle."

"That bad?"

"It's bad and she's plenty pissed. She made me raise up on her. I could've strangled her, but my conscience wouldn't let me do it."

"Man, I'll have to hurt you myself if you mess with Linda. Every time I've ever come to the crib, she's treated me with respect and offered me food to eat. She could've damn well been my momma. I have mad respect for Linda. Keep your paws off of her."

Tyrone laughed softly, although he didn't like that Pucci was reading him for going off on his cousin. But Pucci was right. Linda had, for most of his life, been his mother, especially since the woman who'd provided him the birth canal that brought him to the existence he was forced to live, did nothing more than that. If he hated anyone, it was his biological mother.

CHAPTER 74

*I*t was eleven p.m. and Linda found herself heading to El Pollo Loco to get a chicken avocado quesadilla and two crunchy chicken tacos. If the day hadn't turned out as it had, she would've cooked her own meal with all of the Christmas trimmings. She was famished, but she wouldn't have gone if it weren't for Tyrone.

Linda drove casually, intentionally not pushing the speedometer over the speed limit. All seemed quiet and she hadn't noticed anything out of the ordinary. As she neared Madison Street, Linda happened to look into her rearview mirror and noticed a car that seemed to be trailing not too far behind.

She turned into the drive-thru at El Pollo Loco. Glancing back, she noticed that the car that she believed was trailing her slowed down at the entrance to the fast-food restaurant but moved forward.

Linda ordered her food, paid for it, and waited at the last window to receive it. Before she knew what happened, two plainclothes cops were upon her with their weapons drawn. The server in the drive-thru lane dropped Linda's food on the ground when she saw the revolvers pointed at her customer.

"Riverside Police Department, pull up some and let down your window with your left hand," the cop shouted through the window on the passenger side. Linda complied. One of the officers moved to the driver's side of the vehicle. "Now hold your hands up and get out when I open the door."

Rage and anger replaced Linda's relaxed countenance. When the door handle moved and the door was jerked open, she eased out slowly from her vehicle, her hands now held high in the air. They frisked her without an ounce of sensitivity.

"Pop the trunk," the second officer shouted. "Pop the trunk now." Linda reached in. "Keep the left hand up."

Sweat poured from Linda's brow as she reached in and pulled the lever to release the door to the trunk of her car. She wasn't sure why Tyrone thought it was a good idea to hide in it, but this appeared to be the end of the road. Now she was going to be taken to jail as an accessory and accomplice to all of Tyrone's mess. She let out a sigh. And then in the next instant, a puzzled look crossed her face.

"No one is in the trunk." The officer slammed the trunk down and kicked the tire. "Damn, I was sure he'd be in there, waiting for the appropriate moment to get out undetected." The officer hit the trunk again. Next he opened the back door. Finding nothing, he cursed to high heavens.

The officers withdrew their guns, while Linda looked at them stoically, her insides on broil.

"Where is Tyrone Rogers?" the officer who had told her to get out of the car asked, his jowls shaking against a crimson-red face.

Linda's answer was short and tart. "I haven't seen him since earlier today."

"You've been home all day. So why is it that you chose to drive all the way down here in the middle of the night to get something to eat? You have more than three fast-food restaurants close to your house."

"So, you've been spying on me? You've been watching my house all day?"

"Ma'am, don't answer a question with a question. My patience is spent. Now, why did you come all the way down here to get something to eat?"

"I wanted a damn chicken avocado quesadilla and none of the three fast-food restaurants that I passed on the way here serves what I wanted. There can't be a crime in getting something to eat."

"Who were you ordering for? Is Tyrone at your house?" As if a light bulb had gone off in the officer's head, he turned, walked back to the drive-thru window, and banged on it.

The server looked scared and took her time opening up the window. After the cop hit it an additional two times, the young Hispanic girl opened up the window.

"The last order, the one you dropped, what was it?"

"A chicken avocado quesadilla and two crunchy chicken tacos," the young lady rattled off and then shut the window as fast as she could.

The officer turned back to Linda. "Were you planning on eating that by yourself?"

"All by myself," Linda said with contempt. "You see, after the door to my house was pushed in and the police riddled my place with bullets and knocked everything down in sight, my nerves were rattled. I had every intention of going out today to get a nice Christmas meal. However, what I went through this morning threw me for a loop. At ten-thirty, I realized I hadn't eaten anything all day and my stomach begged to be fed. Does that satisfy you, officer? Earlier, I told your chief, or whatever he is, that I didn't know anything about what Tyrone is up to. And I still don't."

"Let her go," the officer said. "If I see, hear, or find out that you've aided and abetted a fugitive of the law, I will arrest you, lock you up, throw away the key, and make sure you're prosecuted to the inth degree of the law so that you'll never see daylight again."

Linda didn't say a word. She quietly got back into her car and started to drive away when the server hollered out of the window, waving her hand.

"Ma'am, *te hice otra orden de comida!*"

"What?"

"I made you another order of food."

Linda looked at the young Hispanic girl. "I'm not hungry anymore. You eat it." And Linda got back in her car and drove off.

CHAPTER 75

*T*yrone temporarily nursed a scratch as he jumped from yard to yard, across wooden fences, misjudging the height of the last fence that scratched his arm up good when he dove into a neighbor's backyard. He'd convinced Linda to drive to her favorite Mexican chicken place with him in the trunk, after which he'd jump out and make a run for it. At least that's what he told her. But he had other plans.

He told Linda he had her keys. However, when they went into the garage, Tyrone said he thought he had them but didn't, which prompted Linda to go back into the house. Before she left, he pretended to get into the trunk, but the moment she was inside the house, Tyrone, dressed in all black, slid outside through the side door and crouched low by the side of the house until he knew she was gone. He saw headlights come on and then several cars suddenly move in the direction Linda was traveling.

"Damn," Tyrone said, as he wiped small droplets of blood from his left arm that had now saturated his shirt. He couldn't stop now. As soon as the cops realized that he wasn't in the car, they would be circling back and he wanted to be long gone.

Tyrone continued to run and kept to the alleyways as best he could. When he felt that he wasn't being followed, he stopped and called Pucci.

"What's up, man?" Pucci whispered.

"Look, Pucci, I'm on the run."

"Where are you?"

Tyrone gave him a description of where he was hiding.

"I'll have somebody pick you up. They're probably watching me too. You can't come here."

"Okay. I'll need a ride to L.A. I can manage once I get there."

"Give me a few minutes to hit my cousin up. You'll have to peel off some green stuff in order for him to take you all the way to L.A."

"No problem. Send him here as quick as you can. When the cops realize I'm not in the car with Linda, they'll have a dragnet over the city."

"Okay. I'm on it."

"Oh, and Pucci, I need for you to check and see if Skye Culbertson is still at Cedars. I want her put out of commission."

"All right, but right now, time is ticking. You need my cousin. Will call you right back."

"Okay." And the line was dead.

Tyrone continued to nurse his arm. The blood had stopped oozing and he was glad. He stayed hidden in the shadows of the alleyway behind a couple of industrial-type garbage cans. Within three minutes of his last call, Pucci was calling him back.

"My cousin, Rock, will be there in ten to fifteen minutes. It's going to cost you."

"No problem as long as I get out of here and to L.A. He'll get what I think I owe him."

"Don't mess with Rock, Ty. The brother can be pretty mean. He's from the mean side of the hood and got all of that prison anger built up inside."

"I said I'll take care of Rock. There's no need to worry."

"All right. Safe travels to L.A."

"Thanks, Pucci."

Within fifteen minutes, a blue Toyota Camry turned into the alleyway. It crept slowly as if searching for something. When it got close to where Tyrone was hiding, he lifted his head and the car stopped.

When the door flew open, Tyrone immediately got up and slipped inside. And the car drove away.

"Thanks, Rock. I appreciate this man."

"Any friend of Pucci's is a friend of mine," Rock said in a deep, guttural voice. "Where in L.A. do you want to be dropped?"

"Off of Figueroa Street on West Gage."

"I got a lot of people in South Central. I know the area well."

Tyrone didn't want to say anything else. In fact, he was going to have Rock drop him off close to where he wanted to go. The last thing he needed was someone to pinpoint his exact location. Although Rock was a thug from the hood, if push came to shove, he probably wouldn't hesitate to drop a dime on him, if it meant his survival.

They rode in silence for the next thirty minutes or so. "The Harbor Freeway is coming up soon, bro. That will cost you a hundred."

"A hundred dollars for a forty-five-minute ride?"

"I've got to make a roundtrip. I put myself at risk for you. I hear the PoPo wants your ass real bad. A hundred is a small fee for my services—especially this being a holiday. Rates are higher."

Tyrone pulled out his wallet and pulled out a hundred-dollar bill and gave it to Rock.

"Don't you have any twenties? Folks be looking at me strange if I come up in the liquor store with a hundred-dollar bill. Everyone knows I'm a felon."

"Take it or leave it."

"Nigga, I don't like your attitude. Pucci said you were cool and all, but I beg to differ." Rock took the hundred-dollar bill. "If you need another ride, tell Pucci not to call me. I can't stand ungrateful, running-from-the-law niggas."

Without another word tossed between them, Rock pulled to the curb when he reached their destination. Tyrone eased out of the car, slammed the door behind him, and disappeared into the night.

CHAPTER 76

*T*he air was crisp and all was quiet in the city. All of Henderson's guests were up and ready to start the day, especially now that Skye would be discharged from the hospital.

Henderson watched as his sons reluctantly packed their backpacks, trying to delay the moment when their mother would pick them up. They had begged into the night to stay with Henderson, but he wanted to do the right thing so that he could have future visits from his sons, although C. J. would only be several hours away up the coast.

As he prepared to get breakfast for the family, C. J. ran into the kitchen with his cell phone extended to his dad.

"Who is it?" Henderson asked.

"It's Mom. I asked if we could spend the day with you. She said she had to talk with you first."

Henderson took the phone from C. J. and reluctantly spoke to Stacy. "Good morning."

"Good morning, Corlis. The boys told me that they're having a good time."

"They are and I'm enjoying them as well."

"Your sons asked if they could spend the day with you, and I'm okay with it, if it's all right with you. I will pick them up at eight this evening."

"Sure they can stay. They are my sons, too. I'll make sure they're ready at eight."

"Okay. Let me speak with C. J. again. And I'll see you later this evening."

"Sure." Henderson handed the phone back to C. J. who was beaming as he left the room.

Henderson smiled in spite of himself. He was surrounded by family and that made him happy. He was anxious to get the day started, which included picking up Skye.

Skye was anxious to go home and be surrounded by family. Her dutiful friend, Jaylin, was by her side, assisting her with getting dressed and being presentable when the gang arrived to pick her up.

"You're a lucky woman, Skye," Jaylin said, as she tightened Skye's hair.

"If you're talking about lucky in that I have a friend in you, you're absolutely right. I wouldn't be where I am without you."

"Yes, you would." Jaylin brushed away Skye's comment with her hand. "You have the confidence to be whatever you want to be. All I did was help to bring it out of you. Look at you, the few years that you've been in L.A. You've been in several movies and were a regular on a hit sitcom. And while I won't tell anybody, you were L.A.'s hottest stripper."

"You ought to quit, Jaye. You've never even seen me hit the poles. But I could work it with the best of them. Those days are completely over, though. Okay, I don't want to reminisce about that; I want to look good for my man and my family."

"Well, your hair is fixed and I think you look gorgeous in your brown tweed slacks and brown swing blouse."

"Thanks for the Christmas present. It goes well with my engagement ring." Skye stuck out her hand and admired her ring. She smiled.

"How do you feel?"

"I'm a little sore but not enough to stay in the hospital another day. The doctor has released me, and I can't wait for Henderson to get here."

"Henderson is a little old for my taste, but he's a fine catch, Skye. He loves you."

"And I love everything about him. He listens when I talk. He's caring and sensitive to my needs. Even the hostile side of me has calmed all the way down. Henderson understands me, and I'm sure his age is a factor. But Jaye, that man can throw down in the bedroom. He gives new meaning to the phrase *wear you out*. Making love to my man is probably what 'Thriller' meant to Michael Jackson. I'll admit, though, I wasn't all into sex like I am now. Henderson and I make love, and, Jaye, he makes love to me all the way down into my inner core."

"Too much information, but I'm glad you're happy. Uhmm, you go on, Ms. Skye. Go on and be Mr. Henderson's love thing and let him work his magic on you."

"It is like that, and I can't wait for his hands to hold me and touch me all over."

"You're feeling much better, and I got the picture. You're the only one, present company included, that has a fantastic man like Henderson. Don't gloat or I'll crack another one of your ribs and make your hospital stay longer." The ladies laughed. "I'm happy for you."

The door to Skye's room suddenly opened. Half expecting to see Henderson, Skye jumped up, ready to embrace her man.

"May I help you?" Jaylin asked, acting as if she were the sergeant-at-arms as the tall, scruffy black man, who wore blue scrubs, entered the room.

The gentleman scanned the room and then made his apologies.

"I'm sorry; I must have the wrong room." And then he stared at Skye. "Are you going home today, ma'am?"

Skye looked at the man with inquisitive eyes. "No, I'm going for a walk."

"Ohh, okay," the visitor said, his eyes still wandering. "I beg your pardon. Have a good day." And he left the room.

"I didn't like him, Jaye. There was something strange about his demeanor that I can't immediately put my finger on."

"I didn't like him, either. Sit tight. Where is that officer who's supposed to be guarding your door? I'm going to alert the nurses' station."

"Don't leave me, Jaye. I'm scared. Rico is still walking around somewhere and he may make another attempt to kill me."

"Don't say that, Skye. I'll call instead."

Jaylin picked up the phone and called the nurses' station. Before she could barely turn around and hang up the telephone, an armed officer entered the room.

"We're checking our surveillance cameras now to see if we can locate the person you said came into your room," the officer said. "We thought he was one of the orderlies since he had on blue scrubs. I'll stay with you in the event the person in question decides to return."

"Where were you?" Jaylin asked. "You were supposed to be guarding the door. Although the man had hospital scrubs on, he was suspicious-acting."

"I stepped away for a second to take a call. We're glad that you were both alert, though."

Skye called Henderson to advise him of what was going on. And they waited.

CHAPTER 77

For the next thirty minutes, they waited. Skye's nerves were on pins and needles, along with Jaylin's. The first report indicated there was no sign that the intruder was still in the hospital; after all hallways, stairwells, bathrooms, closets, empty hospital rooms, cafeterias, and pharmacies had been checked and rechecked. Yes, the intruder was spotted on several surveillance tapes, but it had appeared that he had exited the hospital and was nowhere to be found.

Security was tight. The LAPD sent more reinforcements to the hospital to stave off what could possibly be a massacre if Tyrone Rogers was truly hell-bent on obliterating Skye Culbertson from the face of the earth. Skye had become a risk that the hospital didn't need. Their allegiance was to all patients, but the risk of incident would go away as soon as Skye was completely discharged.

An hour after the intruder paid a visit to Skye, Henderson arrived at the hospital. He rushed to her side and held her tight, not wanting to let go.

"I tried to get here as fast as I could. The traffic was terrible and I had to go through an intense body search to get into the hospital."

"I'm glad you're here. Jaye and I were scared to death."

"Your mother is worried stiff after I told her what happened. It was best that she stayed at the house in the event things turned ugly."

"Henderson, I'm concerned about what may happen after you

leave here," Jaylin piped in. "If this is indeed the work of Rico, he has spies everywhere and he's not going to stop until he does something horrible to Skye. I don't understand it. Skye took the fall for him when she was arrested in his stolen vehicle. She owes his sorry butt nothing."

Skye put both hands up. "He's mad that I put his whole operation in jeopardy. Hell, I didn't even know I was driving a stolen vehicle until I was busted. And to think that I was being followed, which only means to me that Rico... Tyrone, or whatever his real name, is had to have had some inkling that the police was on to him. He'd never asked me to drive one of his cars before. Why then? I wasn't running an illegal business, and he deserves whatever he gets. And don't forget, the asshole stole all of my money. He was a liar from the jump; the truth was never in him."

"I'm going to do everything in my power to protect you, Skye. He's going to have to come with a full army to get to you."

Skye smiled. "How did I get so lucky to find a man like you, Corlis Henderson?"

"I'm the lucky one. Are you ready to go?"

"Yeah, I'm good and ready."

A police escort followed the trio to their cars in the parking garage. Skye hated saying goodbye to Jaylin. She had been so supportive of her during her hospitalization. Jaylin had to take care of some personal business but promised to hook up in a day or two. She got in her car and drove away.

Henderson helped Skye into his Lexus, went to the driver's side, and prepared to get in. As Henderson opened the car door, a bullet whizzed by him and shattered the glass on the driver's side window. The police escort, who was on his way back to the hospital, suddenly turned around and shouted at two guys who ducked behind a car two rows over. Before he could get off another round, another bullet whizzed by and hit the tank on Henderson's car.

Panic-stricken eyewitnesses scrambled for safety while Henderson nearly hurdled over the front end of his car to help rescue Skye. She was scrambling to get out of the car when the back side burst into flames. Henderson pulled Skye out of the car, rolled over onto the cement, and covered her with his body. With the help of a Good Samaritan who happened to be getting out of his car at the same time, they were able to move safely away from the vehicle.

"I'm a doctor, Dr. Garrett Sullivan," the gentleman said.

"There's a gunman in the garage who's after my fiancée. She was released from the hospital minutes ago. She has several rib fractures and I'll need to get her to safety...back into the hospital, but I'm not sure if the gunman has left."

"My medical bag is in my car. Stay down on the pavement while I'll try and retrieve it. I'll be able to check her pulse and monitor her condition, if I'm successful."

"I'm all right," Skye managed to say as she gasped for breath.

"Don't talk, miss. Be as still as you can."

Skye nodded.

The police had the hospital surrounded and on lockdown. Traffic was immediately blocked off from entering the parking garage, and those who'd already entered were told to take cover.

Henderson watched as his car was engulfed in flames, the red inferno charring the interior and the frame, while it also licked the concrete above. All he could do was watch.

While the car burned, a volley of shots rang out from several weapons. Every vehicle that stood between the gunmen, the police, and the SWAT team was riddled with bullets. The rapid fire that emitted from the guns lit up the garage like the Fourth of July. It continued for the next two to three minutes.

"I got him," someone shouted, and then another round of shots went off.

In less than five minutes flat, two fire trucks arrived along with other safety personnel. The police flagged them and rerouted them from the war zone that was taking place.

It had become an all-out assault until the head of the SWAT team, who'd taken charge, raised his hand. Several members of his team ran through the parking garage like the assault team they were, although proceeding with caution and with their weapons drawn. A hand from one of the team members went straight up into the air.

"Three men down. There doesn't appear to be anyone else."

Even still, the SWAT team, in cooperation with the police, took the liberty to search every inch of the garage to make sure.

"It seems to be over," Henderson said to Skye. "How do you feel?"

"I'm hurt, but I want to go home."

"Let's get you back into the hospital and checked out," Dr. Sullivan said. "It would be better to know that you didn't hurt your ribs all over again. The scrapes on your arms will heal, but the external is what I'm concerned about. Your body was tossed and turned and it's better to be safe than sorry."

Henderson reached down and kissed Skye's cheek. "I agree with the good doctor. Thanks, Dr. Sullivan, for being in the right place at the right time."

"Yes, I was where I was supposed to be."

One of the members of the police department held up what appeared to be a wallet.

"I'm going to walk over there and see what's going on," Henderson said.

"Don't leave me."

"Dr. Sullivan will be with you, Skye."

Henderson walked toward the group of officers. When he walked up, one of the officers held out his arm. "You can't go beyond this point. It's a crime scene."

"The perpetrators were after my fiancée. It was my car they shot up."

"I'm sorry, sir," the officer said to Henderson. "I can tell you that three men are dead. We're waiting for the coroner to arrive. In fact, he's on his way in now."

"Can you tell me who the persons are? That would mean a lot, especially to my fiancée."

"I can't release any names at this time."

The police officer who escorted Henderson and Skye looked up. He saw Henderson and headed in his direction. Once he was upon Henderson, he put his arm around his shoulder and walked a short distance from the site where police tape was now being placed.

"Tyrone Rogers was one of the three. I saw the driver's license myself. I'm sure you wanted to know. But don't go anywhere yet. The police will need your statements."

"Thank you," Henderson said, feeling a moment of relief. Now, maybe Skye's life would return to normal.

CHAPTER 78

When Skye and Henderson entered the Emergency Room, Jaylin was sitting in the waiting room, her knuckles white from rubbing them so much. Jaylin jumped up when she saw them and ran to Skye.

"I was about to exit the hospital when they blocked the entrance. They said there was a shootout in the parking garage. My heart was doing double somersaults. Immediately, I knew that that asshole Rico had somehow got to you. This is the first place I came to in the event that…that something happened to you."

Skye smiled. "God is good. He spared my life again. For sure he's trying to tell me something."

Jaylin looked at Henderson and then Skye. "So why are you in the ER?"

"To make sure I didn't suffer any more damage to my ribs. Girl, you wouldn't believe that the Lord sent a doctor to my rescue. When the bullet hit the car…"

Jaylin gasped. "A bullet hit the car?"

"And the car burst into flames," Henderson offered.

"Oh my goodness. You guys…you guys could've been killed."

"I'm sending up praises now," Skye said. "And as I was saying, God placed this doctor at the scene who kept me calm while all the shooting was taking place. My hero, of course, is my future husband who pulled me from the car, along with the doctor."

Jaylin put her hand over her mouth. "Damn, girl, until I met you, I didn't know what drama was. You've played in some of the best movies in Hollywood since you've been in L.A. called *Your Life*."

"Rico is dead."

"For real, Skye?"

"The police officer told Henderson."

Henderson nodded his head. "They're calling us, Skye," he said. "Let's get checked out and hopefully you'll still get to go home."

"Okay."

"Don't you go anywhere, Jaye. We're going to need a ride home."

"You know me; I'm not going anywhere."

Skye was released to go home a couple of hours later. Rest was what the doctor ordered. There wasn't any additional trauma to her ribs. The scrapes to her arms that she received as she was being pulled from the car were cleaned and bandaged. Skye was ready to go home to her family.

CHAPTER 79

Everyone was happy to see Skye when she walked through the door. Nona gave her a big hug, not wanting to let go.

"We heard the news on TV. What happened?" Nona asked, catching her breath.

"Believe it or not, we had a police escort," Henderson said, finally flopping down in the nearest chair in the family room. "Jaye had gotten in her car and driven off, and while we were still getting into the car, a gunshot rang out from nowhere. And before we knew it, the officer who had escorted us to the car shot back. And then there was more gunfire and my gas tank was hit."

"Gas tank?" Whitney's mouth flew wide open.

"Yes, the gas tank and my car burst into flames while Skye was trying to get out. A doctor who was coming on duty helped me to get Skye out of the car before it was totally engulfed in flames. My heart is still beating fast from the memory."

"Thank God you're fine," Nona said, hugging Skye some more.

"Skye has got to rest if she is to stay at home."

"I feel fine, Corlis. I do. I want to stay up awhile."

"Okay," Jaylin warned. "We don't want you to have to go back to Cedars. It has too many bad memories."

"You and Corlis are too overprotective."

"It's for your own good. If we plan to get married soon, I need you to be in tip-top shape." Everyone laughed.

"Hi, Ms. Skye," C. J. said, coming from another room followed by Torian.

"Hi, C. J. Hi, Torian. I didn't know you were still here."

"I'm going to take the guys out and do some men stuff. You're welcome to come along, Jeffrey."

"You and your guys need alone time. I'll stay here and keep the women happy."

"Okay. You're in good hands, Skye."

"Thanks, babe." Skye threw Henderson a kiss, and he and the boys left.

"So," Nona began, "with all that has happened, will you be returning to Junction City?"

Skye looked thoughtfully at her mother. "I love you, Mother, but I can't go back to Junction City to live. I've made a new life here in L.A."

"But with all that's happened to you, are you sure you won't reconsider?"

"Rico is dead. He can't bother me ever again. I don't know why he was so incensed with me. He took from me and he made my life miserable. But I don't have to worry about that anymore. We've talked about you coming to live in L.A. Have you thought any more about it?"

Nona got up and walked around. She wrung her hands two or three times before stopping to look at Skye. "It sounds good, but Junction City is all I know—my job, my few friends from church. I'd be lost in a big city like Los Angeles."

"I'll go to church with you and you can find another job."

"What about my pension? I've banked a lot of years at Walmart and I want to reap the benefits."

"Mother, you sound so dependent. You can retire if you want to with all the years you've given those people."

"I am; in fact, I think you're a lot like me. Let me think about it, but I do have one request."

"What?"

"That you come home to get married."

"Yes," Whitney shouted. "I'll give you the biggest bridal shower ever."

"I've lost track of the few friends I had."

"I have plenty of friends who'll bring presents, and, of course, Jaye will be coming. Right, Jaye?"

Jaylin looked at Whitney with a smile. "If you say I am, then I guess so."

"We'll see, Mother. I'll have to heal first," Skye interjected.

All heads turned when the doorbell rang.

"I'll get it," Jaye offered.

"Why don't I answer the door?" Jeffrey said, especially with all that had gone on.

"Rico is dead. He's not coming back," Jaylin said. "I got it."

The impatient person on the other side of the door continued to ring the doorbell. Jaylin jerked it open and stared into the face of a beautiful, black woman, who stared equally as hard at her. The woman's hair was short and molded to her head on one side, while the other half looked as if she was missing part of a pageboy. She wore a pair of black designer shoes and a red, stretched-knit short dress that was form-fitted to her body, as well as black leggings that amplified the natural shape of her youthful-looking legs.

The woman sized Jaylin up and walked into the house uninvited. "Is my ex-husband here?" Stacy sneered, scanning the house. "I've come to pick up my sons. Thank God I got here in time."

"No, he isn't here," Jaylin said, enunciating her words so they wouldn't be misconstrued.

"Well, where is he? Where are my sons? And who in the hell are you?" Stacy started to walk past, but Jaylin stuck her foot out and moved directly in front of her.

"I said Henderson isn't here and neither are his sons." Jaylin put her hands on her hips.

"What's your name? Are you Corlis' new whip?"

"My name is Jaylin Scott and whatever my relationship is to Henderson is none of your damn business."

Stacy rolled back on her hips and gave Jaylin a dirty look. "Be glad I packed my patience when I came here this afternoon. I haven't got time to fool up with Corlis' baby hoes."

It was Jaylin's time to step back. She puckered her lips to say something but must've thought better of it. "I'm nobody's hoe." Jaylin threw her hands up in Stacy's face for emphasis. "I told you, Henderson isn't here and I'd be more than happy to let him…"

Before Jaylin could finish her sentence, Skye walked up holding her back.

"Oh, Lord, I've got to get my boys. Is Corlis running a whorehouse up in here?"

Skye took center stage. "So that you aren't misinformed about who I am, my name is Skye Culbertson—actress and fiancée of Mr. Corlis Henderson."

Stacy's eyes bulged as they shifted between Skye and Jaylin.

"Whoever in the hell you are, you need to beat it. There aren't any hoes up in here. I'm recovering from a bad accident and you're disturbing my peace."

"What's wrong?" Nona asked, now approaching the group of women from the rear. "Skye, you should be resting. All I hear is raised voices."

"It's okay, Mother. This is Corlis' ex-wife and she's leaving now. Corlis has taken his sons for an outing—father and sons. He'll be back before the time you said you'd pick the boys up."

Stacy's face was contorted and ready for war. "Call him now and tell him that I'm here to pick up my sons."

Nona stepped in front of Skye. "I don't know you and don't care to, but if you holler at my daughter like that one more time, I'm going to give you something to holler about. You heard my daughter. Your sons are out with their father. You can pick them up at eight. Now it's time for you to go."

"Uhh…"

"There's nothing else for you to say," Nona said. "It's time for you to go. If you'd come here with a different attitude, things might have been different. But I've been around a long time, and I'm not putting up with any bull today." Nona stood in front of Stacy until she backed up, turned around and walked out of the door.

"You haven't heard the last of me."

As soon as Stacy's body was on the other side of the door, Nona slammed it in her face. "Mess with me and you're going to see," she said to the door.

"Mother, I didn't know you had it in you."

"You stood up to that bitch. Oops, I'm sorry Mrs. Taylor."

"It's all right, Jaye; she was definitely a bitch and a half." The ladies laughed. "But I'm a mother who still protects her young. Corlis is going to have to put that woman in check, Skye. Maybe Mother needs to move to California and take charge."

Skye, Jaylin and Nona laughed hysterically.

"You told her, Mother." Skye kissed Nona. "I love you and I hope you will change your mind and come out and stay with us."

Nona smiled. "I'll give it some more thought."

CHAPTER 80

The flint hills of Junction City, Kansas loomed large in the background, while the tall, white tower that announced to visitors that they were approaching Ft. Riley Army Base was visible to the many men and women who were stationed there. It was a brisk spring day, and for a change, there wasn't a cloud in the sky—perfect weather for a bridal party.

The date had been set. Skye Culbertson would become Mrs. Corlis Henderson the following weekend. And as Skye's sister, Whitney, had promised, she threw the biggest bridal shower that Junction City or Ft. Riley, Kansas had ever seen.

The Officer's Club was decorated like a Hollywood set. There were black and white balloons, streamers, placards that looked like movie film that had the words "Hollywood Skye" embossed on them that adorned the room. Tables were dressed with white linen table-cloths, black placemats and napkins, and white china plates. Each centerpiece was a cluster of red roses, cut low and placed in a medium square crystal vase. It made each table come alive.

A white cupcake stand made in the shape of a flower cart held more than 200 cupcakes in eight different flavors—Red Velvet, Mudslide, Carrot Cake, Raspberry Truffle, Cookies and Cream, Pineapple Upside, Strawberry Shortcake, and a sinful Chocolate Divine. Two eight-foot tables showcased an abundance of heavy hors d'oeuvres that might be served at an elegant Hollywood bash, along with a tasty punch that was Whitney's secret. She had out-done herself with the help of Henderson. And to set it all off, a red carpet was placed at the entrance to the room so that Skye would not only be ready for her walk down the aisle the following week but as practice when she'd go to her first Emmy awards show. She'd landed a starring role in a new Tyler Perry television series that would run on OWN television network. Her career was taking off and blossoming.

Besides Nona, Whitney and her friends, and Nona's church friends, several of Skye's old friends from high school came to join in the festivities. After all, their old friend was a celebrity. Jeffrey, Henderson, and Skye's brother, Jermaine, were also in attendance. But what made her most happy was to have Jaylin by her side. Jaylin had introduced her to L.A. and helped her survive the tumultuous times that had thrust Skye into true womanhood. Skye would cherish their friendship forever.

With everyone assembled, Whitney stood up front with Nona at her side. She took a knife and gently hit the side of a tall champagne glass to get everyone's attention.

"Thank you all for coming to celebrate my sister, Skye's, up-coming nuptials. Yes, Skye is getting married…again." Laughter. "I'm so glad she chose to come home to Kansas to do so, and today we honor her with a pre-celebration—her first bridal shower. We're going to play some games to see how well you know the bride and groom—that may be a little difficult for some of you—but the questions, I promise, aren't difficult.

"As many of you know, my sister is also an actress—the reason for the movie motifs that are displayed throughout the room. She played in a sitcom a couple of years ago and had a few roles in several movies. But before we eat all of this wonderful food, par-take of the games, and Skye opens all of these wonderful gifts you brought her, I have a special surprise."

The room was silent.

"Tyler Perry, come on out."

The room erupted, the clapping getting louder and louder. Tyler Perry, in all of his glory, acted like regular people. He came to the front of the room, waving to everyone, finally stopping to give Skye a kiss on the cheek. He smiled as he turned toward the audience.

"Good afternoon."

"Good afternoon," the crowd echoed back.

"I feel blessed to be with you today to help jump-start Skye into the next chapter of her journey. I'm doing something I rarely do and that is attending functions that are given by my cast members. But I felt I had to be here with all that Skye has been through.

"I look forward to working with you, Skye. You're a true star in every sense of the word. I wish you and Corlis a wonderful wedding day and that your life together will be forever. Thank you for giving me space to come and do this. I won't be able to stay, but I'm glad I came.

"Oh, and here's a little something to get that honeymoon started—an all-expense paid honeymoon to Jamaica. All the details are inside the envelope. To you and Corlis...all the best." Tyler reached down and gave Skye a kiss. He then turned to Whitney and Nona and kissed them both on the cheek, shook Henderson's hand, and then was gone.

The crowd went wild—whistling, clapping their hands, and fanning themselves.

"Alrighty now," Whitney began. "Ladies, pick your lips up off the floor. I've got to pick mine up first." The room roared again with laughter. "I was one-hundred percent sure that you'd enjoy that wonderful surprise. My mother is going to say grace, and then we can eat. Mother, here's the mike."

Nona said a special prayer, grateful that her daughter, Skye, was doing well and had come home to get married. Nona prayed bless-

ings over her family and for the families of all who were in attendance. Skye hadn't heard her mother pray like that in years.

When Nona finished, Skye was told to sit in her chair and food
would be brought to her. As the partygoers raced to the tables to
fill their plates with food, Skye looked up and saw him in her
peripheral vision. It was as if he had appeared out of nowhere;
she was sure that he hadn't been in the room the whole time Tyler
Perry was speaking. Now, he walked toward her, dressed in a military uniform with Sergeant First Class stripes sewn on his shoulders.
He was gorgeous and much better-looking than the day she'd
first met him.

"Hello, Skye."

"Hello, Bryan." Skye looked around the room for Henderson.
"What are you doing here? This is a surprise; I didn't expect to
see you again."

"I'm stationed at Fort Riley. Who would've thought that I'd run
into your sister who looks so much like you? I thought I was seeing
a mirage, and I had to speak to her. That was when she told me
about the bridal shower and to stop by if I felt compelled to."

"Compelled to?"

"Those were your sister's exact words."

"Oh." Skye's mind drifted. It went to a place several years ago
when she'd met Bryan and talked him in to marrying her. Her mind
wandered to the post chapel where they'd hurriedly said their vows
with people looking on that she didn't even know, except for her
mother who was against the whole idea of her marrying someone
she'd met only two weeks prior. But she wouldn't listen and she'd
paid for it.

"Are you all right?" Bryan asked, touching her arm.

"Yeah, yeah, I'm fine. I couldn't help but recall the first time I
met you."

"Oh, yes, I will never forget."

"I see you made rank—Sergeant First Class. That was fast; two promotions in a three-year period. You're on your way."

"You inspired me to be the best that I could be. I've never forgotten what you said about helping me get to Sergeant Major status. Sometimes I wished I had tried harder to make us work."

"It was doomed from the start, Bryan. You knew it and I knew it. No one forces someone to marry them. I was hot to trot the day I drove to this base with my mind set on getting away from this place. I was going to get a military man like my father."

"Yeah, and it didn't hurt that you were wearing those tight jeans and that top that exposed…"

"You don't mind if I interrupt?" Henderson said, handing Skye a plate of food.

"No, not at all." Bryan extended his hand. "I'm Bryan Culbertson, Skye's ex-husband."

At first, Henderson ignored Bryan's outstretched hand but thought better of it. "I'm Corlis Henderson, Skye's fiancé."

"Congratulations to the both of you."

"Thank you," Skye and Henderson said simultaneously.

"I'm not going to stay. My wife is waiting for me at home. Since Whitney asked me to stop by, I wanted to see you again. Oh, I'm a father now."

"Oh," was all Skye could muster. She wondered if his wife was the woman she'd caught him in bed with long ago. It didn't matter; she had the love of her life. She watched as Bryan walked away.

"You're not having second thoughts, are you?"

"No, baby, you're all the man I need. But I'm glad that I was able to look him in the eyes and feel no regret about how our marriage ended. I've purged the past from my system."

Henderson kissed her on the lips. "I'm glad for you."

"Skye," Jaylin said, walking up to the couple, "who was that fine brother you were talking to? I thought there were only hillbillies in this part of the country. Girl, you need to introduce me to him."

"That was my ex, Jaye. Whitney ran into him on base and invited him to my bridal shower. He's stationed at Fort Riley—the place where I met him. Can you believe that?"

"Damn, just my luck. I guess I'll have to go back to L.A. and settle for a good Cali boy."

"You're crazy, Jaye."

"No crazier than you. This is a beautiful day and I can't wait for you guys to get married and make me an auntie."

"You may already be."

"What are you talking about?"

"You heard her, Jaye," Henderson said with a smile. "We're having a baby. All that loving after she got well. We haven't told anyone yet."

"But as soon as we say 'I do,' I'm telling my mother. She's going to go crazy."

"You guys had this planned. Have a baby so Mother Dearest will go back to California with you and be your live-in babysitter."

"It wasn't planned that way, but you're in the ballpark. Right, baby?"

Henderson kissed Skye on the lips. "I don't think we'll get any protests from Nona."

"Oh sookie, sookie, now," Jaylin said. "This news is cause for celebration—a toast to Skye, Henderson, and the bundle of joy baking in the oven."

CHAPTER 81

And the twain became one.

ABOUT THE AUTHOR

Suzetta Perkins is the author of *Behind the Veil*, *A Love So Deep*, *EX-Terminator: Life after Marriage*, *Déjà Vu*, *Nobody Stays the Same*, *At the End of the Day*, *In My Rearview Mirror* and *Silver Bullets*. She is also the cofounder and president of the Sistahs Book Club. Visit www.SuzettaPerkins.com, Facebook/Suzetta Perkins Fan Page, and Twitter @authorsue, to learn more.

DISCUSSION QUESTIONS

Skye Taylor-Culbertson suffered several challenges in her life that made her an emotional wreck—challenges that she was unable to cope with. While some of the challenges, such as dealing with the death of her father, made you feel sorry for her, others were self-inflicted and made you want to knock some sense into her head.

1. Skye was a daddy's girl and held him in high-esteem. Do you believe her father's death was the cause of her irrational behavior?

2. Did Skye's mother contribute to her emotional instability? Why or why not?

3. I've had a fixation with men in uniform. I married a soldier, although he was my sweetheart before he went into the service. What was your reaction to Skye's approach to getting Bryan Culbertson's attention?

4. Bryan made the ultimate sacrifice, albeit a stupid one. He could've walked away and left Skye standing on the sidewalk where he met her. Was he intimidated by her? Do you know of a similar situation in real life?

5. Skye and Bryan's marriage was doomed for failure. Although Skye should've realized that as well, what drove her to pursue

the marriage? What signs were present before she got married that let you know that it would be a short one?

6. All of the military benefits Skye reaped couldn't keep her disaster of a marriage together. How long did the marriage last and what was the last straw?

7. Did Skye getting on a bus bound for Los Angeles surprise you? Why or why not?

8. While writing this story, Skye made me an emotional wreck. I couldn't be sure what she was going to do next. Yes, I wrote the book, but my characters on many occasions dictate what I write. So, I jeopardized Skye's character by introducing her to Rico Tillman. What were your thoughts about Rico? As a young girl trying to get a break in Hollywood, would you have been as gullible...trusted him?

9. Skye tells her friend Jaylin that Rico hasn't slept with her, although he's wined and dined her. Do you feel that because a man/woman does something nice for you that you should reciprocate with sexual favors? Why do you think Rico hasn't slept with Skye?

10. Naiveté was Skye's downfall. Do you believe that being a friend to Jaylin helped Skye's awkwardness in the big city of Los Angeles?

11. What were some of the things Skye did that let you know that she wasn't ready for big city life?

12. When did Skye begin to grow up?

IF YOU ENJOYED "HOLLYWOOD SKYE," BE SURE TO LOOK FOR

Silver Bullets

BY SUZETTA PERKINS

AVAILABLE FROM STREBOR BOOKS

One For The Queen

Queenie Jackson threw her designer pocketbook on the pink, Queen Anne sofa, kicked off her black Manolo pumps, let out a sigh, and plopped down on the sofa next to her bag. She was exhausted from having to sing her solo part over and over again until she got it right during choir rehearsal at Shiloh Baptist Church. However, her exhaustion stemmed from a heated argument with her best friend and the choir director, Emma Wilcox, who said she'd seen her boo, Linden, slipping into Minnie Smith's house.

A squeaking sound came from the kitchen. Queenie jumped up from her seat and ran toward the kitchen in her stocking feet. She grabbed her chest when she saw Linden's butt, body bent over, extracting food from her refrigerator, as if he paid the bills at her residence. Linden was Queenie's on again, off again boyfriend. She was through with him—his fake brown contacts and perfect body, except for the slight limp incurred from his days of playing basketball—and didn't want to see him tonight or any other night.

"What are you doing here, Linden?" Queenie asked, her hands hugging her pleasingly plump hips. "You scared the hell out of me, and, furthermore, you can't ride up in here anytime you feel like it." Queenie shook her finger in his face. "I'm not that kind of sistah. This is my house, and you're going to respect my space. I want my spare key before you leave here tonight."

"Now hold your horses, Red. I don't know what's wrong with you, but I'm not going anywhere tonight but in your bed. I had a hard day at work. There's got to be something in this refrigerator that will give me a boost of energy so we can…throw down in the bedroom tonight."

Queenie stared at the six-foot, nut-brown, bald-headed brother, with the light-brown eyes thanks to his special brand of contacts. "I'm not in the mood tonight, sugah. You tail has got to go."

"Look, Red, I can whip it on you tonight. I've got the blue pills in my back pocket ready to rock-n-roll when you give the word. You might as well call that job of yours and tell them you won't be seeing them tomorrow. I'm going to be keeping you up all night long. Now give me some of that sweet, brown sugar."

Queenie slammed the refrigerator door shut. She tried to push her argument with Emma to the back of her mind. However, vivid images of Linden creeping inside Minnie's house formed in her head and wouldn't let go. "I don't care if you have red, green, pink, or blue pills, you won't be touching my sheets tonight. Give me my key and get your sorry-ass-behind out of my house now. Go to Minnie's since you seem to be so comfortable with her and she apparently has what you need. I'm nobody's stopover station."

The look on Linden's face didn't faze Queenie one bit. "I don't know what you're talking about, Red. Your old-ass, gossiping girlfriends run their mouths and tell lies every chance they get. Yeah, I was over at Minnie's…"

Slap.

Linden rubbed the side of his face with his hand. His eyes jutted out of his face like they'd been blown up with an air pump. "Hell, what you go and do that for, Red?"

"For fifteen minutes I stood in front of Emma and called her a liar—told her she didn't know what the hell she was talking about. Then she made me sing my solo over and over again although I was on key. And now you've got the audacity to stand in front of me and say that you were at Minnie's house?"

"Red, it wasn't like that at all. I went over to Minnie's house to connect her television cable. I didn't want to get caught supplying free cable to the sister. She's strapped for money and I said that I'd do her this favor but it had to be after the sun went down. Now you owe me an apology."

"It ain't that simple, Linden. Everybody's strapped for money. I bet you switched on her cable box all right."

"I'm telling the truth, Red. I love you, and if you weren't so damn stubborn, I'd marry you tomorrow."

Queenie softened a little. "Marry me? Did you hear what you said? Do you truly mean that, Linden?"

"Have I ever lied to you, Red? Girl, I'd kiss the ground you walk on and drink your bath water, too."

"You have a funny way of showing it. I've waited for an eternity for you to make your intentions known. You come in and out of my house like it's Home Depot…"

"Stop, Red, I'm serious about my love for you."

"I want to believe you, Linden, but you still have to go home tonight. There's a consequence for your actions. Next time, you'll remember to tell me before you step in another woman's home to do some housework. The argument I had with Emma tonight was no joke. Give me a kiss and my key. You can come by tomorrow; I have an early day at work…"

"You've got to be kidding. I'm horny as a…"

"Take a cold shower when you get home. My key, a kiss, and I'll see you tomorrow."

Wednesday Special

Before she could get the key out of the door, Emma Wilcox could smell the grease from the fried chicken her husband, Billy, had prepared for dinner. Every Wednesday night was fried chicken night. You could swear on your mother's grave that Billy was going to have crisp, golden-fried chicken sitting on a platter on Wednesdays—fifty-two weeks a year. Billy was a retired mess-hall cook for the United States Army where he proudly served Uncle Sam for twenty-four years.

Emma pushed through the front door and headed for the family room. She flung herself onto the sofa, which didn't protest her added weight. Even after three children, now adults, Emma was in remarkable shape. But it was her hazel eyes that defined her. With those and her processed bleached-blonde hair, she could still turn heads—from the young to the old ones. And if she wasn't so hung up on Jesus and Billy, she might have given a few of them a run for their money, especially since Billy was almost non-existent in the love making department.

As dutifully as always, Billy appeared in the room to take off her shoes and rub her feet. "You're tense, Emma. Those sisters give you a hard time at choir rehearsal tonight?"

"Only one sister was a thorn in my side tonight. I can't believe Queenie had the nerve to rock back on her heels, point her finger in my face, and call me a bold-faced liar."

"What did you say to Queenie to make her so mad? Queenie doesn't usually go off unless somebody hits her atomic bomb button."

Emma looked at her husband: fifty-six to her fifty-five; together since junior high; married the day after high school graduation. Having enlisted in the army right after, Billy had taken care of her for the next thirty-six years. He'd provided for her and their children as he moved up the mess hall ranks. He'd been admired and held in high regard as a cook, receiving many medals of commendation for his culinary skills in war and peace time.

Billy had been a little freak when they first got married. At one point, Emma thought they were going to have an army platoon full of kids. But she remembered her mother's words admonishing her to not let any man keep her barefoot and pregnant.

"A man will saddle you with a whole bunch of kids," Emma's mother had warned, "that you'll have to stay home and take care of while his tail run the streets behind some other young thing that has no baby bruises all over her body and makes him feel young. Take care of yourself—your appearance—and always be sure to make your man happy. That's how you keep them."

Emma's mother's words always resonated with her and she made sure that she took her daily birth control pill until she was ready to have another income tax deduction.

"I didn't say anything to her, Billy," she said now. "Queenie's an angry woman."

"I still say that you must have said something to her."

Emma eased off the sofa and laid her hands on her hips. "Yeah, I told her something that she needed to know."

Billy backed up. Although Emma was usually a gentle soul, he recognized this side of her.

"I told Queenie that I saw her man sneaking into Minnie Smith's house."

"Why did you go and do a fool thing like that, Emma? You knew Queenie was going to blow up in your face."

"She had a right to know. Linden Robinson has been sucking up all of her joy and great hospitality with no intention whatsoever to make an honest woman out of her."

"Well, it's none of your business, Emma. You need not stick your nose where it doesn't belong."

"Let me tell you something, Billy Wilcox. I'm a good looking black woman and I still got it. I see how the men at church watch me and how big Mike-next-door's eyes get when I go to close the blinds in my bra and panties. All I'd have to do is make one gesture, and they'd come running. But you're lucky, Billy Wilcox. You're lucky that I love the Lord and your sorry black behind that can't get his dipstick up and don't remember the first, middle, or last thing about pleasuring his woman. You're too happy frying chicken."

"You're wrong for that, Emma. Apologize now. I'll be damned if I'll have my wife belittling me in my home that I keep clean so she doesn't have to prepare every meal that she throws down in her belly, so she can relax and get off of her feet when she gets home from work at night. Yeah, I love to cook, but mess with me, sister, and this will be the last Wednesday you'll have fried damn chicken."

Billy was so mad he hadn't realized Emma had fallen onto the couch, laughing her head off.

"Billy, I think I lit a fire under your ass tonight. You are so cute when you get mad."

"Why did you have to go and insult my manhood like that, Emma? Why? I've been faithful to you all the years we've been married."

"Uhm-hmm."

"You can uhm-hmm all you want. I didn't say I never looked at anybody. I have. You're supposed to look at pretty things, but I always kept my hands to myself. The only place I've put my hands beside you is inside hogs, chickens, and cows to clean out their guts. And that wasn't even as much fun as making babies with you."

"Our babies are grown, Billy. That was a long time ago. The question is what have you done for me lately?"

"I clean your damn house, cook your dinner, and make your bath water. Dinner is served unless you don't want the Wednesday special. And if you don't want the Wednesday special, then you are plumb out of luck. Take it or leave."

If Emma wasn't a praying woman, she'd leave Billy and his fried chicken that very moment. Oh, it would be wonderful to feel the touch of a man who'd make her feel like a real woman. But after the foreplay and lovemaking were over, she'd want him to be gone. Emma was fifty-five and she didn't have time to babysit or play kindergarten teacher.

She'd keep Billy in spite of his shortcomings, no pun intended. He was a good man, who loved God and their children. She owed him. Maybe she'd surprise him one night—maybe on a Wednesday—and cook him up something special.

Looking Good

Queenie was glad it was Saturday. Her Monday through Friday job as an editor at *The News & Observer*—Raleigh, North Carolina's local newspaper—had taken a toll on her this week.

She had run herself ragged, verifying and editing stories that were serious headliners; stories that sold more newspapers in one week on the newsstands than the previous two weeks. That's how news went. Some weeks the papers were filled with fluff about old-money politicians and their thousand-dollar plate political fundraising dinners or Hollywood's bad kids gone further bad. Then a salacious story with all the makings of a major crime movie breaks.

Last week was last week. Today, Queenie set out for her favorite nail salon for her bi-weekly manicure and pedicure. There was nothing like pampering yourself. Queenie always came away with a euphoric feeling when her nails and toes were freshly scrubbed and polished. It made her feel as if she was on top of the world. She also enjoyed catching up with her girlfriends.

She hadn't talked to Emma since the incident at choir rehearsal the other night, but she'd be the bigger person and apologize. After all, Emma was half right. Queenie also looked forward to seeing Yolanda and her younger sister, Connie, as well as "First Lady" Jackie O'Neill.

Decked out in a pair of fuchsia capris that hugged her behind and wouldn't let go, a pair of five-inch, fuchsia stilettos, and a white frilly blouse with ruffles around the collar, Queenie plopped down in her red Jaguar XK Coupe and hit the road. It was a beautiful spring day, exceptionally so for the last week in March.

The spa was located in the Cameron Village part of Raleigh. The ladies loved the area with all of its great shopping opportunities. The tree-lined streets and one-of-a-kind artsy shops, restaurants and cafes were what made the Village quaint and appealing. Queenie arrived at her destination and pulled into a parking space. She spotted Yolanda's Lexus a couple of spaces over.

Queenie latched onto Yolanda like a protective big sister. Yolanda was petite and sported a close-cropped hairdo.

"Hey, girl," Yolanda said, giving Queenie a big hug in return. "You're looking good."

"And so do you," Queenie said. She meant it too; Yolanda's silver and black mane complemented her dark brown complexion and she had a gym body with curves in all the right places. Not bad for a newly divorced fifty-six-year-old woman.

After releasing Yolanda, Queenie turned in Connie's direction and gave her a big hug.

"Hey, Connie, what've you been up to? Preston put a ring on your finger yet?"

"I love you, too, Queenie," Connie said, giving Queenie an extra squeeze.

It was an old joke between them. Connie Maxwell was knocking on a half century. The former pageant winner was still a natural beauty but had not been able to capture a man's heart the way she did those coveted rhinestone tiaras—that is until she met Mr. Preston Alexander.

Preston Alexander was the man of her dreams and came with a pocket-full-of-money, a nice cushy job as a pharmaceutical rep for GlaxoSmithKline, and a three-bedroom cottage at Brier Creek Country Club Cottages. Foremost and of considerable importance, Preston had no baby mamas, no alimony, no child payments. Connie had been with Preston for the past three years, and while their relationship seemed to be at full throttle, there was yet to be a real conversation about marriage.

"Connie doesn't need to get married," Yolanda rushed to say, as they walked into the spa. "She's better off living the single life instead of getting her heart hurt over some man that'll cost her thousands of dollars later on when she decides that saying "I do" and becoming one ain't for her anymore. You see, I don't need a man; it's me and my Jesus."

"Don't hate on me, YoYo," Connie said. "It was you who allowed Eric to turn your happy home into an emotional, dysfunctional wreck. Whenever Preston decides to ask for my hand in marriage, that'll be fine with me. You busy bodies used and abused your exes and that's why they were happy when you threw them out. My man and I are fine, and he's going to be the father of my babies."

"Do you hear yourself, Connie?" Queenie asked, her face all bunched up. "Your eggs are going to turn to powder waiting on that man to propose to you."

Connie poked out her lips. "Come on, Q, that was a mean thing to say."

"All I'm saying is, if you really want to have a baby, there are a lot of orphans out there hoping that someone would love and adopt them. Look at Angelina Jolie and Madonna. Anyway, your biological clock is already doing a slow drag. Menopause is about to catch up to you any minute."

"I'm not trying to save the world, Q. I'm talking about one baby."

"I understand how my sister feels about having her own child," Yolanda said, rushing to defend Connie. "I wish I had more than one. All I'm saying is that she doesn't have to be married to have a baby."

"God don't like ugly, YoYo," Connie said. "I've waited all this time to have a baby with the man who I want to be my baby's father, and I'm not going to compromise my values because you all are operating on a high level of ignorance."

"A high level of what?" Queenie shouted as she looked at Yolanda. "Did your sister say we were ignorant?"

"We're telling you the twenty-first century truth, Connie," Yolanda offered. "I've known you all my life and you yearn for perfection. But if you think Preston Alexander is it, baby you've got it wrong. I like Preston, but you've got to put what Connie wants first. If you want a baby, adopt. Preston hasn't budged one bit when you hinted at marriage, which may be the reason why he's in his house all by himself and has never married. Do the math, sister."

"I think he's got something to hide," Queenie added. "He seems so secretive."

Connie twirled her finger about her head to indicate somebody was crazy. "As I said, someone is operating on a high level of ignorance."

"Saved by the bell," Yolanda said. "Here comes Emma and First Lady."

"Are you all ready for your pedicures?" the nail technician asked, interrupting what might have been a potential free-for-all at Connie's expense.

"Yes, we're ready," Queenie said. "You better be glad I'm ready for my claws to be manicured, Ms. Connie. I was ready to let you have it."

"Leave me and my man alone and we'll be good."